## Erle Stanley Gardner and The Murder Room

>>> This title is part of The Murder Room, our series dedicated to making available out-of-print or hard-to-find titles by classic crime writers.

Crime fiction has always held up a mirror to society. The Victorians were fascinated by sensational murder and the emerging science of detection; now we are obsessed with the forensic detail of violent death. And no other genre has so captivated and enthralled readers.

Vast troves of classic crime writing have for a long time been unavailable to all but the most dedicated frequenters of second-hand bookshops. The advent of digital publishing means that we are now able to bring you the backlists of a huge range of titles by classic and contemporary crime writers, some of which have been out of print for decades.

From the genteel amateur private eyes of the Golden Age and the femmes fatales of pulp fiction, to the morally ambiguous hard-boiled detectives of mid twentieth-century America and their descendants who walk our twenty-first century streets, The Murder Room has it all. >>>

## The Murder Room
### Where Criminal Minds Mee´

themurderroom.com

**Erle Stanley Gardner (1889–1970)**

Born in Malden, Massachusetts, Erle Stanley Gardner left school in 1909 and attended Valparaiso University School of Law in Indiana for just one month before he was suspended for focusing more on his hobby of boxing than his academic studies. Soon after, he settled in California, where he taught himself the law and passed the state bar exam in 1911. The practise of law never held much interest for him, however, apart from as it pertained to trial strategy, and in his spare time he began to write for the pulp magazines that gave Dashiell Hammett and Raymond Chandler their start. Not long after the publication of his first novel, *The Case of the Velvet Claws*, featuring Perry Mason, he gave up his legal practice to write full time. He had one daughter, Grace, with his first wife, Natalie, from whom he later separated. In 1968 Gardner married his long-term secretary, Agnes Jean Bethell, whom he professed to be the real 'Della Street', Perry Mason's sole (although unacknowledged) love interest. He was one of the most successful authors of all time and at the time of his death, in Temecula, California in 1970, is said to have had 135 million copies of his books in print in America alone.

*By Erle Stanley Gardner*
(titles below include only those published in the Murder Room)

## Perry Mason series

The Case of the Sulky Girl (1933)
The Case of the Baited Hook (1940)
The Case of the Borrowed Brunette (1946)
The Case of the Lonely Heiress (1948)
The Case of the Negligent Nymph (1950)
The Case of the Moth-Eaten Mink (1952)
The Case of the Glamorous Ghost (1955)
The Case of the Terrified Typist (1956)
The Case of the Gilded Lily (1956)
The Case of the Lucky Loser (1957)
The Case of the Long-Legged Models (1958)
The Case of the Deadly Toy (1959)
The Case of the Singing Skirt (1959)
The Case of the Duplicate Daughter (1960)

The Case of the Blonde Bonanza (1962)

## Cool and Lam series

The Bigger They Come (1939)
Turn on the Heat (1940)
Gold Comes in Bricks (1940)
Spill the Jackpot (1941)
Double or Quits (1941)
Owls Don't Blink (1942)
Bats Fly at Dusk (1942)
Cats Prowl at Night (1943)
Crows Can't Count (1946)
Fools Die on Friday (1947)
Bedrooms Have Windows (1949)
Some Women Won't Wait (1953)
Beware the Curves (1956)
You Can Die Laughing (1957)
Some Slips Don't Show (1957)
The Count of Nine (1958)
Pass the Gravy (1959)
Kept Women Can't Quit (1960)
Bachelors Get Lonely (1961)
Shills Can't Cash Chips (1961)
Try Anything Once (1962)
Fish or Cut Bait (1963)
Up For Grabs (1964)

Cut Thin to Win (1965)
Widows Wear Weeds (1966)
Traps Need Fresh Bait (1967)
All Grass Isn't Green (1970)

## Doug Selby D.A. series

The D.A. Calls it Murder (1937)
The D.A. Holds a Candle (1938)
The D.A. Draws a Circle (1939)
The D.A. Goes to Trial (1940)
The D.A. Cooks a Goose (1942)
The D.A. Calls a Turn (1944)
The D.A. Takes a Chance
  (1946)
The D.A. Breaks an Egg
  (1949)

## Terry Clane series

Murder Up My Sleeve (1937)
The Case of the Backward
  Mule (1946)

## Gramp Wiggins series

The Case of the Turning Tide
  (1941)
The Case of the Smoking
  Chimney (1943)

Two Clues (two novellas) (1947)

# Murder Up My Sleeve

## Erle Stanley Gardner

An Orion book

Copyright © The Erle Stanley Gardner Trust 1937

This edition published by
The Orion Publishing Group Ltd
Orion House
5 Upper St Martin's Lane
London WC2H 9EA

An Hachette UK company
A CIP catalogue record for this book is available from the British Library

ISBN 978 1 4719 0946 7

www.orionbooks.co.uk

*To*

### KIT KING LOUIS

Ngoh geh pang yieu dak beit chung
meng Sin Sahng

*In memory of a rainy day at
the railroad station in Peiping*

**TERRY CLANE SAT WAITING IN THE OUTER** office of the district attorney; and had no idea why he was waiting, nor for what.

In the background of his immediate memory was the recollection of peremptory knuckles on his door, of men pushing past Yat T'oy, his Chinese servant, and into his bedroom, waiting while he dressed, of being hustled into a police car, which, with screaming siren clearing its way through traffic, had rushed him to the district attorney's office.

Against the background of these hectic and scrambled memories, the irksome waiting in the district attorney's outer office was a period of nerve strain which made the clacking of the wall clock seem a veritable tattoo of accusation.

The blond young woman at the information desk, from time to time, made a surreptitious study of Terry Clane's profile.

Keeping his eyes averted, yet conscious of her scrutiny, Terry wondered whether the district attorney had perhaps instructed her to observe and report upon his demeanor, or if her interest were purely gratuitous.

It was shortly before ten o'clock. Trial deputies bustled importantly from the side doors flanking the long corridor, pushed open the swinging gate and strode across the outer office. As they walked they flung words over their shoulders to the girl who sat at the desk marked "Information."

Terry Clane watched them with detached interest.

"Department Five, People vs. Taylor," a red-headed man said, and hurried out. "Judge Belter, preliminary in the Jackson case," a thin, nervous individual snapped as he too lunged toward the outer door. "Argument on Motion to Quash, People vs. Heinz," remarked a fleshy young man whose perspiring hand clung to his leather briefcase as though he were afraid someone might try to snatch it from his grasp.

The young woman at the information desk made notes on a long sheet of paper containing a typewritten list of names. She checked these names off one at a time. A clock chimed the hour of ten. The frenzied activity of the office ceased. There were no more banging doors, no more hurried steps in the corridor.

The slightly wistful eyes of the young woman glanced once more at Terry Clane.

Clane, swiftly shifting his own eyes, caught and held hers.

"Do you think," he asked, "that such haste actually makes for efficiency?"

"Certainly," she said; then after a moment added, "It's the modern pace."

Clane's nod was deferential, but he said casually, "Exactly, going in circles."

She frowned. "Did you say circles or cycles?"

"Which," he asked, extracting a carved ivory cigarette case from his pocket, "would *you* say?" And, while she was wrestling with that, inquired so casually that he seemed merely making conversation, "What did the district attorney wish to see me about?"

Instinctively she grasped at the understandable question. "I think it's something about . . ." She caught herself mid-sentence.

Far from showing disappointment at his failure to elicit information, Clane calmly pre-empted the conversational lead as she hesitated, making it seem almost as though he had interrupted her. "The modern pace," he said calmly, selecting a cigarette from the case, "defeats its own ends: the public demands that tomorrow's newspapers be on the street tonight, and so misses the real morning news; that fruit be picked green and softened on the fruit stands; that the Christmas numbers of magazines be on the stands the first of November . . . Tell me, wouldn't you like some tree-ripened fruit for a change?"

Her nod was a trifle vague.

"Am I supposed to be a witness to something?" Clane went on smoothly, in the same casual tone, "or have I committed some major crime—a murder, perhaps?"

The dazed young woman was groping for a reply when the buzzer on the switchboard sounded. Her agile fingers clicked keys into place. She said into the transmitter, "Yes, Mr. Dixon." Her finger snapped a key. As she raised her eyes and spoke to Terry Clane, her voice showed relief. "The district attorney will see you now, Mr. Clane—right through that gate, straight down the corridor to the double doors at the end."

Terry Clane smiled his thanks, walked down the long corridor and pushed open the swinging doors. A secretary who sat very rigid behind a desk nodded toward a door marked "Private" and said, "Right through that door, Mr. Clane, please."

Terry opened the door.

Parker Dixon, seated in a massive leather swivel-chair, was signing correspondence. He glanced up, said, "Good morning, Mr. Clane. Take that chair, please." His eyes were back on the letters before he had finished speaking. His pen scrawled a signature. A young woman with tired eyes mechanically blotted that signature while the district attorney was making another. When the correspondence had all been signed, she deposited it gently in a wire basket and tiptoed from the office as though she feared to intrude upon sacred thoughts.

The district attorney looked up.

He was in his early fifties. His lips smiled with the readiness of a veteran politician. His eyes were watchful and did not smile. So completely convincing was his facial cordiality that few persons bothered to notice the cool appraisal of those eyes.

"I'm sorry that it was necessary to bother you,

4

Mr. Clane," Parker Dixon began without other preliminary, "but a matter of great importance makes it necessary to ask certain questions."

"Just what," Clane asked, "is the nature of this matter? Should I feel flattered or frightened?"

The district attorney continued to smile, but his greenish eyes were as watchful as those of a cat studying a caged bird. "Suppose," he said, "you let me ask *my* questions first? If you don't mind, we'll dispense with preliminaries. You see, I've already acquired complete information about your life. Therefore, I only want to ask *you* about certain specific events which took place within the last few hours."

Clane's eyebrows showed courteous surprise. "You've collected *complete* information about my life?" he asked.

"Yes."

"May I ask when your interest in me reached the information-seeking stage?"

The probing eyes caught the reflection of light from a window and seemed to glitter.

"Since about four-thirty this morning. Does *that* mean anything to you, Mr. Clane?"

"Only that your information would, under those circumstances, be woefully incomplete."

The district attorney said, "I'm afraid you underestimate the facilities which are at my disposal."

Somewhat after the manner of a magician producing a rabbit from a hat, he picked up several closely typewritten sheets of paper from his desk; and Terry Clane, realizing that he had played into the other's hand by saying exactly that which he had been expected to say, schooled himself against repeating his blunder.

The district attorney began reading in a low monotone:

"Terrance Clane, age twenty-nine, hair dark, wavy, complexion smooth olive, eyes blue, height five feet eleven, weight one hundred and eighty-five, graduated from the University of California, took law course and was admitted to the California Bar; went to China and then entered the diplomatic service, showed himself an apt student of Chinese language, philosophy and psychology; abruptly resigned from service, disappeared and was reputed to have started for the interior, accompanied by an old Chinese.

"A Communist uprising took place in a district through which he traveled and it was surmised he had been murdered, since no ransom demands were made. Four months ago he appeared in Hongkong, giving only a sketchy account of his wanderings. He shipped by the Dollar Line steamer *President Hoover*, disembarked in San Francisco, looked up a few of his closest friends, maintained a marked reticence about his Chinese adventures. Keeps a bank balance of something less than a thousand dollars in the main branch of the Bank of America at Number One Powell Street, but seems to be free from financial worries. Has a host of Chinese friends in the local district. At night sometimes goes to Chinatown, enters stores, disappears through back doors, and upon such occasions fails to return to his apartment until shortly before dawn.

"Is an adventurer, described by some of his intimates as a bit wild. Is noted in his circle of acquaintances for a scorn of conventions, yet lives a life which is for the most part above reproach.

"Investigation in China indicates that during the period he was missing he had entered a Chinese monastery, posing as a neophyte in order to gain access to ancient temple ruins where gold and gems had been stored. The teachers regarded him as an apt pupil. He is reported to have completed his training, when some incident forced him to flee for the treaty ports."

The district attorney turned the sheet, started to read from a second page, then checked himself and said, "I think I have read enough to illustrate my point."

"Sounds rather bizarre," Terry commented.

"I have every reason to believe it's absolutely accurate, Mr. Clane."

Terry shook his head. His eyes showed quiet amusement. "I never completed my training," he said. "I remained a mere neophyte. Four and a half seconds of concentration was the best I was ever able to accomplish. The masters . . ."

"Four and a half seconds!" the district attorney exclaimed. "Surely you mean hours. Frequently, Mr. Clane, I myself become so absorbed in concentrating upon a legal problem I lose all track of time."

Terry noticed the trace of irritation in the district attorney's voice. It was quite evident that he wanted to get back to the matter in hand, equally evident that he prided himself upon his ability to concentrate. Resenting the fact that he had so easily given the district attorney the verbal opening which had enabled him to produce a typewritten report, read just enough from it to make him vaguely uneasy as to what might be in the balance of the document, Terry whipped a pencil from his pocket, held the point against the top of the desk.

"You *thought* you were concentrating," Clane said. "As a matter of fact, you were bringing only a small portion of your mental powers into focus. For instance, concentrate on the point of that pencil for just two seconds."

Dixon started to say something, then frowned and stared at the point of the pencil. "Now I presume," he said, as Terry put the pencil back in the pocket, "you want me to describe the point of the pencil. Very well, the lead is somewhat softer than the ordinary grade of lead. There's a small place near the point where . . ."

"Pardon me," Terry interrupted, "but what did I do with my left hand while you were concentrating on the pencil held in my right?"

"You kept it in your left coat pocket," Dixon said positively.

Terry smiled. "In China," he said gently, "one who concentrated upon the point of a pencil would be expected to focus *all* of his mental faculties on the point of the pencil. I can assure you, Mr. Dixon, that it isn't easy to do."

Dixon's voice showed irritation. "I didn't send for you to discuss elemental psychology," he snapped.

Terry seemed to be enjoying himself. Obviously, the interview wasn't going just as Dixon had planned it. "Perhaps," he suggested, "since your report is so complete, you might like to add to it the *real* reason I was expelled from the monastery."

The district attorney raised inquiring eyebrows.

"It was," Clane said, "a matter of legs, or, if you are at all old-fashioned, limbs. I am personally very partial to good-looking . . . er . . ." He broke off to study the facial expression of the district attorney and then, with a smile which just missed being patronizing, said, "I think, under the circumstances, 'limbs' would be the proper word."

From the fleeting expression of annoyance which clouded the district attorney's eyes, Clane knew that his shot had told, but he went urbanely on:

"This little Russian girl had drifted in from God knows where. She was a beauty, she was clever as the very devil, and she interfered with my studies. The estimable gentlemen who watched over my progress were quite right in assuming that one who permitted himself to be so easily distracted lacked the moral stamina to put the outer world completely from his thoughts. They suggested that I return to my native land, or, at least, to the treaty ports. I may state, in passing, that subsequent events have convinced me that their judgment in this, as in other matters, was flawless."

The unmistakable frown of annoyance on the district attorney's face showed his irritation at Clane's facetious manner

"Had that statement been included in my report," Dixon said, "I might then have agreed with you in your characterization of it as bizarre."

"Not," Clane pointed out, "if you'd known the Russian."

Dixon ostentatiously dropped the typewritten sheets into a drawer of his desk, suddenly raised his eyes to stare at Terry Clane with what might have been intended as disconcerting steadiness. "I think, Mr. Clane," he said, "we'll dispense with these friendly informalities and remember that this interview is official.

"Last night you attended an informal dinner-dance at the home of B. Stanley Rayborne." He waited only for Clane's nod before going on: "Miss Alma Renton was also there. You were Miss Renton's escort. You left the Rayborne residence about twelve-thirty A.M., did you not?"

"I can't tell you the exact hour," Clane said, his voice and manner stiffly formal.

The district attorney opened another drawer in his desk, took from it a small square of lace-bordered linen. "Do you recognize this?" he asked.

"No," Clane said promptly, almost before the question had left the district attorney's lips.

Parker Dixon frowned. For a moment his lips were as hard as his eyes. "No, no, don't be in a hurry. Take it in your hands, smell the perfume, look at it."

He leaned across the desk, handed the handkerchief

to Clane, who examined it, smelled it, handed it back, and said casually, "Surely you don't attach great importance to a handkerchief?"

"Why not?"

"Oh, I don't know. It's such a conventional thing. On the stage and in books, women are always leaving handkerchiefs behind. One would think that a person of ordinary intelligence who has attended no more than half a dozen mystery plays would certainly be above dropping a handkerchief, unless, of course, she were someone who wished to implicate the owner."

"For one who doesn't recognize a handkerchief," Dixon said dryly, "you're making rather an obvious effort to defend its owner, and, incidentally, I haven't intimated this handkerchief was connected with any crime."

Terry Clane sighed, a sigh which seemed but a degree removed from a yawn. "When a district attorney," he observed, "has me routed from bed and whisked to his office to examine a handkerchief, I assume that his interest is official."

Dixon smiled, not the automatic lip smile he customarily used to disguise the fact that his every move led toward some definite objective, but rather the conciliatory smile of one conceding a point because it does not at the moment suit his convenience to argue over it.

"You will," he said, "notice the initial 'R' embroidered in the handkerchief."

"I noticed it."

"Miss Renton is an artist?"

"I believe so, yes."

"Quite successful?"

"You are referring to success from a monetary or an artistic standpoint?"

"From both."

"I know nothing concerning her income."

"Is that her handkerchief?"

"I'm sure I couldn't say."

"Did you go directly to Miss Renton's apartment after you left the Rayborne residence?"

"That depends on what you mean by 'directly.' "

"Did you take the shortest road?"

"No."

"Where did you go?"

"Is that important?"

"*I* consider it is."

"We drove around a bit."

"Did your drive take you along Grant Avenue in Chinatown?"

"Yes."

"May I ask why?"

"We were talking about the subconscious grouping of colors in the Oriental mind. I drove through Chinatown to illustrate a point I had made."

"Rather an odd hour to make such an illustration, wasn't it?"

"An artist doesn't exactly keep office hours."

"Did Miss Renton seem to have anything on her mind?"

"A young woman of Miss Renton's intelligence always has something on her mind."

"That isn't what I meant. Was she worried? Was she nervous?"

"I didn't think so."

"Did she mention that she was in any particular trouble?"

"No."

"Did she intimate that some person was forcing her to do something against her will?"

"No."

"Miss Renton uses her maiden name in her profession, but she is in fact a widow, is she not?"

"So I understand."

"She was married some seven years ago to a Robert Helford?"

"Yes."

"Where were you when her husband died?"

"In China."

"You knew her before her marriage?"

"No. I met her afterward."

"Through Helford?"

"Yes."

"In other words, Helford was a close friend. After he married, you naturally visited his house on numerous occasions and became acquainted with his wife. Is that right?"

"Yes."

"How long after Helford's marriage did you start for China?"

"About six weeks."

"You left rather suddenly?"

"Yes."

"Can you fix the exact time you left Miss Renton last night?"

"No."

"Can you approximate it?"

"Only vaguely. After all, in calling upon an adult woman who is responsible to no one for her actions, one doesn't sound a curfew."

"I quite understand that," Dixon said. "Nevertheless, I *have* encountered cases, Mr. Clane, in which men were able to fix the time of their departure quite accurately."

"Indeed," Clane muttered, as though the statement were most surprising.

"It must have been *after* one o'clock," Dixon said.

Clane's tone implied that he was delighted to find some point upon which he could agree with his interrogator. "I'm quite certain it must have been," he admitted.

"Was it before two o'clock?"

Clane pursed his lips thoughtfully and said, "It's *so* hard to be accurate in these matters, Mr. Dixon."

There was something ominous in the district attorney's voice as he said, "I'm giving you an hour's leeway, Mr. Clane. I think I'm entitled to an answer to that question, and I think I should warn you that the answer may be important—to you."

"I couldn't say definitely," Clane said.

"But it was before three o'clock in the morning?" Dixon persisted.

"I would say so, yes. In fact, I would place it generally as some time between one and two."

The district attorney's manner relaxed somewhat. "You know a George Levering?" he asked.

"Yes."

"Do you know much about him?"

"I know that he married one of the Renton girls, a sister who died."

"Know anything else about him?"

"Nothing that I consider important."

Parker Dixon's smile was frosty. "Do you know anything about him which *I* might consider important?"

"As to that, I couldn't say."

"Is it true that Cynthia Renton, Alma's sister, has nothing to do with him, but that he imposes upon Alma to the extent of securing substantial 'loans'? Is his life of social idler, polo player, and general society hanger-on largely, if not entirely, supported by these 'loans'?"

"Unfortunately," Terry said with dignity, "Miss Renton has never seen fit to confide in me concerning her more intimate financial affairs. Strange as it may seem, she prefers to keep these exclusively in her own hands."

"That will do," the district attorney said coldly. "There's no call for sarcasm, Mr. Clane."

Terry's calm silence threatened to become an eloquent contradiction.

The district attorney's forefinger slid surreptitiously across the desk, came to rest casually upon a mother-of-pearl button. His eyes remained fastened on Clane's face. Terry's consciousness was focused,

15

not upon the district attorney's face, but upon that which he observed from the corner of his eye: the all but imperceptible raising of the wrist as Dixon pressed the button, two long and two short signals to someone somewhere.

The district attorney opened the drawer of his desk which held the typewritten report and dropped the handkerchief in on top of the papers. He closed the drawer with an air of finality.

"I had hoped you would be more willing to co-operate," he said.

"I am answering your questions," Clane pointed out. "Co-operation implies a definite mutual objective."

The district attorney hesitated a moment, then switched abruptly to another attack.

"You know Jacob Mandra, the bail-bond broker?" he asked.

"I have met him."

"Did you know him *before* you went to China?"

Terry sought to maintain an unyielding formality as a barrier through which the district attorney might not break.

"No. I looked him up after my return in order to verify an opinion I had previously formed."

"Why?"

"He wrote, asking me to pick up a certain object for him, and offering very substantial remuneration."

"What was this object?"

"I'd prefer to have you ask Mr. Mandra."

"Unfortunately, that is impossible."

16

" 'Impossible' is a very definite word."

The district attorney ignored the comment. "By any chance, Mr. Clane, was that object a sleeve gun?"

Terry hesitated for almost three seconds, then said, "Yes, it was a sleeve gun."

"Precisely what *is* a sleeve gun?"

"It's a tube of hollow bamboo, containing a powerful spring and a catch which is released by pressure. A metal-tipped dart can be inserted in the bamboo and pushed back against the tension of the spring until it's engaged by the catch, which holds it in position. The device is some nine inches long. It can readily be inserted up the rather copious sleeve of a Chinese gentleman, or, for that matter, a woman. By resting the forearm on a table or other hard object, the catch is depressed and the dart is released."

"It's a deadly weapon?"

"Very deadly."

"By deadly, I mean it can kill a man?"

"That's the purpose for which it is primarily intended."

"*Did* you procure such a weapon for Mr. Mandra?"

"No."

"Why not?"

"In the first place, they're rather rare, being curios of another phase of Chinese life. In the second place, I was not in China to purchase curios."

"You have seen Jacob Mandra since your return from the Orient?"

"Yes."

"When?"

"About a week after I returned. I had tea with him at his flat on Stockton Street."

"I believe you said you wished to verify certain impressions?"

"Yes."

"What were those impressions?"

"I'm sorry," Clane observed, "but I cannot see the necessity of such questions."

"*I* feel they are very necessary, Mr. Clane."

Clane sighed. "I had a sleeve gun of my own," he said. "If the impressions I had received from Mr. Mandra's correspondence had proven incorrect, I intended to present him with that sleeve gun as a gift."

"Did you present him with it?"

"No."

"By that you mean that the impressions you had drawn from his correspondence were correct?"

"I saw no reason to present him with a sleeve gun."

"*What* were those impressions?"

"I was not entirely certain," Clane said, "that the man wanted the article as a curio."

"You thought he might have wanted it as a weapon?"

"I wouldn't go so far as to say that."

"But you *didn't* give him the sleeve gun?"

"No."

"What was your impression of Mr. Mandra's character?"

Clane raised his eyebrows.

"I can assure you," Dixon said, "I have a reason for asking the question."

"Frankly, the man interested me as well as repelled me. He undoubtedly has a keen mentality, but I doubt if the uses to which he puts his mind are . . . shall we say 'ethical'?"

"Did he say why he wanted the sleeve gun?"

"Merely as a collector. He said a sleeve gun would make a very welcome addition to his collection of death-dealing knickknacks."

"Did you form any opinion as to Mandra's nationality?"

"Not a definite opinion," Clane said. "I'll admit his nationality puzzled me. He has many definitely Oriental characteristics, both physical and mental, yet I don't think he's of Chinese or Japanese extraction."

"Can you tell me some more about the opinion you formed of his character?"

"He's a strange mixture," Clane answered, "having a ruthless cunning as well as a tragic realization of what he's lost by misapplying his rather remarkable natural talents. I consider the nature of the lethal weapons he has collected in his little museum indicates a very definite and sinister trait of character."

"In what way?" Dixon asked, his interest shown by the way in which he snapped out the question.

"I noted," Clane said, "that, while the weapons were all death-dealing, very few of them were weapons of open antagonism. They were, if I might use the

19

word, surreptitious weapons, things which made no noise, daggers which could be concealed in the hem of a garment, blow guns which shot poisoned darts, silken cords of stranglers, and things of that sort.

"You'll understand, of course," Terry went on, "that I'm acting on the assumption you consider my impressions of Jacob Mandra's character sufficiently important to make my answers in a way obligatory."

The district attorney nodded. "You didn't see Jacob Mandra last night?" he asked.

"No."

"At any time yesterday?"

"No."

"Do you know whether Miss Renton knew him?"

"I have no idea."

"Do you know whether Miss Cynthia Renton knew Mandra?"

"No."

"Did either of the sisters ever mention a portrait of Mandra?"

"A portrait?"

"Yes."

"No," Terry said positively.

"Did you ever discuss Mandra with either of the Renton sisters?"

"No."

"You left Miss Alma at her apartment last night?"

"It was early this morning," Clane corrected, "between one and two, or between one and two-thirty. She invited me in for a cup of tea."

"Do you know whether she saw Jacob Mandra yesterday night or early this morning?"

"I'm sure I couldn't answer that question."

"Which means you won't?"

"Not exactly . . . I couldn't tell what she did when I wasn't with her—naturally. And I'm certain she didn't see him when I *was* with her."

Dixon stared steadily at Terry Clane with thoughtful eyes. There was no trace of a smile on his lips. "It might interest you to know," he said slowly, his voice low, his words evenly spaced, "that Jacob Mandra was murdered sometime shortly before three o'clock this morning. The cause of death was a steel-tipped dart which had been shot into his heart by some force which made no noise and which caught him completely by surprise. In short, Mr. Clane, death was probably brought about by the use of a sleeve gun such as you have just described."

Terry Clane met the district attorney's eyes. His own eyes did not change their expression. His face did not move a muscle. "No," he said, "the information does not interest me."

"I have reason to believe," the district attorney went on, "that a young and beautiful Chinese girl called on Mandra in his apartment sometime after midnight."

"Indeed," Terry muttered politely.

"You know many of the better-class Chinese in San Francisco, do you not?"

"Yes."

"Among them, do you know of some young woman who might have called on Mandra?"

"Your question," Terry pointed out in a tone which was almost a rebuke, "contains its own answer. *No* high-class Chinese girl would have called on Mandra at such an hour."

"I am afraid," Dixon said, watching Terry narrowly, "that you aren't taking a very active interest in the matter, Mr. Clane."

"I have answered all your questions."

"Your attitude, however, has been rather . . . shall we say 'aloof'?"

"I believe you were the one," Clane reminded him with unbending formality, "who suggested that, inasmuch as the interview was official, we could dispense with friendly informalities."

Dixon's expression showed that the shot went home. He was evidently finding Terry's cold formality as disconcerting as the demonstration of what Terry had meant by concentration. "You seem highly unconcerned over a very mysterious murder," he charged.

"Frankly, I can't see that it concerns me in the least."

"It perhaps concerns Miss Renton."

"Why don't you ask your questions of Miss Renton then?"

"Because, unfortunately, she can't be found. Her bed wasn't slept in last night, and she isn't in her apartment this morning. Nor can any of her friends tell me anything about her."

"Perhaps, then," Terry said, "I can clarify the situation somewhat by asking you a few questions. Is there any reason to suspect that Miss Renton is mixed up in the Mandra murder?"

Dixon said, "I don't care to answer that question right now."

"Have you any reason to believe that she called on Mandra last night?"

"That, also, is something I prefer not to answer."

"Why did you think *I* could give you any information of value?"

"Because of your correspondence with Mandra about the sleeve gun."

"And the fact that I was with Miss Renton yesterday evening and early this morning had nothing to do with it?"

"I wouldn't say that," the district attorney said slowly and significantly.

Terry sat back in his chair, regarding the official with the polite interest of one who has nothing further to offer save courteous attention.

Parker Dixon spread his hands in a gesture of dismissal. "That is all," he said. "I had hoped you would be willing to give us more co-operation."

Clane got to his feet. "I take it that where information is concerned you act on the assumption it's more blessed to receive than to give."

This time the smile of District Attorney Dixon's lips was reflected in his eyes, as the sparkle of sunlight on arctic waters is reflected from the side of an iceberg.

"It is," he agreed, "the motto of the office. We had hardly hoped to find in you so apt a pupil, Mr. Clane."

Terry suddenly grinned, the cautious formality of his manner seemed to drop from him, as a cloak slipping to the floor. "Well," he said, "if the catechism is ended, let me suggest that you add that bit about the Russian girl to your report. Have you ever tried to concentrate upon an abstract philosophy, when a wanton little devil with a figure so supple it seemed as though her bones would melt under your touch . . . No, no, don't bother to answer. I can see by your eyes that you haven't."

And Terry Clane, managing to make his exit something of a gesture, stepped into the corridor, leaving behind him a somewhat baffled and very exasperated district attorney.

## 2

TERRY CLANE PAUSED ON THE SIDEWALK in front of the building in which the district attorney had his office, ostensibly to light a cigarette.

Standing there, with the flame of the match held in his cupped hands, he took a deep breath, brought the problem of Mandra's murder to the forefront of his mind, and then, using the methods of concentration he had learned in the Orient, brought his thought to a focal point of white-hot concentration upon that one subject.

The noise of traffic in the street faded in his ears from a roar to a dull muffled sound, then became inaudible. The hurrying forms of pedestrians, the steady stream of motor cars dimmed from his vision, until his eyes saw only the flame of the match and became oblivious of all else.

During the space of time which it took the match to burn to his fingers, Terry Clane concentrated.

Jacob Mandra had been murdered. The district attorney suspected Alma Renton of being somehow implicated in that murder. The crime had been perpetrated with a Chinese sleeve gun, a noiseless weapon. The time of the murder, according to Dixon's statement, had been fixed at around three o'clock in the morning. The investigation of Clane had been instituted at four-thirty. The crime, then, must have been discovered almost immediately after it had been committed, and the district attorney's office had promptly concentrated its attention upon Clane. And, since much of the information in the hands of the district attorney could only have been received by cablegram from the consular office in Hongkong, the investigation must have been vigorously conducted.

Terry had left Alma Renton at sometime around one-thirty in the morning. She had then been at her apartment. So far as he knew, she had intended to retire immediately after his departure. If her bed had not been slept in, she must have left her apartment soon after one-thirty, certainly before three o'clock in the morning, the time Mandra had been murdered. The district attorney had very evidently made a determined attempt to question her before questioning Clane. That he had been unable to do so, had been due entirely to his inability to find her. It was, therefore, reasonable to suppose that all her customary haunts had been searched, and searched in vain. Alma's disappearance was, then, no casual matter. It had been deliberately achieved.

And the district attorney had pressed a button on his desk. Somewhere, that button had actuated a buzzer or bell, two longs and two shorts. Very definitely it was a signal to someone to do something. Yet no one had entered the office in response to that signal. Clane surmised, therefore, the district attorney had used this means to arrange for some operative to shadow him.

Clane did not make the mistake of looking back over his shoulder, nor did he hesitate unduly. In that brief interval, while he was holding flame to his cigarette, his mind sifted the salient facts from the confusion of minor developments with smooth efficiency.

It was, therefore, not strange that the detectives, who followed him, both insisted in their later reports that Terry Clane had not in the least suspected he was being shadowed.

His manner had been that of a citizen going openly about his business, without suspicion—and without guilt. He had paused to light a cigarette. The match had evidently gone out, since he had stood for a second or two holding it in his cupped hands, then had taken another match from his pocket, lit the cigarette, purchased a newspaper, called a taxicab, and been driven directly to his apartment house. Not once had he so much as turned his head to look back. He had left the taxicab standing with the motor running, from which the detectives surmised he had intended to resume his travels.

Five minutes later, an aged Chinese, whom the detectives subsequently ascertained to be Yat T'oy, Clane's servant, had appeared with a suit of clothes over his arm. He had delivered these clothes to the cab driver, whereupon the detectives had investigated and discovered that Clane, when he had stepped from the cab, had given the driver a bill and told him to wait for a suit of clothes to be delivered to his tailor.

Clane had telephoned Yat T'oy from the lobby to bring down the clothes. He, himself, had passed through the lobby to the alley in back of the apartment house, where his own car had been parked. He had entered his automobile and driven away. It had all been done simply, naturally and apparently without any ulterior motive.

Such incidents frequently confuse the best of shadows. The district attorney, studying the reports, noted particularly that Clane had not once turned around to look back. Not entirely without some inner misgivings, he absolved Clane of any attempt to shake the shadows from his trail. He was all the more reluctant to announce his decision to his associates, because the memory of his attempt to surprise information from Terry Clane remained in his mind as a coldly dissatisfying morsel. It was not often that the district attorney encountered a witness so bafflingly formal, so completely poised, so thoroughly unsatisfactory.

Clane, in the meantime, drove his car out Bush Street to Gough, turned right on Gough and stopped his car in front of an apartment house. He took the elevator to the top floor, pressed the button of a studio apartment marked "Vera Matthews."

While he could hear sounds of surreptitious motion from behind the door, his ring remained unanswered.

Clane tapped on the panels, and heard a faint noise such as might have been made by cautious feet tiptoeing over a carpeted floor.

"It's Terry, Alma," he called gently.

The bolt shot back, disclosing an unlined, delicately featured face, carefully groomed hair as lustrously blond as dried wheat stalks reflecting the sunlight, and startled gray eyes. "How did you know I was here?" Alma Renton asked, flinging the door open, then closing it behind him after he entered.

He didn't answer her question at once, but, placing his forefinger under her chin, tilted it up so that he could look into her eyes.

"Worrying too hard," he announced, "which is twice as bad as working too hard."

She laughed nervously and pushed him away. "Stop it, Terry," she said. "You make me feel as though you were stripping the clothes from my mind. How *did* you know I was here?"

"Simple," he told her, smiling.

"No, it *wasn't* simple. No one on earth knew I was here."

His voice held a note of banter as, making the motions of pulling up his sleeves, he said, "Observe, I have nothing in either hand and nothing up my sleeves. Now then, no later than last week you mentioned that Vera was going on a vacation and that you were going to water the plants in her window boxes. This would indicate Vera had left you a key. Therefore, when I learned that you were not in any of your usual haunts, I surmised . . ."

"Oh," she interrupted, "*that* was it, was it?"

He shook his head mournfully. "Magicians should never give their tricks away," he proclaimed. "Now, if I had only pretended it was mind-reading you'd have held me in awe. As it is, I'm just an intruder, and you'll tell me to get out."

"The trouble with you, Terry," she said, "that is, *one* of the troubles with you, is that you never forget anything. And I strongly suspect your habit of facetiousness is a mask which covers your moves toward a very definite objective."

"Wrong," he announced. "Pretending to make moves toward a very definite objective is the mask which covers my facetiousness. What are you doing? Busy?"

She hesitated a moment before saying, "Not unless watering flowers is being busy." But her eyes involuntarily shifted toward a closed door.

Clane snapped open his cigarette case, extended it to her with an elaborately casual manner. "Where'd you go after I left you last night?" he asked.

"To bed, silly. It was after one o'clock. What do you think I am, a sleepwalker?"

Terry shook his head as she accepted a cigarette. "Your natural temperament, Alma, is that of a rather serious young lady with responsibilities. When you become flippant, it's a very definite symptom."

"What do you mean, Terry?"

"Every time you try to conceal something," he said, "you unconsciously try to change your personality and imitate Cynthia's happy-go-lucky attitude."

She frowned thoughtfully. "It's not deception, Terry, it's just rebellion at being the balance wheel of the family. Cynthia never bothers to get a serious thought in her head. She's always getting into scrapes and someone's always getting her out . . . What made you think I was trying to conceal something, Terry?"

She placed one of his cigarettes between her lips. He struck a match, held the flame to the cigarette. As she leaned forward, every detail of her features illuminated by the flame of the match, Terry said, "The district attorney told me your bed hadn't been slept in."

Involuntarily, she jerked backward, then, controlling herself, leaned once more toward the match. She raised her hand to his, the better to guide the flame, and he noticed that the tips of her fingers were cold. "You're joking, Terry," she said.

As he gravely shook his head, she added hastily, "I got up early."

"Around five o'clock?" he asked.

Her face flushed indignantly. Before she could speak, he said, "Don't think I'm unduly curious. I mentioned it because I *think* that's when the district attorney's men investigated. It might be well for you to know—in case you're questioned."

She had now recovered from the surprise. Her acting, he decided, if it was acting, was flawless.

"Terry Clane," she said, her voice showing surprised incredulity, "will you kindly tell me *why* the district attorney should be interested in where *I* slept?"

He puffed complacently at his cigarette and said, "He's a funny chap, the district attorney. Likes to lull you into a false sense of security with a pleasant smile. If he questions you, Alma, remember that an atmosphere of cold, precise formality gets his goat. He's grown to place so much reliance on that disarming smile of his that when it doesn't work it leaves him up in the air."

"He questioned you, Terry?"

"At length."

"What about?"

"About you and about Mandra."

"Mandra?"

"Yes, Jacob Mandra. Know him?"

"No, but I've heard of him—a bail broker, isn't he?"

"Yes. Rather mysterious. Some said he was part Chinese, others that he was a Gypsy. An interesting character, wealthy, and crooked as a corkscrew. He was murdered early this morning—around three o'clock."

"Murdered!"

He nodded.

"Did you know him, Terry?"

"I'd met him. He wanted me to get him a sleeve gun. I had one I could have given him, but I thought I'd look him over first. So I ran up and had tea with him."

"And didn't give him the sleeve gun?"

He grinned at her and said, "Stay with it, Alma, you're doing fine. You and the district attorney think of exactly the same questions."

She walked halfway across the room, to seat herself on the arm of a chair. Her face showed only an expression of puzzled interest, but she seated herself abruptly, as though her quivering knees were glad to be relieved of strain.

"How . . . how was he killed?" she asked.

"With a sleeve gun," Terry said, his voice cheerfully unconcerned.

"Terry!"

He waved his hand airily. "Oh, you don't know the half of it yet, Alma. The district attorney's ominously mysterious. He's full of quick questions and dark hints, and . . . Oh, yes, I nearly forgot the handkerchief."

"What handkerchief?"

"The one with the initial 'R' embroidered in the corner. It has rather a distinctive perfume. The district attorney was quite dramatic about it."

She kept her eyes averted. "Did you identify it?" she asked, and this time her voice sounded thin and strained.

"Certainly *not*," he told her. "There are many elements which enter into the identification of a handkerchief: the size, the material, the mesh, the border, the weave, the . . ."

"Terry, be serious! Was it my handkerchief?"

"The perfume was similar to that used by your sister."

"Cynthia wouldn't know him," Alma said positively.

Terry looked at the ceiling and said casually, "Weren't you wearing a smock when I sounded the buzzer?"

"A flower-watering smock, Terry?"

He nodded.

"Don't be silly."

"There's paint on your fingers."

She stared at her hands.

"Not definite smears," he told her, "just a faint stain as though you'd wiped your hands with a turpentine rag when you heard my ring."

Before she realized what he had in mind, he was striding toward the closed door. She flung herself at him, clutching at his arm.

"No! No! Terry," she screamed. "Don't. Please don't! Stop!"

He twisted the knob of the door just as the weight of her body lurched against him. The opening door threw them both off balance. They staggered into the room.

Daylight filtered through a huge window of ground glass, disclosing a large room, the walls hung with canvases. An easel, standing near the center of the room, supported a canvas across which a black drape had been drawn so that it was totally covered. A palette lay on a table near a stool. A smock had been thrown over the back of a chair.

Terry, the first to recover his balance, eluded her clutching hand, reached for the black drape and pulled it to one side.

The canvas was some three feet in length by two

and one-half in width. From it, a face stared at them in coldly cynical appraisal.

It was a face which, once seen, could never be forgotten. And the treatment skillfully accentuated its individuality.

Against a subdued background, the head dissolved into shadows. The features emerged into highlights, to take definite form. The face was swarthy, its expression a strange combination of sneering cynicism and wistful yearning. The nose was long and slightly curved. The mouth was thin and definitely cruel. The eyes dominated the face. They were a silvery-green in color, and they stood out from the somber canvas with attention-compelling power, as clearly conspicuous as patches of coral water against the shore line of a tropical isle.

Terry Clane appraised the painting with critical eyes.

"A wonderful portrait," he said. "I thought you told me you didn't know him."

She clutched at his arm with one hand; the fingers of her other hand dug into his shoulder. With his eyes still on the painting, Clane said, "It's a clever bit of treatment, Alma. When did you do it?"

She stared at him with hurt, helpless eyes. "Terry, *please*," she pleaded.

"Please what?"

"Please don't."

"Don't what?"

"Don't question me about this."

"So far," he told her, "I've gone to considerable

trouble to co-operate with you. And I'm afraid I'll be put to more trouble to give more co-operation. I don't want to *keep* running around in circles in the dark. I might stub my toe."

She clamped her lips into a tight line of obstinate silence.

"How long have you been here?" he asked.

She shook her head.

"How long have you been here?" he repeated.

She hesitated until the compelling power of his silence dragged an answer from her.

"Since about four o'clock this morning . . . Oh, Terry, please don't make me tell you. You can make me tell you. You know it and I know it. You've always had that power over me. You can make me do anything. I can't keep anything from you and never could. Before you went to China . . . that night . . ." She choked into silence.

"Why not tell me, Alma, and let me help?" he asked tenderly.

"No. No! You mustn't! Terry, for God's sake, keep out of this!"

"But I've already been dragged into it, Alma."

"No, you haven't. You've just been questioned. That doesn't mean a thing. Promise me that you'll take a plane and get out of town."

"That wouldn't get me out of it, Alma," he said. "That would get me into it that much deeper. And I'm not going to run away and leave you to fight this thing alone. Now tell me what it is. Come on, let's have it out. You didn't kill him, did you?"

"Of course not."

"Do you know who did?"

"No," she said swiftly, her tone savage, "of course not . . . Oh, Terry, I need you so d-d-d-damn much. Why is it I can't ever have you when I need you most?"

He opened his arms and she clung to him like a child, clinging to its mother in the dark.

"Alma," he said, "quit trembling and talk to me. Tell me what it's all about, and I'm going to help you."

She was silent for a few moments while her fingers dug into his shoulders, her cheek pressed against the lapel of his coat. Then she pushed herself free and laughed. There was a little catch in her laugh, but her eyes were defiant.

"No, Terry," she said, "you're not going to help me, and that's final."

"But I *am* going to help you."

"And I say you're not."

He drew her to him, and she raised hungry, quivering lips to his; then once more freed herself.

He motioned toward the portrait. "Tell me about this, Alma."

"No."

"Look here, Alma, are you trying to shield George Levering in this thing?"

"Terry, I'm not going to talk with you. I'm not going to say another word."

He stared for several seconds moodily at the picture, then said grimly, "All right, Alma. Perhaps it'll

be better that way. But understand this: I'm going to
see this thing through, and I'm going to help you.
Perhaps it would be better if you didn't tell me *any*
of the facts. If you did, it might tie my hands. But
understand this, Alma, my help is for you, and for
you alone. And if you're trying to shield someone, or
trying to shoulder responsibility which rightly be-
longs to someone else, I'm going to rip the lid off.
I'm not going to let you be made the goat. And that
goes for Levering, Cynthia and everyone else!"

He strode through the door from the studio into
the living room, picked up his hat and pulled it firmly
into place.

"Terry," she called sharply, as his fingers closed
about the knob of the corridor door. "Oh, Terry, if
you only understood. If you *only* knew . . ."

"Don't worry," he interrupted grimly, "you may
not approve of the understanding part, but you'll
have to admit I'll ferret out the facts. And when I do,
whoever's taking you for a ride had better get out
from under."

He slammed the door, leaving her standing there,
watching after him with heart-hungry eyes.

Where San Francisco's Stockton Street emerges
from the north side of the tunnel, it becomes as much
a part of China as though it were directly under the
domination of the Dragon.

Chinese curio stores, offering rare objects of Oriental art, exhibit smartly dressed show windows for the
benefit of tourists. Rubbing elbows with their more

pretentious neighbors, are little shops given over to supplying the demands of the Chinese trade. Here can be found rare drugs from the Orient, sliced deer-horn tips for strength and courage, *gen-ts'en* for the building of blood, if one but refrains from eating any earth-grown vegetable while the blood is building. On the corners are open-air stalls where one may buy Chinese sweet-meats, dried shrimps, and the peculiar, dark brown hemispherical chunks which look like bits of maple sugar but are, in reality, dried abalonies.

Back of the spacious display windows of the front streets are crowded domiciles where Chinese huddle together like swarming bees. When a people have lived for crowded generations in cities where space is at a premium, and have learned to be happy in a sardine-like existence, habit naturally gravitates them into close and odoriferous juxtaposition when left to their own devices.

Here are plain doorways which white men will never open, long flights of stairs leading to corridors where numerous doors give an atmosphere of spacious privacy. But these doors all open into common halls where families dwell in a harmonious congestion impossible for the Western mind to comprehend.

Terry Clane opened an unmarked door and climbed two flights of gloomy stairs flanked by banisters on which countless human hands had left a mahogany-like veneer. He walked to the end of a passage and turned the knob of a door which seemed even more shabby and dirty than those of its neighbors. The door swung on noiseless hinges to disclose yet another

39

closed portal. This one, however, was a massive door of carved teakwood.

Terry pressed a button. From the interior came the sounds of a jangling bell. A moment later a Chinese servant, whose face was as seamed and wrinkled as the outer shell of a dried lychee nut, surveyed him with eyes far too self-controlled to give the faintest flicker of expression.

The man stood to one side, and Clane entered a deep-carpeted hallway, turned sharply to the left, through a doorway, and stepped around a screen.

Chu Kee was too imbued with Oriental superstition to occupy any room in which a door was on a straight line with the window, or in which two doors were directly opposite. And, to make assurance doubly sure, he had even gone so far as to place a folding screen just inside the door.

For it is a well-known fact that those unattached and dishonored spirits known as "Homeless Ghosts," destined to wail through the twilight of after-life, can travel only in straight lines. Such ghosts cannot cross a zigzag bridge, nor can they round the corner of a screen. Moreover, they cannot lift their leaden feet from the floor to climb over a six-inch beam set in a dark corridor.

Chu Kee had a mind sufficiently logical to pay close attention to Occidental arguments illustrating the fallacy of these beliefs; but he was sufficiently steeped in the lore of his race to neglect none of the time-honored precautions.

When Chu Kee saw Terry, he gravely removed the

huge, horn-rimmed spectacles which windowed his eyes and, by so doing, paid Terry the implied compliment of setting aside his years, in acknowledgment of the younger man's wisdom.

Terry clasped his hands in front of him, shook them gently in the Chinese manner of greeting.

"As sunshine warms the dying leaves of Autumn, so you have given new life to my heart," said Chu Kee in Cantonese.

Terry answered in the same language. "It is I who have come to bask in the sunlight of your great wisdom."

Chu Kee gravely indicated the seat which was reserved for the most honored guest. Had Terry conformed to strict Chinese etiquette, regardless of the urgency of his visit, he would have taken time to protest that he was unworthy of such a chair and made a pretense of seating himself in some other, allowing his host the opportunity to make many flattering speeches. But Terry had no time to waste with the intricacies of Chinese etiquette, and so, lest his failure to do so should seem curt, he served tactful notice upon his host by switching to the English language, which enabled him to come at once to the object of his visit without giving offense.

"Where's Sou Ha?" he asked.

Chu Kee tapped a gong. A carved panel slid back in the wall. The wrinkled face of a servant regarded him impassively. Chu Kee breathed the name of his daughter. The panel slid shut. A few moments later, a door opened.

The name of a Chinese daughter represents that which the daughter stands for in the mind of her father. Sou Ha, as nearly as the language of the white man can give it meaning, signifies "Embroidered Halo."

Terry got to his feet as she entered the room, delicate as a flower petal, as freshly tonic as dawn in the mountains. Her eyes, black as wet obsidian, regarded him appraisingly. The lips which smiled at him had been daringly emphasized with lipstick. The long tapering fingers touched his hand in greeting. "Why the official summons? I was only delaying to make myself beautiful."

"Lily-gilder!" he accused. "Painter of roses, would you add to perfection?"

She laughed, and the sound of her laughter was like the tinkling of strips of glass dangling from a Chinese wind lantern.

Without using a word, by the simple dignity of a gesture, Chu Kee asserted the prerogative of his years and dominated the conversation. This moon-faced Chinese, who could blandly mask his thoughts beneath a suave coating of Oriental evasion, could also gear himself to the life of an Occidental business world. His hand, with its long, fat fingers, the nails encased in golden sheaths studded with bits of jade, gestured to chairs. When they were seated, he said to Terry, "Speak, my son."

Picking up his spectacles from the desk, he adjusted them to his eyes, thereby signifying that he too had put aside the niceties of Chinese etiquette.

"You knew Jacob Mandra?" Clane asked.

Embroidered Halo stiffened in her chair for a moment, but as Clane's eyes turned to her, she showed only that courteous interest which one must give a guest, while she waited, as becomes a dutiful daughter, for her father to be the first to speak.

"He is a bail-bond broker," Chu Kee said in an English which had no accent, yet held just the faint suggestion of hissing sibilants.

"I knew him," Sou Ha remarked tonelessly.

"What about him?" Chu Kee asked. "Are you, my son, in the power of this one? I have heard that he is evil."

Terry Clane had spoken of Jacob Mandra in the past tense. The papers had, as yet, said nothing about his death. And Sou Ha herself had used the same tense.

It was as though she realized the trend of his thoughts. "Is he dead, then?" she asked.

"I didn't say so."

"But you asked if we *knew* him."

Terry nodded and said nothing.

Chu Kee's face, as benignly bland as a June moon, was turned politely toward Clane, and Terry knew that, were the Chinese to sit there for hours, his expression would not change by so much as a line. But Sou Ha's eyes were narrowed. Watching her from the corner of his eye, Clane thought her nostrils were slightly dilated.

Terry strove to make his voice highly impersonal. "When I last saw you," he said to Chu Kee, "you mentioned that an increasing amount of opium was finding its way into Chinatown; that no longer were only the very aged men wooing the poppy, but the young men were being taught to embrace a vice toward which they had an hereditary weakness."

Sou Ha said quickly, "That's right, Father. You remember you told Terry that you thought some white man was at the bottom of the thing, and that when his identity was learned our people would deal with him in their own way."

The calmly courteous lines of the placid face remained serenely untroubled as Chu Kee shifted his eyes to his daughter. But in that shifting glance there was a parental rebuke too subtle for the eye of the ordinary Occidental, yet as deadly in its significance as though it had been a blow. He switched back to the Chinese language.

"One of the compensations of life, my daughter," he said smoothly, "is that when the eye of the parent becomes dim and his memory uncertain, he may have dutiful children to lend him the sharp vision of youth and the quickness of perception which is the property only of the very young."

Terry Clane knew better than to turn his eyes toward Sou Ha by even the fraction of an inch. So far as any external evidence was concerned, he saw nothing significant in the remarks of Chu Kee. Pretending to look straight ahead, with all his attention nevertheless focused upon what he could see from the corner of his eye, he observed Sou Ha stiffen into rigid immobility.

"Did you," Clane asked, "ever locate the white man who was back of this opium ring?"

In the pause which followed, the Chinese girl was as a delicate statue carved from old ivory. Terry Clane knew that she would not speak again until given permission to do so.

Chu Kee managed to convey surprise without raising his eyebrows or appreciably changing the tone of his voice. "You mean that this man was Jacob Mandra?" he asked.

"I didn't say that."

"If *you* have any information about the head of the poppy ring, I trust the bonds of friendship between us will loosen your tongue," Chu Kee observed, speaking once more in Chinese.

Clane said slowly, "*I* have no information. I merely asked a question."

"No information whatever?" Chu Kee inquired, and, while his tone was casually courteous, Clane sensed that the answer might somehow be momentous.

"I have no information."

Chu Kee didn't move, but Sou Ha almost imperceptibly settled herself in her chair. It was as though she had expelled a breath she had been holding.

Terry Clane, knowing then that despite the friendship which existed between Chu Kee and himself, the Chinese had thrown up a barrier between them in this matter, and that he would never get any information save such as he might surprise from them, turned his eyes deliberately to Sou Ha.

"Did *you*," he asked, "know anything about this man?"

Under the steady impact of his gaze she became perfectly wooden. The animation faded from her eyes. Her face was a mask. It was as though she had switched off all her animation and left him only a lifeless exterior upon which to gaze.

Terry got to his feet, bowed.

"*If it will set your mind at rest*," he said significantly to Chu Kee, "there is, so far as I know, no evidence connecting Jacob Mandra in any way with anything Chinese, other than the fact that some young and beautiful Chinese woman is said to have called upon him shortly before his death; and that he was killed by a Chinese weapon."

"The wise person," Chu Kee replied, "always seeks to keep his mind at rest. It is a saying of our race that the biggest ships can sail only upon the placid rivers . . . And will you not stay for tea and melon seeds? I have been remiss in my hospitality. More and more, as I live in this Western world, I find my sense of values becoming warped. I sometimes forget that the personal contacts in life are of greater value than the things which are accomplished through those contacts."

Terry Clane shook his clasped hands in grateful refusal of the invitation.

"Time races onward," he said, "and I must keep pace with the sun."

Chu Kee arose. Solemnly, he removed his glasses. Terry Clane bowed once more and backed through the door of the room. It was as he turned to face the teakwood door which led to the shabby corridor, that he heard the rustle of silks behind him and turned to encounter Sou Ha's glittering eyes.

He noted the half-parted redness of her lips, the spots of delicate color which appeared beneath the smooth skin like the waxen texture of a rose petal.

Her hand reached for his arm; the long tapering fingers rested lightly on the sleeve of his coat.

"Tell me," she asked, "do you, then, love her so much?"

"Who?" Terry inquired, his voice showing genuine surprise.

"The Paint Lady," she said.

Terry's quick interest showed in his voice. "What do *you* know of *her?*" he asked.

She stood as though he had struck her. Slowly her lips closed, her face became utterly inanimate.

"Please don't misunderstand me, Embroidered Halo," he pleaded.

She said nothing, but held unseeing eyes focused steadily upon his face.

He bent to kiss her forehead, and might as well have kissed a wooden image.

She was still standing there as he opened the door and slipped into the shabby corridor with its myriad smells.

## 3

IT LACKED TEN MINUTES OF NOON WHEN
Yat T'oy silently intruded upon Terry Clane.

Clane, stretched out in a wicker chair in the solar-
ium, raised the strip of cloth which covered his eyes
against the glare of the sun. Yat T'oy's parchment-
like skin, seamed by innumerable wrinkles, hung
loosely from his cheekbones, but stretched tightly
across his forehead. Age had shrunk his frame until
he was a bare five feet in height, but his glittering
eyes missed nothing.

"What is it, Yat T'oy?" Clane asked.

"The man with sunburnt skin and pale eyes, whose
name tangles my tongue, awaits you," he said in Cantonese. "It is the man who talks always of horses and
money."

"That will be Levering," Clane said in English.
"Tell him to wait for a few minutes. He wouldn't call
at this hour, Yat T'oy, unless he wanted something.
Letting him wait will do him good." And to illustrate
his point, Terry quoted the Chinese proverb that, the
longer meat stews, the more tender it grows.

Yat T'oy did not smile, but a general softening of
the lines of his mouth indicated his understanding.

Terry gave his visitor ten minutes to stew, and then, entering the living room, found Levering pacing the floor in ill-concealed nervousness.

Terry shook hands, indicated a chair, dropped into another chair, thrust out his feet, crossed his ankles, and said, "Would Scotch and soda help you say what you have to say, Levering?"

"I can say it without any help," Levering blurted.

"Go ahead then, say it."

"You were with Alma last night. You took her to the Rayborne's."

"Yes."

"You didn't drive her directly home. You drove her through Chinatown."

"Quite right."

"You left her at about three-thirty," Levering asserted positively, then stared with his pale, speculative eyes at Clane's sprawled figure.

"So what?" Terry drawled.

"I want to know if you went directly to your apartment after you left her."

"Yes," Terry said, smiling, "I went directly to my apartment *after* I left her."

Levering's face showed swift triumph.

"Thanks a lot," he said, "I just wanted to know."

"But," Terry went on smoothly, "I didn't leave her at about three-thirty. I left her sometime shortly after *one*-thirty."

Levering, who had half risen from his chair, gave an exclamation and dropped back to a sitting position.

"You're mistaken, Clane," he said. "It's very easy to be mistaken upon a matter of time. Think back and you'll remember it was around three-thirty. It just happens that it *may* be important."

Clane shook his head.

"Well," Levering suggested, "you could at least *say* it was. You could make your recollection agree with Alma's, couldn't you?"

Clane picked up a striker, tapped a bowl-shaped gong which sent melodious notes throbbing through the apartment. A door opened and Yat T'oy stood in the doorway, his wrinkled countenance impassive, his eyes bright and alert.

"I'm going to have a glass of plain soda. *You'd* better have some Scotch and soda, Levering."

"Very well," Levering agreed sullenly, and waited until the door had closed before he said to Clane, "Why *can't* you make it three-thirty? Why can't you do *that* much for Alma?"

"Because," Terry said, "I wouldn't like to change the story I've told."

Levering missed the significance of the remark.

"You know Alma well enough to know she's on the square. You'd just be backing up her story."

Yat T'oy appeared with a siphon of soda water, a bottle of Scotch, ice cubes, and glasses, placed them upon a coffee table and withdrew. Terry waited until the door had clicked shut and Levering had started mixing a drink.

"I'm afraid," he said to Levering, "that the district attorney had my story taken down in short-hand."

Levering had splashed a generous portion of Scotch over the ice cubes in his glass. He was add-ing charged water from the siphon when the signifi-cance of Terry's remark dawned upon him. His pale eyes widened with consternation.

"The district attorney!" he exclaimed.

Terry nodded.

Levering raised his elbow, gulped down the con-tents of his glass as though feeling in immediate need of a stimulant.

Without giving him a chance to recover his com-posure, Terry went on smoothly, "And, by the way, when you leave here you'll probably be shadowed, so don't go to Alma."

"But *I* don't know where Alma is," Levering blurted, and then pattered out frightened questions: "When did the district attorney grill you? What did you tell him? What makes you think *I'll* be shad-owed?"

"Well," Terry said, staring in amused scrutiny at his visitor, "let's see if we can't deduce what *must* have happened. The district attorney tells me that Alma has disappeared and that her bed wasn't slept in last night. I left her shortly after one-thirty this morning. You drop in to see me and very casually remark that I left her at about three-thirty. Evi-dently you hoped that I wouldn't be quite clear as to the time I had left her. You figured you could make the positive statement that it had been after three-thirty this morning, and that my mind would absorb the suggestion, retain it as a definite impression, and repeat it later. Therefore, Levering, I would say *you* knew of some reason why it would be important to have it appear I'd left her after three o'clock instead of an hour and a half earlier."

Levering jumped to his feet. "That insinuation," he said, "is a dirty crack, and you have no right to make it!"

"To make what insinuation?"

"The one you just made."

"Why not?"

"Oh, I'm not going to argue with you . . . Dammit, Clane, I'm strong for Alma. You know that. I'd lay down my life for her."

"Yes," Terry said, "you're as attached to her as a kid is to Santa Claus at Christmas time. But, tell me, when did *you* last see her?"

"I had a cocktail with her about five o'clock yesterday evening."

"And, if you haven't seen her since, how did you know that it was important to make me believe I'd been with her until three-thirty this morning?"

Levering cleared his throat, started to say something, grabbed for his glass and poured more liquor into it, then said sullenly, "I saw Cynthia."

"When?"

"This morning."

"And what did Cynthia have to say?"

"Cynthia asked me where Alma was last night. I told her she was with you. Cynthia said she thought you'd probably have driven Alma through China-town, since you'd been telling her some stuff about Chinese colors. She thought it'd be a good idea for me to impress it on your mind that you hadn't left Alma until sometime around three-thirty."

"Did she," Terry asked, "say *why* she thought it would be well to establish this fact?"

"No . . . Now suppose you answer my questions. Why's the district attorney interested in what you were doing or what time you left Alma?"

"That," Terry said, "is something that isn't en-tirely clear in my own mind. I think you'd better ask the district attorney."

"In other words, you don't trust me enough to con-fide in me, is that right?"

"In other words, I have nothing to confide."

"Haven't you some inkling?"

"Inklings," Terry said, "are dangerous. Was there anything else you wanted, Levering?"

Levering got to his feet and said savagely, "Oh hell! I know you don't like me. You made that very apparent when I was here with Alma night before last. You think I'm a cross between a gigolo and a sponge. Well, some day you're going to find out how wrong you are."

Having drawn himself up with dignity, he delayed starting toward the door long enough to gulp down the last of his drink. Then, with no word of farewell, he crossed the room, opened the door and slammed it shut behind him. A moment later Terry heard the clang of the elevator door.

Stepping to the window, he stared down the street.

He saw nothing which impressed him as unusual, save a paneled delivery truck which was parked near the curb just behind Levering's flashy sport roadster.

Terry sighed with relief as he saw Levering emerge from the apartment house and cross the sidewalk to his roadster, without being accosted by any official-appearing pedestrians.

Levering's hand was reaching for the ignition switch of his car when a broad-shouldered man jumped from the rear of the paneled delivery truck, and walked with swift purpose to Levering's car. He placed a foot on the running board of the roadster, just as Levering was reaching for the gear shift.

Terry saw Levering's startled motion of apprehensive surprise, as the man pulled back his coat lapel. He saw the man march with slow deliberation around the front of the roadster and climb in beside Levering.

The roadster slid from the curb and turned to the left at the first street intersection.

Terry Clane pressed a buzzer button which summoned Yat T'oy. When he heard the door open and the shuffle of the Chinese servant's feet, he said over his shoulder, his eyes regarding the delivery truck in moody appraisal, "You may remove Levering's glass, Yat T'oy."

# 4

AN HOUR AFTER LEVERING LEFT, CYNTHIA
Renton brought Terry the noon edition of the newspaper containing the account of Mandra's murder.

"Hello, Owl," she called as soon as Yat T'oy had
opened the door. "We're due for a council of war.
What's this about my handkerchief?"

Without waiting for an answer, she came breezing
into the room and inquired, "How about a drink?"

Terry nodded to Yat T'oy.

Cynthia swung about to face the Chinese and said
with a grin, "You savvy Tom Collins?"

Yat T'oy did her the honor of matching her grin.

"*Heap* savvy," he said.

"A little more soda for me," Terry ordered.

"Drinking plain soda, Owl?"

"Oh, I use enough Scotch to give it flavor. This is
an unexpected pleasure."

"Liar," she told him. "You've been staying right
here in this apartment because you expected me,
haven't you?"

"Well," he admitted, "I thought it barely possible
you *might* show up."

"Because of the handkerchief?" she asked.

55

"That and other things."

"What other things?"

His eyes met hers steadily. "A portrait," he said. "A portrait of a dead man."

Her lips, delicate and expressive, turned up just the right amount to register a casual smile, but there was worry in the depths of her hazel eyes. Abruptly, she ceased smiling, and perched herself on the corner of a table, swinging one foot in little nervous circles.

"Oh hell," she said, "I'm not going to keep stalling with *you*. I'm scared. You'll find it out sooner or later, so I might as well admit it now."

"That," he told her, "is better."

Her features showed a faint resemblance to her sister's, but the nose was turned up more than Alma's and her hair was spun copper. She seemed as full of potential motion as a humming bird.

"Come on," Terry urged her, "get over in the chair and sit down. Somehow, I always think of you as being on the move. I don't think I've ever seen you when you weren't in a hurry."

"You sound just like the speed cop on the Bay Shore Route," she said. But she moved over into the chair opposite Terry, crossed her knees, glanced down at her stockings, said, "Not too much, I hope . . . Well, just to be on the safe side . . ." And she pulled her skirt down another inch. "How's this?" she asked. "You see, I've got to learn to hit the pose just right: innocent maiden—shocked at tragedy— seeking information from one-time lawyer . . . No, I like you better when I call you Owl. Since you've been dabbling around in this Chinese stuff you're like a tree full of owls.

"Don't stare at me like that, Terry Clane! Honestly, I'm all cut up over this business, and you make me feel as though you were looking right through my mask of flippancy into what's going on inside. I don't like it, and yet, somehow, at a time like this I *do* like it. I'm depending on it."

"Why the mask, then?"

"I'm darned if I know. It's just because there's a part of me that's too much *me* to be dragged out for everyone to see. So I began by throwing up a screen of wise cracks; and now it's got to be a habit. Go on, Owl, be a nice boy and tell me about the handkerchief."

"The district attorney," he told her, "showed me a handkerchief. It was embroidered with an 'R.' It had rather a distinctive perfume. It was *very* similar to the perfume you use. If I'd known where I could have reached you, I'd have warned you not to come here, but Alma wouldn't answer the telephone at Vera Matthews' place and no one seemed to know where you were. I've ditched shadows once today and made it seem accidental. Twice in a row would be tempting fate."

"Fate being the minions of the law?" she asked.

"As represented by a very cold and suspicious district attorney," he told her. "What do you know of the murder, Cynthia?"

"It's a long story, Owl . . . Why would you have warned me not to come here?"

"Because," he told her, "George Levering was here a little while ago, and when he left a detective drove away with him. I'm mentioning it because I want you to know what to expect. And, by the way, Cynthia, did you suggest that Levering come here to see if he couldn't make me believe I'd been with Alma until three-thirty?"

"Something like that, yes."

"Why?"

"I wanted to keep Alma out of it."

"Why Alma?"

"Oh, I don't know, except that I didn't want her to become involved."

"Any *particular* reason?"

"No," she said definitely, "Alma's out of it. I thought an alibi might help her but *she* doesn't need one."

Yat T'oy opened the door, shuffled in with clinking ice and beaded glasses. Cynthia tasted her drink, smiled at the Chinese and said, "You *heap* savvy Tom Collins, Yat T'oy."

It wasn't until the grinning servant had left the room that the light died from her eyes.

"Tell me, Terry," she asked, "do you think I can take it?"

"It depends," he told her, "on how much you have to take. Can I help?"

"Yes, of course. That's why I came. Will you?"

"My ears," he told her, "are at your service."

She frowned. "That's one of those Oriental things that sound swell until you stop to analyze them," she remarked. "Putting your ears at my service is very polite and very Chinesey, but it isn't like saying 'yes.'"

Terry laughed outright. "After all," he said, "you must make allowances for environment. In Chinese there is no word for 'yes.' Therefore, one expresses its equivalent by various means."

"Terry, is that true? Isn't there any word for 'yes' in Chinese?"

"Not in the general sense that we use it. That is, not in Cantonese dialect. They use '*Hai*' or '*Hai loh*,' meaning 'it is.' But Chinese etiquette generally forbids a short form of affirmative. The so-called Mandarin language has . . . However, you didn't come here to listen to a dissertation on the Chinese language. Tell me, what's on your mind?"

She surveyed him thoughtfully for several seconds and then said, "Terry, I'm about to unburden myself of a serious utterance. I trust it won't besmirch my reputation for perpetual flippancy."

"Go ahead," he invited.

"What you've just told me," she said, "accounts for a lot of the change in you since you've been in China. You're baffling, and darned if I don't believe it's all due to the fact you've forgotten how to say 'yes'!"

"Yes?" he asked mockingly.

"Yes," she said emphatically.

"And you came all the way up here to talk with me about this?" he inquired with exaggerated courtesy.

Her eyes clouded. "I came up here to talk with you about the murder."

"Sparring around, stalling for time isn't going to help any, Cynthia," he said kindly.

She spread out the newspaper. "I don't know how much of the evidence is being held back, but this gives a fairly complete account of the crime. Shall I read it?"

"No. Give me a summary. Never mind the newspaper embroidery, and try to forget that you're you and I'm me. Be coldly efficient."

"Do you want me to be entirely impersonal?" she asked.

"Yes, while you've giving me the facts."

She sighed docilely, raised her thumb and forefinger to her right temple, twisted her hand and made a clicking noise with her tongue against the roof of her mouth.

"Turning off the personality," she explained, in answer to his inquiring eyes. . . . "Don't look at me like that, Owl. Must you see my mind entirely naked?"

"It's the facts that I want unadorned," he explained. "It always helps to have them that way."

"Very well, Owl, prepare your ears, as the Chinese would probably say. It's too bad your stomach isn't big enough so you could sit cross-legged and hold it on your lap . . . No, no, Owl, don't be sore. I'm just fighting a preliminary with myself . . . All right, here we go into the main event.

"Bong! That's the gong."

She sighed, started speaking in a flat, mechanical monotone. "Mandra," she said, "had a gorgeous flat in an apartment building which he owned on the fringe of Chinatown. If you're interested in a floor plan, there's a sketch in the newspaper.

"The main thing is that this flat was really a combination of two big apartments and was arranged so he could have absolute privacy. Sam White, a onetime Negro heavyweight, was Mandra's bodyguard. There was a Japanese cook, a K. Tanigosha. Tanigosha went to bed early. Sam White never went to bed until after Mandra told him to.

"The three rooms where Mandra slept and did his work were separated from the rest of the flat by a locked door. Sam White guarded that locked door. No one could see Mandra except by passing Sam White.

"There was an exit door equipped with a lock which experts claim was practically burglar-proof. Mandra is supposed to have held the only key to that lock. He never admitted visitors through the exit door. But *he* could come and go as he pleased."

Terry, watching her closely, said, "Why all the emphasis on the lay-out of the apartment, Cynthia?"

"Because I think it's important," she said. "Last night Mandra went into his private suite at about eleven o'clock. The newspaper mentions that 'a young woman, whose identity is known to the authorities,' had an appointment with Mandra at eleven-thirty. Sam White says he didn't see this young woman leave.

"At quarter past two," she went on, "a woman with the high collar of a fur coat turned up around her neck so it concealed most of her face, asked Sam White to tell Mandra that a friend of Juanita's wished to see him on important business. According to the newspaper, Sam White saw this woman's eyes and says she's Chinese, and young. He could tell she was an Oriental from her eyes, and her voice sounded more Chinese than Japanese.

"There's a telephone White uses in announcing visitors. He rang Mandra and told him about the girl. Mandra said to send her in. She stayed until two forty-five. That's White's story."

"White saw her leave?" Terry asked.

"Yes."

"And during the time she was in there, where was this woman who had entered at eleven-thirty?"

"That's one of the things the newspaper says is 'unexplained'," she told him, staring at him steadily.

Watching her eyes, he said slowly, "You're telling me now what the *newspaper* has to say?"

"Yes, because the newspaper sets forth all the evidence the authorities have."

"Could Mandra have let this other girl out through the exit door?" Clane asked.

"He could if he'd wanted to," she said, "but the newspaper emphasizes that Mandra never, under any circumstances, used that door for such a purpose. And you must remember that Mandra had three rooms in this inner apartment."

"Now let's get this straight," Clane said, his eyes

fixing her with unwinking scrutiny, "this Chinese girl gave no name?"

"No."

"But said she was a friend of Juanita's?"

"Yes."

"Who's Juanita?"

"That's just it. No one knows."

"How about Sam White, the bodyguard? Does he know?"

"No, he says he doesn't."

"Go on," Terry said, "tell me the rest of it."

Cynthia consulted the newspaper.

"Doing that to refresh your recollection," Terry asked, "or to hide your facial expression?"

She laughed nervously and said, "Both. Don't interrupt me, Owl, let me do it my own way."

"All right, go on."

"At ten minutes to three a tenant in the building went out to get a cup of coffee. He distinctly remembers that this door from Mandra's private rooms to the corridor was closed when he passed it. He came back at five minutes past three. At that time, the door was not only unlocked but partially open. The tenant had never seen this door open. Naturally curious, he looked through, into the room, and saw someone slumped forward over a table. He decided the man was either dead or drunk, and telephoned the police. A radio car arrived shortly afterwards. The body was that of Mandra. He was dead. Sam White, the Negro bodyguard, was still waiting outside the other door to Mandra's rooms."

"White had a key to that door?" Terry asked.

"Yes, he had one key and Mandra had one."

"Who opened the door when the Chinese girl left?"

"The Chinese girl did. It had a spring lock which could be opened from the inside. She opened it and White heard her say, 'Good night, Mr. Mandra.' Then she pulled the door shut behind her and White showed her out."

"That was at two forty-five?"

"Yes."

"Then," Terry said, "if the tenant's statement is correct, Mandra must have been alive and opened that corridor door after she left."

"Yes," Cynthia said dubiously, "*if* the witness is correct in saying it was locked when he went out. But the door *might* have been unlocked, you know, and a current of air *could* have swung it open afterwards. And, of course, it wouldn't have been *impossible* for this Chinese girl to have called good night to a dead man."

"We still haven't accounted for the young woman who entered the apartment at eleven-thirty."

"At two o'clock," Cynthia continued, "an artist who lived in the building met a young woman coming down the stairs to the street. This woman was carrying an oil painting in such a way that it concealed everything except her feet and ankles. Apparently the paint on the canvas was still wet, because she was carrying it holding it by the edges, with the painted part held out straight in front of her. It was a large canvas. The woman found it awkward to handle, so this artist who was coming up the stairs flattened himself against the side of the staircase to leave her plenty of room.

"Because he was an artist, he noticed the canvas particularly. He saw that it was an excellent portrait of Jacob Mandra. As he describes it, the back of the head merged into a dark background, while the face caught the highlights. The eyes dominated the portrait."

"And this was at two o'clock?"

"Yes."

"Then," Terry said slowly, "*if* this was the young woman who had entered Mandra's apartment at eleven-thirty, Mandra *must* have violated his custom and let her out through that corridor door—or else the bodyguard must have been asleep. It's not impossible, you know, for a Negro bodyguard to doze off for forty winks."

She put down the paper to stare at him steadily.

"That's all the evidence the police have," she said slowly. "White swears he was sitting where no one could have left the room without his knowing it."

"So far," he reminded her, "we've been talking about *the newspaper* account of the crime."

She raised her eyes to his. "And I knew *that* was coming," she said.

"Having anticipated the question," he told her, "you have perhaps anticipated the answer?"

She nodded and said, "If you mean trying to think up some lie that'll hold water, I have."

"And what's the best one you've been able to think up, Cynthia?"

"Not a one, Owl. I'm afraid I'll have to stick with the truth."

"Which is . . . ?"

She sucked in her breath, as though about to start a long speech, then slowly exhaled, shook her head, grinned and said, "No good, Owl, you'd better ask questions."

"You knew Mandra?"

"Yes."

"And Alma knew him?"

"No."

He raised his eyebrows in silent interrogation, and she shook her head defiantly and said, "She really *didn't* know him."

"The portrait?" he asked. "Wasn't she the one who painted that?"

"No, I was."

"*You* were?"

She nodded. "I'd been working on it for some time. Last night I went to his place about eleven-thirty. The portrait was finished, save for a few finishing touches. Sam White let me in. I left an hour before Mandra was killed. I'm the woman the artist saw carrying the portrait down the stairs."

"Do the police know you were there?"

"Certainly," she said. "They've been looking for me all day, and I've been hiding out because I was scared. They *had* to know about me, you see. Sam

White knows me and knows what I was doing. And then there's the matter of the handkerchief."

"Yours?" he asked.

"Yes."

"Did you leave it?"

"I guess so."

"Go on," he invited. "Suppose you begin at the beginning and tell me the whole story. Tell me what hold Mandra had on you."

"He fascinated me."

"What hold did he have on you?"

"What makes you think he had a hold?"

"I feel certain he must have."

"It happened a month ago. I was driving while I was tight—not drunk, but I'd been drinking. I hit a man. It wasn't my fault. I can drive just as well after half a dozen cocktails as I can when I'm cold sober, but try and tell that to a judge or a jury.

"Get me straight, Owl, I didn't pull a hit-and-run act—not where it would count—but there was a car not over a hundred yards behind me, and another one coming toward me. This man was wearing dark clothes. Honestly, Owl, I don't know *where* he came from. That man just sprang up out of nowhere and stood in front of me, fascinated by my headlights.

"I wasn't going very fast, but I was moving along at the usual rate of speed. You know, it's one of those places where there's a legal speed of around fifteen miles an hour, and no one ever pays any attention to it. I suppose I was hitting twenty-five or thirty. The car behind me was traveling at about the same clip, and the one that was coming toward me was coming pretty fast. It was foggy and the streets were wet. I could have put on my brakes, but I don't think I could have stopped in time. Honestly, Owl, he was right in front of me. How he got there I don't know. The car that was coming toward me didn't leave me very much room to maneuver, but I swung the wheel to the left as far as I dared, and then flipped it back to the right so I could skid the hind end around him. I thought I was going to miss him, but, all of a sudden, I felt that peculiar quivering jar which comes when you've struck something animate, even if it's just a chicken or a rabbit."

She became silent for a moment, and her eyes showed how unpleasant was the picture her memory conjured up.

"You ran for it?" Terry asked, in a voice which was utterly devoid of expression.

"Of course not," she snapped, "not then. Don't be silly, Owl. But remember, I hadn't used the brakes. I'd tried to dodge. I slammed into the curb and that threw me into a skid. Now, get the picture, Owl. There were three cars on the road—mine, the one that was coming toward me, and the one coming behind me. I went forty or fifty yards before I got my car back in the road, under control and stopped. Then I got out and looked back. The car that had been coming behind me had stopped, and someone was picking the man up. The other car, the one that had been coming toward me, evidently hadn't seen what had happened, and had kept on going. Remember, I'd had two or three cocktails, not enough to make me tight, but enough to give me a breath. And I felt like the devil, Owl. I was frightened—not the deep solemn scare I have now, but the awful wanting-to-run kind of scare you get when someone jumps out at you unexpectedly in the dark ... Oh, *you* wouldn't know what I mean. But, anyway, I was frightened."

"And you ran away?" he asked.

"Now don't be like that, Owl! I got out of my car and ran back. I wanted to do everything I could to help the man. The car that had stopped behind me was a sedan. A man had been driving it, and he was lifting someone into his car when I came up. I said, 'Oh, is he badly hurt? I didn't see him. He jumped out right in front of my headlights.' And, Owl, that man turned around and started to abuse me. He said I was drunk; that I'd been driving too fast and had been driving all over the street. He said he was going to report me to the police for drunken driving. I was furious, but I was too concerned about whether the man was badly hurt to let myself go and get mad. The man who was handling him said he was a doctor himself and that he was going to go directly to his office, which was half a dozen blocks back down the road. He gave me a card with his name and address on it, a Dr. Sedler."

"Do you still have the card?" Terry asked.

"Not the card, but his name's in the telephone directory. I looked it up later."

"Well go on, what happened?"

"This Dr. Sedler climbed into his car and told me to follow him down to his office; that he was going to have me arrested. He spun the car in the middle of the block and started back.

"Now, remember, Owl, he hadn't asked for my name. He hadn't been driving close enough behind me to see the license number on my car, and he hadn't asked to see my driving license or anything. He was a doctor. He was taking the man back to his office, and was going to see that he had immediate medical attention. And he was one of those fanatics who think just because a woman takes a cocktail she's a dissolute character. He'd smelled liquor on my breath, and that was enough for him. He'd have sworn I'd been racing down the street like mad and was dead drunk.

"I walked back to my car and looked it over. There wasn't so much as a dent on it. I didn't think the man could possibly be seriously hurt, and I didn't see any reason why I should go back there and be browbeaten and blackmailed. I was fully covered by insurance, and I decided to wait until I saw how badly the man was hurt before I did one single thing. So I got in my car and drove up to my apartment. I realize now, of course, what I should have done. I *should* have telephoned my own doctor and had him go right out to Dr. Sedler's place and make an independent examination, and I should have had him put me through a sobriety test. But I was just too rattled. You know, Owl, I was frightened and mad and worried, all at the same time."

"So what *did* you do?" he asked.

"I rang up the traffic department and asked them if they had any report of injuries sustained by a man knocked down by a car, and gave them the address where the accident took place. I told them I'd been driving past and thought I'd seen a man knocked down, and of course I gave them a false name and address over the telephone. They looked up their records and said they didn't have any accident reported from that vicinity. So then I felt certain the man had just been stunned, or more probably drunk. So I decided to keep in touch with the traffic department and if the accident was ever reported, I'd go to see the man."

"Then what happened?" Terry asked.

"For a day or two nothing happened. And then Mandra telephoned."

"What did he want?"

"Wanted me to call and see him."

"What did you tell him?"

"I told him to go roll his hoop down some other alley. And then he told me he was a bail-bond broker and that I was implicated in a hit-and-run case."

"What did you do?" he asked.

"Hung onto the telephone receiver until I thought I'd squeeze my finger marks into it. But I managed to laugh into the transmitter and tell him he was crazy."

"But you went to see him."

"Yes."

"Did you pay him money?"

"Not then."

"Did he ask for any?"

"Not directly. He said the man had suffered a spinal injury and any moment a warrant might be issued for my arrest; that I'd better have things all fixed up so I could get a bond just as soon as I was arrested. Otherwise, he said, I'd be thrown in with a lot of disreputable women. I told him I thought that would be swell, that I thought disreputable women were a lot more interesting than reputable ones. So he changed his tune and started telling me about how awful jails were: cold, clammy cells, inadequate sanitary facilities, filthy washbowls. That was what got me, Owl—the dirty washbowls. The man was clever, I tell you, horribly clever!"

"Did he tell you how *he* knew you'd been driving the car?"

"Not in so many words. I gathered some of the police officers stood in with him on those cases where there was a chance to make money on bail bonds. He said the police were making an under-cover investigation. A witness I hadn't seen had got my license number, but he'd got one figure wrong. He'd read the last figure as a seven instead of a one. Mandra had done some fast checking on license numbers and picked me."

"Did he tell you the case might be fixed up?"

"No, *I* asked him to try and fix it up, and I told him I wanted to see the man and see that he had the best possible medical attention."

"Then what?"

"He told me I'd better let him handle that end of

it, that I'd better keep in the background until after he'd seen the witnesses. Then he sent for me again. He thought the case could be squared. I'd given him a couple of thousand to get the best doctors money could buy."

"How about your insurance? Didn't you make a claim?"

"No. Mandra said that I could collect from the insurance company for what I'd paid out after the criminal responsibility business had been fixed up. He said the victim had no heirs and that if he died I was never to disclose my connection with the case. While he lived, I was to get the best doctors money could buy for him. Then after the criminal end had been disposed of, I could have my insurance company make a settlement of damages. But if the man should die, the police would go after me for manslaughter—if they could be sure I was the one who had been driving the car. But Mandra was handling that end of it. You know how those things go—officers give bail brokers tips, and the brokers give them money. Oh, Owl, it was such a mess! If I could have helped the man I'd struck by going to jail, I'd have gone in a minute. But, my gosh, it was his fault. He'd jumped right into my car. If it hadn't been for that fanatical doctor there'd have been nothing to it."

"Did Mandra give you the name of the man who had been hit?"

"Not then. He did later—a William Shield, who lived on Howard Street."

"Did you ever see this man, Shield?"

"Yes. Mandra took me out to see him. He seemed to be suffering a lot. Mandra took me in as a welfare worker. Shield didn't know who I was."

"That was on Howard Street?"

"Yes, it was somewhere in the eighteen-hundred block on the left-hand side of the street."

"Didn't you realize this was all a blackmailing scheme?"

"Not then. Last night I suddenly saw the whole thing. I was furious. I threatened to tell the police and have Mandra arrested."

Terry shook his head slowly. "The police must never know about this," he said.

"No one knows, except you, Owl."

"You didn't let anyone know you were seeing Mandra?"

"Alma knew."

"You told her about it?"

"Not about the hold Mandra had on me. I just told her he liked some of my painting and had arranged to sit for a portrait."

"Go on."

"Mandra fascinated the painter in me. Honestly, Terry, I couldn't get over his face—particularly the eyes. I liked to watch him when he was in a darkened room, his face blending into the background, his eyes reflecting the light. I think he knew it. He was a dramatic devil, alive to all those little things. I wanted to paint him.

"I suppose you know about my art education. It's a family scandal. Some of the Continental instructors were kind enough to say I had more talent than Alma, but I couldn't stand the routine of training. I never *could* stand discipline. I painted things that interested me; things that didn't interest me I didn't want to paint. As a result, I've done half a dozen canvases. They've been bizarre things; I think they've been compelling—but they've been full of technical faults; no one knew it better than I. It's one of the few things Alma and I really quarreled about. She wanted me to develop technique by a carefully planned course of training. I couldn't do it. But I *wanted* to paint Mandra. Something about his face made my fingers itch to get at a paint brush, just as music makes your feet jiggle."

"And you painted him?"

"Yes."

"And then left with the canvas?"

"Yes, when I realized the whole automobile accident business had been a plant, I took the canvas and left."

"Where's the picture now?" Terry asked.

"Alma has it. I brought it to her and asked her to touch up the background for me."

"You didn't go back to Mandra's after you left at two o'clock?"

"Certainly not."

"Mandra was alive when you left?"

"*Very* much alive."

Terry indicated the newspaper. "Who," he asked, "was the last person to see Mandra alive?"

"No one knows," she said, moistening her lips.

Terry regarded her thoughtfully. "Where were you when the Chinese girl called?"

She finished the last of her drink.

"Apparently," she said, speaking very rapidly, "I must have been on my way to Alma's place. I left with the painting at two o'clock and I must have arrived at Alma's around two-twenty or two-thirty."

"And the person who discovered the body at three o'clock found the corridor door unlocked and open?"

"Yes."

"Whom do *you* suspect?" Terry asked suddenly. And his eyes seemed to hold hers by some physical force.

"I . . . er . . . no one, of course."

Terry leaned back in his chair. "You have several men friends," he told her. "For instance, there's Stubby Nash. Stubby, I believe, resents even the purely platonic friendship which I claim with you. How did *he* feel about Mandra?"

"He didn't know anything about Mandra."

"Are you certain?"

Her stare was defiant. "Yes," she said. "And don't kid yourself about *your* friendship being so platonic. You've been studying some goofy stuff about concentration in China. It's changed you a bit on the surface, but only on the surface. Underneath, you're just the same old adventurer! Don't pull that platonic stuff on me!"

He laughed and said, "Tell me some more, Cynthia."

Her eyes regarded him in slow appraisal. There were smoldering fires in their depths.

"Go on," she invited, "try to laugh it off. You can't make it stick. You're a born adventurer, Terry Clane, and you couldn't settle down if your life depended on it, and you're fifty years too young to have a platonic friendship with me."

Terry didn't answer her. Taking his cigarette case from his pocket, he extended it to her.

"Don't you think I should have another drink?" she asked, as she took a cigarette.

He held a match for her, and said, "No, not when you start being primitive, and besides, you've got to keep your mind clear."

"I'm not primitive, only observing. Anyhow, I can think better with two drinks than I can with one."

He studied her with thoughtful, speculative eyes. "You might feel better for an hour, but, after that hour, you'd wish it had been only one drink."

"Good Lord, Owl, will it be more than an hour?"

"That depends. My own interview lasted for about fifteen minutes."

"And you think mine's going to last longer?"

"It may."

"Why, I've nothing to tell!"

Terry puffed on his cigarette. "Which may," he remarked, "make the interview take that much longer."

She laughed nervously, jumped from her chair,

walked to a mirror, gave her lips deft attention with lipstick and fingertip.

"Well," she said, "it's like a cold shower: I may as well take the plunge. I'm leaving you the paper. You can read about it. Wish me luck, will you?"

He walked with her to the elevator. "Luck," he said.

She took inventory of him with grave eyes as she was waiting for the cage. "Some day," she told him, "you're going to forget this business of being a friend of the family and make a pass at me, and when you do . . ."

The elevator cage slid to a stop and the door opened. She stepped inside, turned and caught the expression in his eyes.

"Sort of floored you with that one, didn't I, Owl? Never mind, remember that your Chinese language has no word for 'yes.' That *should* be your margin of safety. But don't . . ."

The elevator door interposed a sliding barrier between them, shutting the last of her words from his ears.

Terry watched her from the window. The light delivery truck was still parked at the curb. A man jumped from it as Cynthia climbed in behind the wheel of her sport convertible. He walked swiftly to the side of Cynthia's car and pulled back the lapel of his coat.

She said something to him. The man shook his head. Cynthia tilted up her chin, made some swift comment, and the man laughed outright.

This much Terry could see. And he also saw that, despite the man's laughter, he seated himself beside Cynthia in the car, and indicated the direction in which she was to drive.

For the space of some ten seconds after the car had purred away from the curb, Terry stood at the window, staring down into the street with unseeing eyes.

# 5

**INSPECTOR JIM MALLOY OF THE HOMICIDE** squad was full of genial good nature.

"Nice place you have here," he said. "Brought the furniture over from China, didn't you?"

"Most of it," Terry admitted.

"Nice apartment. Nice view. Like these odd apartments. Were you ever in Mandra's place?"

"Yes."

"A funny sort of place, wasn't it? Mandra owned the building. All the other apartments in it were cheap dumps. Mandra's place was fixed up like a million dollars. They say that's the way rich Chinese live, shabby outside stuff, luxurious inside fittings. Too bad about the murder. Sorry they bothered you to go to the district attorney's office, but you know how those things go. Mandra was killed with a sleeve gun and his correspondence showed you'd been writing about a sleeve gun. So the D.A. thought you might give him some information."

"No bother at all," Terry replied. "I was glad to do anything I could. How about a Scotch and soda?"

"Never use 'em on duty."

"And this, I take it," Terry asked, smiling, "is a duty call?"

"Well, you might put it that way. You see, we're interested in this sleeve gun business. We can't find out much about them. We thought perhaps you could tell us a little more."

"Are you *certain*," Terry asked, "that the murder was committed with a sleeve gun?"

By way of answer, Malloy took from his pocket a glass test tube, the end of which had been sealed with a strip of adhesive tape on which was written a date, number, and signature. Sealing wax had been affixed to the adhesive tape. Within the glass test tube, a small dart some five and a half inches long rattled against the glass as Malloy handed it over.

Terry studied it carefully. "That," he said, "is undoubtedly Chinese in workmanship. As nearly as I can tell, it's a dart from a sleeve gun. I've never seen such a dart used for any other purpose."

"That's the do-funny that did the job," Malloy asserted. "It was a dead-center shot. Struck him right in the heart. He went out like a light. I wanted to ask you a few questions about sleeve guns. How accurate are they?"

"At very short ranges they're quite accurate. The gun can be fastened to the forearm if desired, then a downward pressure of the arm on a table top or other solid object releases the dart."

"Deadly little things. Could a woman use one?"

"Certainly, if she wore long, loose sleeves."

"Do you have a sleeve gun I can look at?"

"There's one in that case back of you. You may inspect it if you wish."

"Wonder if you'd mind if we borrowed it for a little while. We'd promise to return it in good condition."

Terry approached the glass-covered case, pulled on the knob of the door, then stood motionless.

"What's the matter?" Malloy asked.

Terry took a key from his pocket, unlocked the door, surveyed the empty corner.

"A sleeve gun *was* here," he said, "over in this corner of the shelf. It's gone now."

Malloy's voice was rich with sympathy. "Well, *ain't that too bad!*" he said, pushing forward. "Anything else gone?"

"No."

"How about darts? Did you have some darts with it?"

"Yes, I had three . . . There are two left."

Malloy's big hand reached into the case and picked up the two darts. His tongue clicked against the roof of his mouth, making sounds of audible sympathy.

"That sure *is* too bad," he repeated, "and I know how hard it is to get one of these things, because we've been trying all day to locate one. What do you suppose could have happened to it?"

"I'm sure I don't know," Terry told him, "and if you're intending to compare the two darts with the one in the test tube, there's no need to stall around. From what I can see they appear to be absolutely identical."

"They do, don't they!" Malloy exclaimed in apparent surprise, as though the idea had just occurred to him. He held the test tube in one hand, the two darts in the other. "Same length, same type of workmanship, same sort of metal point, apparently about the same weight. Tell me, Clane, if a man had a sleeve gun tied to his arm and missed the first shot, it would be pretty hard to reload and try again, wouldn't it?"

"Virtually impossible," Clane agreed.

"Therefore, a man only needs one shot. If that does the work, it's plenty. If it doesn't, a whole pocket full of darts wouldn't help. What I'm getting at is that shooting one of these things isn't like using an automatic revolver, where it pays to carry an extra clip of shells."

"It's a one-shot weapon," Clane admitted.

"So, if a man was going to commit a murder he would take only one dart. He wouldn't have any need for the other two."

"Quite correct," Clane conceded, with just a trace of irritation in his voice. "And having committed the murder, if he owned the sleeve gun, he would then restore it to the place from which he had taken it."

"Sure," Malloy said, "sure he would. But he couldn't restore the dart."

"Naturally."

"Therefore, if he was a *smart* man he'd figure it would be better to have both the sleeve gun *and* one dart missing than to just have one dart missing."

Malloy's warm brown eyes were absolutely devoid of guile.

"You weren't by any chance thinking, were you," Clane asked, "that . . . ?"

Malloy interrupted, making those clucking noises with his tongue against the roof of his mouth. "Tkk, tkk . . . don't give it a thought, Clane! Don't give it a thought! We were just talking about what a smart man would do *if* he was committing a murder. But people like you and me don't commit murders. It takes a person with a goofy streak in him to kill a man . . . Unless it's a woman does the job. There's no accounting for what a woman'll do. Emotional, you know. It's sure too bad about your sleeve gun! You haven't loaned it to anyone?"

"No."

"Then it must have been stolen."

"That," Clane said, "would seem a fair inference."

"And by someone who'd have a chance to open the door of that glass case without being caught. Now, how many people have the run of your apartment, Clane? Not that I want to be sticking my nose into your business, I just want to get this thing straight. How many?"

"Very few. I haven't been back from China long enough to make many new friends."

"The Renton woman who paints?"

"She's been here, yes."

"Some Chinese girl, perhaps?"

"Perhaps."

"Now don't get high hat, Clane. That's what the police are for, you know, to recover stolen property. Suppose you give me a description of this gun. Perhaps you could draw a sketch so we'd know more about what we had to hunt for."

Clane picked up a pad of paper, took a pencil and started a rapid sketch. "I described it in detail to the district attorney this morning, but this will give you a little better idea, seeing it in the form of a sketch. It's a tube of bamboo with a powerful spring and rather a peculiar catch. As nearly as I can remember it, this is the way the catch.looks."

Malloy studied the sketch carefully, folded it, slipped it in his pocket, held the two darts in his hand for a moment and then said, "There ought to be some way of identifying these darts of yours so we don't get 'em mixed up with the dart that was used in the murder. Would you mind writing your initials on the wood and then I'll write my initials right after yours."

Without a word, Terry initialed the small wooden shaft of each dart. Inspector Malloy put his own initials after Terry's.

"Say," Malloy remarked, after he had slipped the two darts into an envelope which he took from his pocket, "how about the Chink here . . . you know, your servant? Would he perhaps have borrowed that sleeve gun?"

"Not a chance. I'd trust Yat T'oy with my life."

"Sure, sure," Malloy agreed, "but would you trust him with someone else's life, someone perhaps who was planning to do you some harm?"

"But Mandra wasn't planning to do me any harm."

"Mandra was a funny one," Malloy said meditatively. "I've known him ever since he got his start in the bail-bond business. That's going onto twenty years. You couldn't say just what he *was* planning. He was a queer one. Of course, I shouldn't speak ill of the dead, but I *will* say this: there's lots of people could have had a motive for murdering Jacob Mandra. That man was clever. He knew people's weaknesses. *You* might learn a lot about human nature by figuring people's good points, Clane; Mandra learned what *he* knew by figuring people's bad points; and I don't know but what Mandra knew more than you or me, at that. You see, people have more weak points than good points. A man ain't as good as his strongest point. He's as bad as his weakest point. Well, I'll be moving on. Sorry to have bothered you."

"Not at all," Terry said. "By the way, Inspector, there's a light delivery truck parked downstairs, and whenever anyone leaves my apartment a man steps out of that delivery truck, flashes a badge, and takes that person somewhere."

Inspector Malloy's brown eyes widened. "Is *that* so?" he asked. "Well, now, ain't *that* something!"

"Have you any idea how long it's going to continue?"

"Why, I couldn't say a thing about it," Malloy said. He walked to the window, moving his ponderous bulk on tiptoe, as a hunter stalking his quarry. His forefinger pointed down at the paneled delivery truck.

"Is that the one?" he asked in a hoarse whisper, as

though the truck might become alarmed and rush into flight.

"That's the one."

"Well," Malloy said, "can you beat that!" His eyes radiated sympathy. "You say they nabbed *everyone* who's been here today?"

"Everyone."

"Well now," Malloy said, "I'll have to look into that. Don't you do a thing about that, Mr. Clane. You just leave it to me and I'll find out about it."

He shook hands and left the apartment. After he had descended in the elevator, Terry moved to the window. Malloy emerged from the lobby, but studiously avoided the light delivery truck which remained parked at the curb. Nor did any mysterious person emerge from it to accost him.

Terry summoned Yat T'oy.

"Yat T'oy," he said, speaking in Chinese, "you will ride in a taxicab and perform an errand."

"What is the errand the Master wishes?"

Terry scribbled an address on a piece of paper. "This," he said, "is the address of George Levering, the man with sunburnt skin and pale eyes. Go to this address and ask Mr. Levering if it will be convenient for him to have dinner with your master."

"And the Master does not wish to use the speak-listen wire?" asked Yat T'oy, using the Chinese idiom for telephone.

"The Master does not wish to use the speak-listen wire. And if any men should be watching Levering's apartment, or making a search of the room, you will report to me at once."

Silently Yat T'oy turned and shuffled from the room. Terry Clane telephoned for a cab. When the cab arrived, he watched Yat T'oy leave the door of the apartment house and shuffle across the sidewalk. As the Chinese reached the cab door, a man jumped from the delivery truck, stepped forward, pulled back the lapel of his coat, pushed Yat T'oy into the taxicab, climbed in beside him, and leaned forward to speak to the driver. The cab drove off.

"Well," Terry mused, staring down at the sinister body of the covered truck, "since you boys are acting so smart, I've given you a *real* tough nut to crack."

Thoughtfully, Terry Clane divested himself of his clothes, took a cold shower and a brisk rub. He had just finished knotting his necktie when the telephone rang. A young woman's voice said crisply, "Mr. Clane? Just a moment. Hold the line, please, the district attorney wishes to speak with you."

A second later, Clane heard a metallic click, then the voice of Parker Dixon saying, "I'm sorry to bother you again, Mr. Clane, but if you'll come up here right away I think it will be well worth your while."

Clane hesitated. "It's hardly convenient," he said, "to . . ."

"It's *most* important," Dixon interrupted. "I don't wish to seem insistent, but I know you're anxious to help us clear up this matter, and . . ." He paused, waiting significantly, and Clane said wearily, "Oh, very well, I'll be up."

"Right away?"

"Right away."

Clane summoned a cab, went to the district attorney's office. This time there was no waiting. Five seconds after he entered the outer door, he was being ushered into the district attorney's private office.

Dixon, seated behind the desk, smiled. It was as though he had merely relaxed, and the muscles of his face had automatically turned on the smile. Inspector Jim Malloy, for all of his big bulk, got to his feet with cat-like quickness, and, with hand outstretched in genial welcome, crossed the office.

"Well, well, Mr. Clane!" he exclaimed, grasping Terry's hand and pumping it up and down. "This is an outrage—twice in one day. When the district attorney told me that we needed you, you know what the first thing I said was? I said, 'Now that's just too bad!' But it's one of those things. Come over and sit down . . . No, not that chair, this one here close to the desk. Sit down and be comfortable. I think perhaps we've got some good news for you. You know, the police department takes a lot of kicks, but sometimes we really do good work. Here it was, just an hour ago you were telling me about that sleeve gun being stolen and now . . ."

"I'll handle it, Jim," Parker Dixon interrupted.

Abruptly, with no preliminaries, he shoved a bamboo tube across the desk to Terry Clane and asked, "Is this your sleeve gun?"

And, with that question, the office suddenly became very silent. Terry sensed that the men were holding their breaths as they fastened their eyes upon him.

Slowly, Terry extended his hand to the sleeve gun.

Holding the sleeve gun in his hand, Terry strove to exclude his surroundings from his mind. Inspector Malloy, on one side, and District Attorney Dixon on the other, watching his every move, hoping that they might surprise some expression on his face which would incriminate him, were impediments to his concentration, and he strove to relegate them to his mental background while he focused his mind upon the problem of the sleeve gun.

He felt certain it was his sleeve gun.

Had it been found at the scene of the crime, they would have asked him to identify it on the occasion of his first visit to the office. Had it been discovered upon one of the suspects who had been taken to the office for questioning, they wouldn't have been so keen upon getting an identification of the gun, unless it had perchance been found in the possession of Yat T'oy.

Giving this matter careful thought while he turned the sleeve gun over and over in his fingers as though looking for some mark of identification, Terry decided the probabilities were very much against such a major indiscretion on the part of Yat T'oy.

"Well," the district attorney said, "I think you've looked at it from *every* angle, Mr. Clane."

Terry raised his eyes and smiled. "I was hoping,"

he said, "to find some mark of identification which I could remember, but I can't do it."

"You mean to say you can't identify this gun!"

"Frankly, I can't. I think it's mine, but I wouldn't want to say positively."

"It looks like yours?"

"Yes."

"And your best judgment is that it *is* yours?" Dixon asked, leaning slightly forward.

Terry shook his head. "Of course," he said slowly, "you understand that these things are made by hand. Each one is individual. Observe, for instance, there's a blemish in the wood here, a dark stain here, a little crack here, and the brass end is, as you'll see, not perfectly round. These are all distinguishing marks which identify *this* gun. Yet I can't *remember* them as having been on *my* gun."

"Gee, that's too bad," Malloy said. "I was hoping we could turn it over to you. I'm sure it's yours, and if you could just identify it, we could turn it over, and that'd be all there'd be to it."

"Of course," Terry pointed out, "now that I've handled it, my fingerprints would be on it anyway, but you might have been able to identify it by . . ."

"No," Malloy interrupted, "there weren't *any* fingerprints on it, not a one. It had been wiped clean, and . . ."

The district attorney said sternly, "That's all right, Inspector, *I'll* handle it."

Malloy lapsed into silence. Dixon turned to Clane. "You haven't any idea when, how, or by whom this weapon was taken from your collection, Mr. Clane?"

"No, I haven't. I can't, of course, say whether it did or did not come from my collection."

"I believe the glass door of your curio case was locked when you discovered the sleeve gun was missing?"

"Yes."

"When you tried to open that door Malloy tells me you simply twisted the knob and seemed rather surprised the door didn't open."

"That's true."

"Then you hadn't expected to find the door locked?"

"No."

"Therefore, someone else must have locked it?"

"Of course," Clane pointed out, "memory is a tricky thing at best, and whether that door was locked or unlocked would ordinarily be a matter so trivial . . ."

"No need to apologize," the district attorney interrupted. "We understand the circumstances perfectly. You're giving us your best recollection."

"My best recollection is that the door was unlocked the last time I had occasion to look into the cabinet."

"You carry a key to it on your key ring?"

"Yes."

"Who else has a key to it?"

"Yat T'oy, my servant."

"How long has he been with you?"

"Three years."

"He was with you in China?"

"Yes."

"Has he changed his name since leaving China?"

Clane smiled and said, "If you're referring to the name on his papers, don't think he's traveling under an alias, Yat T'oy is something of a nickname. It means 'Little One'."

"Do you know if he knew Jacob Mandra?"

"No, I would have no way of knowing."

"You didn't take him with you when you went to call on Mandra?"

"No, I would hardly take a servant with me."

"Isn't he more than a servant? Isn't he a friend?"

"In a way, yes."

"And you can't give us any more help with this sleeve gun?"

"I can't positively identify it, if that's what you're referring to."

"That's what I'm referring to."

"No."

"Look here, Clane, you're morally certain that's your gun."

"I *think* it is my gun, yes."

"Then, why not identify it?"

"Because I can't. . . . May I ask where you found it?"

As soon as he had asked the question, Clane realized that it was the question for which these men had been waiting. Dixon slowly pushed back his chair, got to his feet, strode to the overstuffed leather chair which Terry had occupied on the occasion of his first visit, extended a dramatic, rigidly pointing forefinger, and said solemnly, "Mr. Clane, that sleeve gun was discovered about half an hour ago by Inspector Malloy. It had been shoved down between the cushions of this chair."

"You have no means of knowing just *when* it had been inserted in those cushions?" Terry asked.

"It might have been placed there at any time after the murder," Dixon said.

"Am I to understand," Clane asked, "that you feel it's possible *I* might have had the gun in *my* possession when I was calling on you this morning and surreptitiously inserted it in the cushions of the chair?"

"It is quite possible."

"Well," Terry retorted, "I didn't put it there."

"Have you any idea who did?"

"No."

Inspector Malloy exchanged a significant glance with the district attorney. "Very well," Dixon said with cold formality, "that will be all, Mr. Clane. Please don't leave town without first getting permission from me."

"I'm to consider myself in custody?" Clane asked.

"Not at all," Inspector Malloy interposed hastily. "You're a witness, Mr. Clane. And you're in a position to co-operate with us."

"And," the district attorney added dryly, "we want to be assured of your *continued* co-operation, Mr. Clane."

# 6

TERRY STOPPED TWICE ON THE WAY BACK
to his apartment to call the number of Vera Matthews' studio. Neither call was answered. As he left
the second public pay station and returned to his
waiting cab, he said to the driver, "Wait here for a
minute," and settled back against the cushions.

The driver stared at him curiously. "You mean
you want me to wait right here at the curb?"

"Yes."

"Shall I shut off the motor?"

"No."

Terry focused his eyes upon the glittering metal
bracket which held the rear-view mirror in place over
the windshield, and sought to apply the lessons in
concentration he had learned in the Orient.

To his chagrin, he was momentarily unable to
overcome the distraction of his surroundings. The
throbbing vibrations of the cab, the pounding heels
of streaming pedestrians, the raucous blast of horns,
the shrill of traffic whistles, all impinged upon his
consciousness. And, when he sought to focus his mind
into a narrow beam of concentration which he could
turn at will upon the various subjects which he

wished to consider, he found those distractions sufficiently insistent to split his attention into the minor foci which his Oriental teacher had warned him to avoid as a mental plague.

His consciousness jumped unbidden back to the surroundings of the monastery, the forbidding bleak walls, the barren snow-capped mountains in the distance, the rushing cataracts . . . the interior of his cell . . . the monotonous diet of rice and dried fish . . . the little Russian girl whose laughing eyes and red lips haunted his memory with the illusive vagueness of incense smoke wafted by a sudden draft.

Then his thoughts ran through the whole gamut of memories, the treasure of the old city, the journey to the monastery, the bandits, the strange personality of the master: the calmly serene forehead, the steady eyes, the aura of power which clung to him as the misty clouds hung of a morning to the snow-capped mountain peaks. Terry recalled the teachings this man had expounded in the calm monotone of one who relies upon a logic so powerful that he needs no trick of expression to drive his statements home. . . . "The mind is a good servant, but a poor master. Undisciplined, it is like a child who has never been taught obedience. Memory should be the servant of the consciousness. Too often it becomes the master. The undisciplined mind refuses to focus upon any one thing, but splits itself into hundreds of minor foci. These foci are fed by observation and memory, sapping from the reason a part of its latent power, just as irrigation ditches take water from rivers.

Any man past forty, who lives in the environment of modern civilization, has acquired so many parasitic thought foci that he cannot concentrate with more than thirty per cent of his conscious attention. Anxiety over business, the memories of domestic inharmonies are thin trickles of wasted mental energy which sap the power from his mind."

Terry had never been able to penetrate the past of this mysterious Master. Nor had he ever learned the man's age. The man could speak faultless English when he chose, and could converse with equal fluency in several of the Chinese dialects. He apparently had experienced and learned to scorn the environment of civilization. He spent his days, serenely tranquil, in the mountain fastness, teaching such pupils as were sufficiently earnest in their pursuit of knowledge to make the long and difficult pilgrimage to the monastery.

The cab driver shifted in his seat, and surveyed Terry's scowling concentration with apprehensive eyes.

Abruptly, Terry laughed.

"What is it?" the driver asked, his voice showing relief at the sound of Terry's amused, tolerant laughter.

"I just happened to catch sight of my face in the rear-view mirror," Terry explained. "It frightened me."

The cab driver nodded. "It looked sorta like . . . well I didn't know . . . I seen a crazy guy stare that way once . . . No offense, mister!"

"What's your name?" Terry asked.

"Sam Lebowitz."

"Well, Sam," Terry said, "if you ever want to learn to concentrate, one of the first things to remember is that the frowning scowl is *not* a sign of concentration, but an evidence of weakness. True concentration comes with complete physical and mental tranquillity. The face which is twisted into a frown is merely reflecting the futile effort of a mind which is filled with turmoil—if you get what I mean, Sammy, my boy."

The cab driver said, "Jeez, buddy, if you want to go to a doctor . . ."

Terry chuckled and settled back against the cushions. "It must have been that last cocktail," he explained, and was amused to watch the expression of relief which flooded the face of the cab driver. "Just wait here a minute or two longer, Sammy, and give me a chance to collect my faculties."

Lebowitz settled down in the seat, fished a cigarette from his pocket, looked at the clicking meter with satisfaction, and said soothingly, "Just as you say, boss." He was accustomed to taking drunks in his stride.

Terry once more raised his eyes to the rear-view mirror. This time there was no frown on his face. He might have been sleeping with his eyes open, so far as any outward evidence of muscular attention was concerned.

He breathed with steady rhythm, making no effort whatever to concentrate his attention, until he had first gathered all of his mental forces into a pooled reserve of calm concentration. Then—when the mental irritants of marginal consciousness had been blotted from his attention, when he became completely oblivious of the streaming pedestrians, the waiting cab driver, the idling motor—Terry brought up before his mind, in orderly sequence, the things which he wished to consider, with the care of a biologist examining slides under a microscope.

First, he reviewed, in order, the persons who might have possessed themselves of his sleeve gun: Yat T'oy, whose loyalty was unquestioned, but who would have thought little of murdering someone who was trying to harm either Terry or someone dear to him; Levering, whose cunning enmity would stop at nothing; Sou Ha, who would have given her life to have protected him, yet who might have been trapped by some unforeseen development into committing a murder—for Sou Ha, despite her Western veneer, was of the Orient, and her mental processes placed the saving of "face" far above anything else. Had Mandra sought to humiliate Chu Kee, her father, by getting Sou Ha into his power, it was quite possible that the Chinese girl would have gone to Mandra's apartment, ostensibly demure and complacent, but in reality armed with a truly Oriental weapon, and determined to use it.

Then there was Alma Renton, who would have gone to any lengths to have kept her sister, Cynthia, from being called upon to pay the price which life so inexorably exacts from those who would take it too lightly.

Then, lastly, there was Cynthia Renton, a volcano of primitive complexes, an emotional enigma who would no more submit to mental domination than an eagle would permit itself to be caged.

Terry's consciousness, considering each of these five in turn, realized that, in every instance, there were logical grounds for suspicion, and with the calm finality of a logic which is functioning impersonally, knew that he could never possess himself of the answer until he had first learned far more of the background which surrounded the dead bail-bond broker than had so far been contributed by any of the persons with whom he had talked.

As Malloy had so truthfully observed, Mandra had built up his knowledge of character by ferreting out and capitalizing upon human weaknesses, and Mandra's most ingenious application of mental torture had been applied through the leverage of a certain William Shield, a mysterious and shadowy individual who had been an essential part of Mandra's influence over Cynthia.

Clane brought his mind to focus on the manner in which Mandra had obtained his hold upon Cynthia. Cynthia Renton was high-strung, impulsive, and nervous, but she was not a fool, and Mandra had certainly been far too clever to have played her for one.

Moreover, it was improbable that so elaborate a scheme had been worked by the dead broker merely in order to give him a hold over some one woman who had perhaps fascinated him. It was a scheme which demanded a smoothly functioning organization which, once built up, would offer possibilities of continued operation. There must, of course, be some man whose spine had been injured, since Cynthia had been taken to see this man and her own doctors would apparently have been permitted to have made an investigation.

Obviously, a man so seriously injured would hardy be one to go out on the highways and execute extemporaneous acrobatics in front of oncoming motor cars. The fact that a doctor had been so readily available to pick up the "injured" person, leaving the driver of the car in such an advantageous position for guilty flight, spoke of carefully laid plans, and painstaking attention to detail.

Such a scheme would, then, necessitate the co-operation of one of those doctors who practiced in the twilight zone of professional ethics. This doctor would be a point of continuing contact with the victim. There would, therefore, be a man who had suffered a severe spinal injury at some time in his life, a trained tumbler who could mimic the motions of a man struck by a speeding automobile, and a clever, disreputable doctor. The doctor and the tumbler would have been carefully selected because they had, among other things, the cunning intelligence necessary to enable them to mulct their victims. The man with the spinal injury could not have been chosen in advance. He would be some person whom fate had thrown into Mandra's path. Obviously then, he should be the weakest mental link in the chain of deception.

Having decided that such was the case, Terry promptly mapped out a plan of campaign. He leaned forward and told Sam Lebowitz to go to the eighteen-hundred block on Howard Street. Arriving there, he instructed the cabbie to wait for him, and started a tour of exploration. There was a cigar store a few doors from the corner, and Terry, casually purchasing cigarettes, said, "I'm looking for a William Shield."

"Don't know him," the watery-eyed individual behind the counter said as he made change.

"He's a cripple, lives here in the block somewhere."

"Oh, I think I know the chap you mean. Try the rooming house in the middle of the block on the left."

Terry thanked him, stood in the doorway of the tobacco shop long enough to tear open the package and fill his carved ivory cigarette case, while he located the rooming house the man had referred to. He walked to it, entered a musty corridor, and knocked on a door marked, "OFFICE," which opened a scant two inches, to disclose a ribbon-wide view of a big-boned woman with lusterless blond hair, holding a soiled wrapper tightly about her throat with a big flabby hand.

"You have a William Shield here?"

"What do you want with him?"

"I want to see him."

"What about?"

"Business."

"What kind of business?"

"I have some good news for him."

"What sort of good news?"

"I'm afraid I can't tell you Mr. Shield's private affairs."

"Oh you can't, can't you?"

"Is Mr. Shield here?"

"No."

"Where is he?"

"I don't know."

"One of Mr. Shield's investments has turned out rather well," Terry ventured.

"Investments! You mean one of his lottery tickets?"

Terry shrugged his shoulders.

The door opened another inch or two. The woman's glittering eyes surveyed him from head to foot. Suddenly she said, "He ain't here any more. Try the Shamrock Rooms on Third Street."

The door slammed.

Terry's cab took him to the Shamrock Rooms on Third Street, where he learned that William Shield was a cripple who had been there for two weeks and had moved without leaving a forwarding address.

Terry frowned thoughtfully and decided to switch his attack to the doctor, who, Cynthia had said, was listed in the telephone directory. William Shield might change his residence with each case, but Dr. Sedler would, at least, be permanent. He would, however, be of sufficient intelligence to be a dangerous adversary. Any advantage to be gained from Dr. Sedler's accessibility would be more than offset by the cunning intelligence of a medical man who made his living by keeping one jump ahead of legal retribution.

Terry Clane paid off his taxicab in front of a three-storied frame house which had, with the passing years, lost its status as a "palatial residence" and degenerated into a semi-business property. It still maintained its impressive lines, but the cheek-by-jowl proximity of tailoring establishments and delicatessen stores conspired to emphasize the atmosphere of unpainted neglect which surrounded it.

The huge plate glass windows of what had once been a living room now blazoned, in letters which were just a bit too large, the sign "P. C. SEDLER, M.D." There was also a painted metal sign attached to iron uprights which were thrust into the strip of lawn in front of the building.

Terry Clane climbed the short flight of stairs which led to the cemented porch and opened a door marked "Entrance to Doctor's office." A jangling bell in an inner room signaled Terry's passage across the threshold.

The entrance room was a huge affair, with chairs to accommodate patients crowded arm to arm along the wall. There were only two people in the office: two girls who might have been sisters, despite the fact that they sat at opposite corners of the office. They were both young, slender, attractive. Both were holding magazines. Both raised anxious eyes as Clane opened the door, then abruptly shifted their eyes back to the magazines, apparently finding the reading matter of absorbing interest. Clane walked toward the center of the office, stood by the table, and waited. Neither one of the young women looked up.

The door marked "Private" at the end of the office opened to disclose a tall bony man of forty-five, about whose forehead was strapped a circular reflector. He wore a clean white smock with short sleeves, and his bare thin arms and hands were redolent of antiseptic. A cross light on his face emphasized the high cheek-bones, the cat-fish-like mouth, and the bony jaw.

"Dr. Sedler?" Terry asked.

"Yes."

"I'm in a hurry," Terry said, glancing uncertainly at the two young women. "I want to see you at once."

"A professional consultation?" Dr. Sedler inquired in cold, measured tones.

Terry said, "Both yes and no."

"Come in," Dr. Sedler invited.

He stood to one side, and Clane walked the length of the reception room, through the door, and into an office containing tiers of steel filing cases banked against one wall. An open door beyond showed a white-tiled operating room where lights beat down upon a surgeon's operating table. Dr. Sedler jack-knifed himself into a chair in front of the desk, motioned Terry Clane to another chair, and surveyed his visitor with shrewdly calculating eyes.

Clane seated himself and assumed an air of nervousness.

"Go ahead," Dr. Sedler said, "we're alone."

Clane said, "Evidently you don't remember me, Doctor."

The eyes searched his face as Sedler said, "What's the name?"

Terry shook his head and said, "The name won't help you, Doctor. Surely you must remember that night when the man got in front of my headlights. You were coming along behind me, picked him up and brought him here for treatment. You told me to follow you here, but . . . I . . . I . . ."

Dr. Sedler's mouth was a long, thin, straight line, which gave no hint of sympathy. His eyes studied Clane as though seeking to find the most advantageous spot for a surgical incision.

"You were drunk," he said.

Clane shook his head and said, "No, I wasn't drunk."

"I distinctly smelled the odor of liquor on your breath. Don't tell me you weren't drunk, young man. I'm a physician and surgeon. I've followed my profession too long not to recognize intoxication when I see it. You had no business driving a car. You were even too drunk to follow my car, as I instructed. Now you show up and, I presume, want to make a lot of explanations and excuses. I don't care to listen to them."

Terry said contritely, "I wanted to make certain that the man was all right. You see, Doctor, you were wrong about my condition, and after I walked back to my car I looked it over carefully. There wasn't so much as a dent on the fenders. I couldn't possibly have struck this man much of a blow. He showed up right in front of the headlights and stood there. I swerved to try and avoid him. He jumped to one side and I thought he was in the clear, but I felt a jarring impact and looked back to see him rolling over in the street. He must have lost his footing when he tried to jump, and my fender barely grazed his shoulder. He *couldn't* have been seriously injured."

The surgical calm of impersonal appraisal with which the doctor stared at Terry was as effective as though he had openly sneered.

"Not injured, eh?" he said.

"Not seriously. He couldn't have been."

The doctor took a leather key container from his pocket, selected a key, unlocked a drawer in his desk, pulled out three negatives. "Come over here to the light," he said.

Terry stepped over to the light and peered over the doctor's shoulder at the X-rays.

"See those? Those are vertebræ. See this?" indicating a shadowy line with the point of a pencil. "That's a fracture-dislocation. Do you know what that means?"

"You mean it's . . . ?"

"Exactly," Dr. Sedler snapped. "I mean it's a broken back. And you can thank your lucky stars that it wasn't the third cervical; otherwise there would have been an impingement of the phrenic nerve, a complete respiratory paralysis and suffocation due to inability to actuate the motor reflexes of the diaphragm. Young man, you're in a most unenviable position. Your failure to follow me to my office or to report the accident to the police is an additional fact which will militate against you."

"But I'm insured . . ."

"Insurance be damned!" Dr. Sedler interrupted. "I'm not dealing with dollars and cents; I'm dealing with human lives. Do you know what it means for a man to be bedridden all the rest of his life, to have his legs paralyzed, to have to wear his neck in a cushioned brace so he can't turn his head?—to be unable to eat, sleep, relax with any normal enjoyment? You make me sick, talking about insurance! I've given this man medical attention because I picked him up, and became interested in his case. But *you*, young man, have a criminal responsibility. The prognosis is not at all certain. In the event of death, you'll be guilty of manslaughter. In any event, you're a hit-and-run driver, and an intoxicated driver . . . What's your name?"

Terry evaded the question. "Of course, Doctor, I . . ."

"What's your name?"

Terry said slowly, "If you're going to adopt that attitude, Doctor, I don't think I care to disclose my name."

Dr. Sedler's face showed incredulous surprise.

"You have struck down a man while driving while intoxicated; you have failed to show even the human interest in him which a decent human being would have shown an injured dog; and *now* you have the temerity to stand before me and tell me you are not going to give me your name!"

"Exactly," Terry said, getting to his feet with some show of indignation. "I wasn't drunk, and if you'd taken time to make a reasonably thorough examination of me, you'd have known it. You smelled liquor and jumped to the conclusion I was drunk. I'd had one or two cocktails, and that's all. I was able to drive then, just as well as I can now. But you wouldn't listen to me. You started shooting off your face. I didn't think then, and I don't think now, that the man was seriously injured. I don't know just what your racket is, but I propose to find out. Personally, I think that man jumped up in front of my headlights. How do I know that the whole thing isn't a fake? How do I know that it isn't some sort of a frame-up? Those X-rays, for all I know, could be fifty years old!"

Dr. Sedler got to his feet with the calm, deliberate finality of an executioner. He took off his smock, hung it up, put on a coat and hat.

"I have," he said, "just one answer to make to that. I'm going to show you the results of your criminal carelessness. My car's at the curb. We go out this way."

He led the way through the operating room, through a series of treatment rooms, and out a back door. It was growing dark, a fog swirled overhead on the wings of an ocean breeze. A light sedan was parked at the curb. Dr. Sedler jerked the door open, slid in behind the steering wheel, switched on the headlights and ignition. Terry seated himself and jerked the door shut.

Dr. Sedler gave his attention to piloting the car. Terry settled back against the cushions, lighting a cigarette. Sedler turned into a main boulevard, drove rapidly for a dozen blocks, slowed, turned to the left, into a street given over for the most part to dingy one-story business establishments. A glass-enclosed sign bearing the letters "ROOMS," and illuminated by three incandescents, protruded from a somber two-story building which stretched the length of a deep lot. An occasional front and side window showed as an orange-colored oblong. Toward the rear, a row of dull red illumination marked the location of a fire escape. Dr. Sedler slid his car in close to the curb and said, "We get out here. If you wish, you can pose as a doctor. It may help you to realize there's nothing I'm trying to conceal."

He led the way into the rooming house, up a flight of stairs, past a desk on which appeared the painted legend, "Ring for Manager." Dr. Sedler marched down a long, smelly corridor, paused before a door and knocked twice, then, after a moment, twice more. He stood waiting, frowned, and said, "I wonder . . ."

A querulous voice from behind the door called, "Come in. It's unlocked."

Dr. Sedler opened the door.

"I brought a man to see you, Bill," he said.

Terry stepped through the open door and into the room. Dr. Sedler closed the door behind him. The room was cold, cheerless, and drab, furnished with a cheap iron bedstead, painted table, rickety chairs, and faded carpets. An electric light, hanging from a twisted green drop cord, furnished meager illumination. An emaciated form was half reclining in the bed. The face seemed as drably white as the painted metal of the bed. A leather-padded, steel brace, clamped around the man's shoulders, held his head firmly in position.

In the far corner of the room, occupying a straight-backed chair, which had been tilted so that its back was against the wall, a man sat with the heels of his shoes hooked over the rungs of the chair.

He looked up from a movie magazine he had been reading. His eyes showed interest. His jaw, chewing gum with nervous rapidity, hesitated for a second, and then went on with its rapid, mechanical mastication.

Dr. Sedler nodded to the man in bed and said, "Bill, here's a man come to look you over. He thinks he may be able to help you."

The cripple said, in the drab tone of one who has been bedridden for a long time, "Do you suppose he can do anything for me, Doc?"

"Oh, sure," the doctor said cheerfully. "It's just going to take a little time, that's all, Bill."

The man who had been reading the movie magazine pushed the back of his head against the wall, made a quick jerking motion with his neck, and flipped himself forward. He was standing erect before the front legs of the chair hit the floor. Dr. Sedler said, more by way of explanation than introduction, "Fred Stevens, a friend of Bill's, who's acting as nurse. How are you feeling, Bill?"

"Just about the same, Doc. I don't seem to get no better."

"Well, you aren't getting any worse, are you?"

"I *couldn't* get no worse, Doc."

Dr. Sedler pulled the covers up from the foot of the bed, to expose the man's feet, waxy-white and seemingly inanimate. "Let's see you wiggle your toes, Bill."

The face of the man on the bed twisted in a spasm of effort. The feet remained utterly without motion.

"That's fine!" Dr. Sedler exclaimed enthusiastically. "You're getting a little motion there now. Did you see his big toe wiggle, Fred?"

Fred Stevens said mechanically, as though he had been reciting something he had learned by rote, "Yeah, I seen it move, Doc."

The patient said dubiously, "I couldn't *feel* it move."

"Of course not," Sedler assured him. "That will come later."

"When can I walk?"

"Well, I can't tell exactly. That's going to be quite a little while, yet."

"When can I take this steel harness off?" the bedridden man asked, in that same expressionless voice. "I get so tired of having to be in one position all the time. I just feel numb all over. Honestly, Doc, these muscles have got so badly cramped they feel just like my legs—you know, no feeling at all."

"Oh well," Sedler said cheerfully, "you *could* be a lot worse, Bill. You could be dead, you know."

"I wouldn't be so bad if I was dead, Doc. This business of being dead but still being alive is what gets me."

Fred Stevens came forward. He walked with the smooth co-ordination of a restless panther crossing its cage.

"Listen, Doc," he said, vigorously chewing gum, "would you mind stepping in my room for a minute before you go? I've got a pain I want to ask you about."

"Sure, Fred, sure," Dr. Sedler said. "In fact, we'll go in there right now. I just wanted to look in on Bill and see how he was coming along. I'm pleased to see the improvement he's making."

Stevens opened a door which led to another room similar to the one in which Bill lay. Dr. Sedler, following Stevens into that room, said casually to Terry, "Would you mind stepping in here?"

When Terry had joined them, Stevens carefully closed the door and said in a low voice, "I ain't got no pain, Doc. That was just a stall. I want you to tell me about Bill. You know as well as I do those toes didn't move."

"Of course they didn't," Dr. Sedler admitted. "I'm afraid they'll never move, but we've got to keep his mental outlook hopeful."

"How much longer?"

Dr. Sedler shrugged his shoulders.

"Well, listen, Doc. *I've* got to get out and get some work. I can't just stay here twenty-four hours a day. I've used up all the dough I had salted away for a rainy day. Gee, I don't ever get out no more. I'm just here with him all the time. I have to wait on him hand and foot. He can't get up. He can't do nothing."

Dr. Sedler pulled a wallet from his pocket. "I'm hoping we can get some kind of a settlement so we can put him in a hospital where he can have the right kind of attention. Here's some money that'll help carry you over, Fred. Make it last as long as you possibly can. And, above all, don't let Bill think his case is hopeless. We'll go out through your door, Fred."

"Thanks for the dough, Doc. Gee, I hate to take it from you, because I know all you're doing to help Bill. And, after all, it ain't any funeral of yours. But it's just one of those things that can't be helped. I've been buying the eats for both of us, and Bill can't seem to get no nourishment out of slum any more. He has to have real chow—steaks and that stuff."

Dr. Sedler placed a sympathetic hand on Stevens' shoulder. "I know, Fred," he said, "I know. We'll just have to be patient and put up with it a little while longer. I don't think it's going to be very much longer. And remember he needs nourishing food."

"Okay, Doc, anything you say."

Dr. Sedler caught Terry Clane's eye, nodded and said, "Well, we'll be getting on. I've got a couple of calls to make, and it's getting late."

Stevens was folding the bills Dr. Sedler had given him, as the doctor opened the corridor door and, followed by Terry, walked down the long corridor, where the threadbare strip of carpet was so thin that the boards beneath echoed to the pound of their feet. Dr. Sedler said nothing until Terry was once more seated beside him in the automobile. Then he said, "That, my dear young man, is the effect of a moment's careless driving on your part. That's what comes of starting out with one cocktail too many and that pleasant feeling of well-being which comes with a little too much alcohol."

Terry looked thoughtful.

"I'm not going to say a word," Dr. Sedler told him. "I'm not going to try to preach. I'm not going to try to find out who you are. I'm going to drop you at any place you say, and leave the matter entirely to your own conscience. Whenever you get ready to get in touch with me again, you may do so. On the other hand, young man, I'm going to warn you that the police are moving heaven and earth investigating this case. Once they've located you, it'll be too late for you to make any financial adjustments in the hope of securing a lighter punishment. Every day that you allow this man to suffer without doing what you can to compensate him for your criminal carelessness is going to make your ultimate punishment that much more severe. Prompt action *might* accomplish something. There are a couple of European surgeons who have evolved a new operating technique which might effect results."

"Look here," Terry said contritely, "suppose I make a cash settlement. Would you be willing to help me cover up with the police?"

"Certainly not. I wouldn't stultify my profession

by compounding a felony. I *might* be willing to remain strictly neutral."

"What do you mean by that?"

"I wouldn't say anything to the police about your visit. In fact, I'd consider the entire matter as between us, a professional confidence. In other words, your connection with it would be a closed chapter so far as I was concerned. That's the most I could do."

"Thanks," Terry said. "If you don't mind, I think I'll get out here at the boulevard."

Dr. Sedler promptly swung his car in to the curb.

"I'm leaving you," he said, as he reached across and opened the door, "to debate the matter with your own conscience. In the meantime, good night."

As Terry reached the curb and closed the door of the car, Dr. Sedler, without once looking back, slammed the car into gear and shot out into traffic. Terry turned down the boulevard for a block, caught a cruising cab, and, four and a half minutes later, was climbing the creaking stairs of the rooming house and pounding his way down the thinly carpeted corridor. He knocked twice. Then, after a moment, twice more. The thin, toneless voice said, "Come in, the door's unlocked."

Terry opened the door.

The emaciated individual, with his head clamped firmly in the steel brace, was propped up in bed. Fred Stevens, seated in the straight-backed chair, tilted against the wall, his heels hooked over the rungs, looked up from a movie magazine and temporarily ceased chewing gum.

"Hello," Stevens said. "You're back. What do you want? Where's Doc?"

"Yes," Clane remarked, seating himself on the foot of the bed, "I'm back. Doc's gone back to his office for a while. We can just leave him out of it. I wanted to talk with you, Bill."

Stevens let the front legs of the chair drop to the floor. His jaw came forward at a slowly belligerent angle. "Say," he asked, "what's the idea?"

Clane said casually, "Have you boys read about Mandra?"

Stevens' eyes, nervous, glittering, apprehensive, shifted to the eyes of the emaciated man on the bed, and held them for a second or two. For a moment, the silence in the room was intense. Then it was the man on the bed who said, in his thin, quavering voice, "I'll do the talking, Fred. Who's Mandra?"

"A bail-bond broker," Terry said.

"I don't know him. Am I supposed to have read about him?"

Fred Stevens got to his feet and took a stealthy, stalking step toward Terry Clane.

Terry caught Fred Stevens' restless eyes and said, "Hold it, Fred."

The man on the bed said in that same quavering tone, "I'll handle this, Fred. Sit down."

Stevens stood poised for a moment on the balls of his feet, then went back to his chair and resumed the nervous, rapid chewing of his gum.

"What about Mandra?" Shield asked in the querulous voice of an invalid.

"Bumped off," Terry said.

"Want us to bust out crying?" Stevens asked.

"Shut up, Fred," Bill said. "This is my meat."

"Crying wouldn't be such a bad idea, at that," Terry said. "If a man bumped off, owing *me* a lot of money I couldn't collect, I'd shed a few tears myself."

Shield laughed bitterly and said, "Mandra was a millionaire. If he owed anybody money it wouldn't be such a hard job to collect." He moved his white, wasted hand in a sweeping gesture which included the stained furniture, the wavy mirror, the spotted paper on the wall, the thin, cold carpet. "Does that look like a millionaire owed *me* money?"

Terry said calmly, "I don't know how much he was paying you, but it should have been at least half. You were taking all the risk. And half of twenty thousand is ten thousand bucks. And that's only one payment. I think there were a couple of others."

Terry watched the pale, expressionless eyes of Bill Shield. Behind him, he could hear the moistly, snapping sound of gum chewing increase in nervous tempo. Shield said, "Just who are you?"

"The name's Clane."

"A detective?"

"No."

"Reporter?"

"No."

"Lawyer?"

"No."

"What then?"

"A business man."

"You ain't talking business."

"I *could* talk business if I had the proper encouragement," Clane said. "You've got some frozen investments with Mandra. If you try to collect, you'll be thrown in jail, charged with conspiracy, using the mails to defraud, and a lot of that stuff."

Fred Stevens ventured a comment, "You said something about twenty thousand . . ."

"Shut up, Fred," Shield interrupted, "and stay shut up. We don't know what you're talking about, Mr. Clane."

"I'll cite just one case," Terry said. "Take that Renton woman, for instance. Out of the twenty thousand she paid Mandra for a settlement, you should have got at least ten. She paid the money last week. I know of another that paid fifteen thousand."

Terry took a carved ivory cigarette case from his pocket and focused his eyes upon the cigarettes as he snapped it open, so that Shield and Stevens could exchange glances over his head. Terry selected a cigarette, tapped it on the edge of the case, and lit a match.

Stevens got to his feet and said, "Listen, buddy, what the hell are you talking about?"

Shield tried to keep his voice steady, but it quavered with excitement. "She never paid any twenty thousand," he asserted.

"My mistake," Terry muttered politely.

"How do *you* know she paid twenty grand?" Stevens asked.

"We won't argue about it," Terry said, leaning back against the enameled white on the foot of the bed, and blowing out cigarette smoke.

Fred Stevens spoke so rapidly that the words all seemed to run together. "Listen, Billy," he said, "if this guy knows about Mandra, and the Renton case, and Doc Sedler, we ain't doing ourselves any good by keeping our traps closed, and *if* that Renton dame dug up twenty grand, Mandra was either crossing Sedler, or Sedler is crossing us."

Shield, on the bed, said slowly to Terry, "What's your interest in this?"

"I'm a business man."

"So's J. P. Morgan. What's your proposition?"

"I think someone's holding out on you boys. I'd like to handle your interests and I'd want half of what I got."

"Half!" Stevens exploded. "My God, *I'll* say you're a business man!"

"Half a loaf is better than no bread," Terry pointed out.

Stevens said, in an ominous voice, "Yes, but *our* bread box ain't empty. We can collect our own bread."

"You can't if you don't even know where the bread is."

"Well, I can damn soon find out."

Terry's laugh was sarcastic. "Go ahead," he said. "Play the sucker to the bitter end. It should come easy for you. You know what'll happen, don't you? About the time you boys get close to home they'll decide they need a fall-guy, and you'll be elected, Fred. You'll be serving time, and all the bread you'll get will be what they give you in solitary."

Stevens moistened his lips with the tip of his tongue and said belligerently, "Any time they try to make me a fall-guy, I'll drag the whole shebang into . . ."

"Shut up, Fred," Shield shouted in a shrill treble voice. "You talk too damn much!"

"No," Terry said, "you wouldn't drag anyone in, Fred. It'd be handled so it looked as though the tip-off had come from the outside; and you wouldn't squeal. Sedler would tell you to sit tight; that he was going to get a mouthpiece and beat the rap, and you'd fall for it. Sedler would get a shyster who'd keep patting you on the back and telling you it was a cinch, until after the judge had refused your motion for a new trial, and you were safely on your way to the Big House."

Shield's eyes were half-closed slits of glittering concentration.

"Listen, Mister," he said, "we're not doing any more talking."

"Well," Terry said, "how about listening?"

"We're not even listening."

"You speak for yourself, Billy," Stevens said. "*I'm* listening."

"No," Shield said, "we've got too many things to consider, Fred. Now listen, Clane, there's a lawyer by the name of Marker in the Cutler Building. You go and make your proposition to him. Put all your cards on the table, and spread everything out cold turkey."

Clane laughed and said, "You want *me* to be the fall-guy, eh? Nothing doing."

"You can talk to a lawyer all right," Shield told him. "That's what lawyers are for. It isn't going to hurt you to speak your piece to a lawyer. They can't hang anything on you for that."

Fred Stevens said, "Listen, Billy, why cut Marker in on this?"

"Because I'm afraid of this guy."

"If Marker comes in on it, he'll want his," Stevens pointed out. "Let's make this guy a reasonable proposition, and . . ."

"Shut up, Fred. You talk too damn much. You always did talk too damn much. This guy smells like a dick to me. How do we know the Renton woman paid any twenty grand? How do we know it ain't just a stall to get us talking? And if it is, God knows, *you've* said enough already."

Terry's laugh was scornful. "Of course the Renton woman paid twenty grand," he said. "And there were lots of others that paid plenty. And those were only the first payments. Did you think Mandra was making all this play for chicken feed? You certainly weren't simple enough to fall for that bail-bond stall, were you? Take the Renton woman, for instance. She didn't get any release, did she? Of course she didn't. She came down and looked you over and went out frightened stiff. She paid Mandra twenty grand, just to square the thing. And she paid Sedler to see that you had the best medical attention money could buy. And she was going to keep on paying. Sedler told her there were a couple of European surgeons who'd worked out a new technique they could use in your case and . . ."

"Now you *know* this guy's on the up-and-up, Bill," Fred Stevens exclaimed. "You know that's Sedler's line . . ."

"Shut up," Shield half screamed. "Don't you see the play, you damn fool? He's a dick. Sedler brought him in here as a hit-and-run. Remember the knock Doc gave on the door, and this fellow gave the same knock when he came back. Of course he knows all about Sedler's line, because Sedler pulled it on him. Now, *will* you keep your trap closed and let me handle this?"

Stevens hesitated, while he regarded Clane in frowning concentration, then slowly went back to his chair and sat down.

Shield said, "You go see Marker, brother."

"I don't want to see Marker."

"We want you to."

"I'm a sharp-shooter," Terry told him. "If I've got to cut some shyster in on it, it's just no dice. Now, I could talk with you boys and work out a nice little business arrangement. You couldn't cross me and I couldn't cross you, because we'd all be in the same boat. But the minute I go to a lawyer, there's nothing to keep him from . . ."

"You go see Marker," Shield interrupted. "*We* ain't doing any more talking."

"Well, you'll listen, won't you?"

"No, we won't listen."

Terry laughed and said, "You'll have to listen. You . . ."

Stevens got to his feet, approached Clane with a cat-like tread. His hand rested on Clane's shoulder and fingertips dug in as though a vise were slowly tightening.

"Listen, buddy," Stevens said, "I'm for you myself. I think you're on the up-and-up. What you say sounds like sense to me. But what Billy says sounds like more sense. You go talk with Marker. And *you start now!*"

"But," Terry said, "can't you see what a fool you'd be to cut a lawyer in . . ."

The fingertips seemed to push through clothes, skin, and muscle, and indent themselves in the bone. "Up," Stevens said, "and out!"

Terry caught the significance of the growing suspicion in the glinting gray eyes, shrugged his shoulders, got to his feet and said nonchalantly, "Well, you boys take a few days to think it over."

"Listen," Stevens said belligerently, "if you try to cross us . . ."

"Shut up, Fred," Shield warned. "He knows where we stand. Put him out."

Fred Stevens pushed Clane into the corridor.

"Buddy," he said, "walk out of here, don't come back, and don't stick around the neighborhood. If you know what's good for you, you'll go to see Ben

Marker. We've got confidence in him, and you'd better have."

Clane smiled affably. Freed of Stevens' gripping fingers, he started down the corridor, pausing only long enough to say, "Once a sucker, always a sucker. Think it over, Fred."

"You go see Marker," Stevens repeated doggedly, stepped back into the bedroom and slammed the door.

Clane walked swiftly down the corridor, down the stairs and out into the foggy evening. He walked briskly to the boulevard, flagged a cruising cab, drove back to the corner across from the rooming house and said to the cab driver, "Go over there against the curb and wait. Turn your lights off, but keep your motor running. Keep watching me. When I raise my right hand, swing around and pick me up. I'll have a following job for you, and I want to be sure I have a cab ready."

"Okay, buddy," the driver told him, folding the two one-dollar bills Terry handed him, "I'll be on the job."

Terry went back to the corner and waited for the space of three cigarettes, at the end of which time he was rewarded by seeing the door of the rooming house disgorge two figures. His head still clamped by the leather-padded brace, the emaciated form of Bill Shield hobbled along with such adept use of crutches and legs that Fred Stevens, walking with the light, quick stride of a trained athlete, was hard-put to keep up.

They had crossed the intersection, and Terry was

about to signal his cab, when some whimsy of fate caused Stevens to turn his eyes toward the waiting taxi. He said something to the man at his side, placed fingers to his lips, and whistled. When the cab driver ignored the signal, Stevens ran lightly across the intersection and down the side street. Clane stepped apprehensively back into the shadows. He heard the mutter of low-voiced conversation between Stevens and the cab driver, then Stevens ran back across the road to confer with Shield in low, excited tones. Suddenly they both turned and retraced their steps to the rooming house, the pound of Shield's crutches bearing witness to the haste of their retreat.

When the door of the rooming house had closed behind them, Terry crossed over to the cab driver.

"What happened?" he asked.

"The guy wanted to hire me, and I told him I couldn't take him no place because I was engaged. He wanted to know what sort of a stall that was, and what had I been hired for, sitting here with my motor running, and I told him that was my business and not his. So then he asked me if the guy I was working for was a young, well-knit chap, dressed in a gray suit . . . In fact, he went on and described you to a T."

"What did you tell him?" Terry asked.

"I told him Naw, that I was working for an old dame with glasses, but I don't think it did no good. He looked at me like he wanted to bust me, and then he beat it back across the street and he and the crippled guy hobbled back to that rooming house."

"I know," Terry said, "I was watching them." He opened the door, climbed into the car and gave the driver the address of his apartment house.

"You don't want me to do that shadowing job?" the driver asked.

Terry shook his head. The merest whimsy of fate had served to alarm his quarry, sending them back into hiding, from which they would emerge only after adequate reconnoissance.

Terry had, however, sowed the seeds of discontent among the conspirators, seeds which he knew would sooner or later sprout in the soil of mutual suspicion, to bear fruit in the shape of action. It remained to be seen whether he could manage to capitalize upon such action, in the brief time which was at his disposal.

"No," he told the cab driver, "we'll forget the shadowing."

## 7

TERRY CLANE NOTICED WITH SATISFAC-
tion that the light delivery truck was no longer
parked at the curb in front of his apartment. He
found Sou Ha waiting for him in the lobby.

"Been here long?" he asked cautiously.

"Not too long. Why?"

"There were some detectives watching the place,"
he said solicitously.

Her laugh was light-hearted. "Oh," she said, "you
mean the truck which was parked at the curb? I
waited across the street until it drove away."

"How did you know they were detectives?" he
asked.

"I didn't, but I saw the paneled delivery truck
with no signs painted on the sides, and the license
plates weren't those of a dealer, so I thought it would
be best to wait. You see, Oh First Born, I come of a
cautious race."

And she laughed again.

"Yat T'oy back?" he asked.

"No one answered my ring. Where did he go?"

"A man stepped from the delivery truck and took
Yat T'oy with him."

She said, "He'll soon be back."

"Why do you think so?"

"Getting information from Yat T'oy is like trying to squeeze water from a dry sponge," she said.

Terry entered the elevator with her, took her to his apartment, opened the door, switched on the lights and realized almost at once that the place had been thoroughly ransacked. Not that they had been crude about it, but there were little things which Terry saw at once—the stone lions of Peiping had been shifted in their positions on the mantel; the huge bronze incense burner showing the three sacred Chinese symbols, had been turned so that the dragon faced to the north.

Terry gave Sou Ha no sign of what he had seen, but indicated a seat for her and said, "Which will you be—Chinese or American?"

She raised delicately arched eyebrows.

"In other words," he said, "shall I bring you melon seeds and tea, or Scotch and soda?"

"I'll be Chinese," she told him, "and since the Little One is not here I'll make the tea."

Together, they entered the kitchenette. Clane produced a package of *Loong Soo Cha*, the "Dragon-Tongue" tea of China. Gravely, he removed the cover, disclosing individually rolled, unbroken tea leaves tied with silken thread into cigar-shaped bundles.

Terry placed water on the stove, and with the sharp blade of his knife cut the silken cords which held one of the packages together. Sou Ha carefully selected the number of leaves she wished to use. Clane filled two small saucers with dried melon seeds. He fitted Chinese cups into the holes of circular-shaped saucers. When the tea had been made, they returned to the living room.

Sou Ha nibbled at the melon seeds with the skill of a canary. In between nibbles, she sipped at the clear, golden fluid. She said nothing.

Terry Clane matched her silence. He had, after a fashion, learned the Chinese language, but no white man can ever quite master the art of eating dried melon seeds, which must be held edgewise between thumb and forefinger, and cracked by a gentle pressure of the teeth. When the edges have been sprung just far enough apart, the tip of the tongue delicately extracts the meat. The slightest moisture upon the fingertips causes the dried seed to become as elusive as a wet eel. Too much or too little pressure upon the edges is likewise fatal.

Sou Ha watched him with appraising eyes.

"Excellent!" she said, finally breaking the silence.

Clane bowed his head in acknowledgment of the compliment, sipped his tea.

"You've not asked me why I came," she reminded him.

He answered her in Cantonese, saying, "One does not question the reason for the rising sun, but is content to bask in the warmth of its rays."

Abruptly, she pushed away the saucer of melon seeds, crossed her knees and said, "Let's forget the Chinese stuff. It's too tedious. I should have had a highball and been American."

"It isn't too late," he remarked.

"No. The tea has been refreshing. But let's quit beating around the bush."

"Have we been beating around the bush?"

"You know we have."

"Since when?"

"Since this morning when you were talking with my father but watching me. That made me furious. I hated you when you left."

"The district attorney," he told her, "questioned me, trying to find out if I knew the identity of the Chinese girl who had called on Jacob Mandra."

"What did you tell him?"

"Practically nothing."

"And why suspect me?"

"I didn't, particularly."

"You acted like it."

"I was," he informed her, "simply looking for some clew . . . By the way, have you seen Juanita since Mandra's death?"

"No. I had intended to . . ." She broke off abruptly and her eyes, black as pools of ink, moved restlessly, then returned to meet his.

"Was that a trap?" she asked.

He said, "Yes, Sou Ha, it was a trap."

She made no attempt now to conceal her feelings. Tears glistened in her eyes. "Is it necessary, then," she asked, "that you must sacrifice my friendship upon the altar of your love?"

He said slowly, "Don't misunderstand me, Sou Ha. Mandra was killed with *my* sleeve gun. The district attorney now has the weapon. It was found concealed in the cushions of a chair in which *I* had been sitting when I was questioned."

"Bear witness," she said softly, "that I came to you voluntarily. This morning when you sought to surprise information from me, I withheld it. That is the nature of my race. This evening, when you need my friendship, I have brought it to you. *I* was the Chinese girl who went to Jacob Mandra's apartment."

"Why did you go?"

"I went to warn him."

"Of what?"

"I wished to warn him that the opium traffic must cease."

"You knew that he was the head of it?"

"Yes."

"And your father knew?"

"Yes."

"You received the information from your father?" She nodded her head.

"Why did you want to warn him? Did you know him?"

"No," she said simply. "I knew the woman he loved."

He became conscious of the boring interest in her eyes and tried to hold his features so they would show no expression when she should mention the name of that woman. Yet, almost at once he realized the futility of trying to evade those probing eyes which were for the moment so smoothly dark it was impossible to distinguish between pupil and iris.

"No, First Born," she said slowly, "it was *not* the painter woman."

"Who was it?"

"Her name is Juanita. She is a dancer."

"And because of her you warned Mandra?"

"Yes."

"Why didn't you let her warn him?"

"Because I could not find her, and it was necessary to take quick action."

"Was your warning too late?"

"My father did not know of his death until you brought the news this morning."

"What happened when you went there?" he asked.

"I explained to the negro that I must see him at once; that I came because I was a friend of Juanita. He opened the door and I entered."

"What time was this?"

Her sudden lapse into Chinese warned him that the answer to his question was, for some hidden reason, taxing her thought process so that speech became for the moment a mechanical reflex of thought. "At three characters past the second hour of the Ox," she said, in Cantonese.

"When did you leave?"

"I was there for fifteen or twenty minutes."

"What happened?"

"I found Mr. Mandra a very wise man. I talked with him and he listened. He knew who I was. He had heard Juanita speak of me."

"Can you take me to this Juanita?" he asked.

She brushed the question aside. "While Mr. Mandra talked with me, he held in his hands a sleeve gun. He asked me if I knew of some Chinese artisan who could make a duplicate of the gun so cunningly that the imitation could not be told from the original. When I took the sleeve gun in my hands to inspect it, a current of air blew one of the doors partially open. Mandra went to the door and closed it, but not before I had seen that which was within the room."

"What was it?"

"The painter woman was lying asleep upon a couch."

"You mean Alma or Cynthia?"

"It is the one with the hazel eyes and the up-turned nose, with whom you had a Chinese dinner in the Blue Dragon. Her hair is the color of copper clouds at sunset."

"That was Cynthia," Terry said, "go on."

"Mr. Mandra listened to me courteously. Before I left, he promised me that he would withdraw from the opium business. There was that about him which I liked. He was strong. He was dishonest, and he was cruel. But he did not lie."

"Sou Ha," he said, "it is important that I see this woman, Juanita, and talk with her."

Her eyes showed the pain in her soul.

"Would you," she asked, "do as much for me as you do for this painter woman?"

He crossed to her side and said, "Perhaps, Em-

134

broidered Halo, that which I am doing is as much for you as for the painter woman."

She raised her face in silent interrogation.

"When the district attorney hears *your* story," Terry explained, "as sooner or later he must hear it, he will realize that there were two people who last saw Mandra alive. One was an American and one a Chinese. Mandra was killed with a Chinese weapon."

"You mean," she asked, "that he must have been killed either by your painter woman or by me?"

"I am talking about what the district attorney will think."

Her face was utterly inscrutable. "Suppose that I *did* kill him," she remarked tonelessly, "and the only way I could save your painter woman from being convicted of that murder was by coming forward and sacrificing myself? Would you ask me to do that, First Born?"

He stared at her intently.

"Tell me," she said with sudden savage insistence.

"Why do you ask me that question?" he countered.

"A mother," she said, "might scar her soul to save her child's doll, knowing that it was but a toy, yet knowing also that it was loved by her child."

He passed it off with a laugh, saying, "But I am not a child, you are not a mother, and the painter woman is not a doll. Come, let us start."

Without a word, she walked to the mirror, adjusted her hat, took a compact from her purse, touched up her cheeks, and applied lipstick with the tip of a deft finger. During all this time she made no comment. When she had quite finished, she turned to him and said, "I am ready."

They went in Terry's car. Sou Ha guided the way into that maze of nondescript streets which lie to the north and west of San Francisco's Chinatown.

"Turn to the right," she said, "and stop at the curb."

Clane spun the steering wheel, braked the car to a stop. Sou Ha opened the door and jumped to the sidewalk before he had switched off the lights and ignition. When he joined her, she slipped her hand possessively through his arm and said, "Remember that on this occasion you are *my* friend, and only my friend."

They climbed two flights of narrow stairs. Smells of garlic and sour wine assailed their nostrils. Odors of Spanish and Italian cooking clung to the corridors like mist to tule-patches. They turned to the right at the head of the stairs on the second floor and walked down a dimly lit hallway. The apartment indicated by Sou Ha was at the back of the house. Her fingers tapped gently on the door.

Almost instantly it was opened.

Terry Clane gazed into eyes which thinly concealed hot emotions, as the crust of cooling lava still holds a reddish warning of that which lies beneath. She was young, he saw, well-formed, dusky of skin, black of hair. She might have been a Gypsy, or perhaps part Spanish or Mexican. She showed no surprise. Her eyes flitted from Sou Ha to him, back to Sou Ha.

"My friend," Sou Ha explained. "I call him 'Sin Sahng,' which is Chinese for 'First Born,' and is applied to teachers. And this," she said to Clane, "is Juanita . . .'"

"Mandra," the other interrupted, as Sou Ha hesitated for a moment.

Sou Ha asked a question with her eyes.

"We were married," the woman said, flinging out the words defiantly, "secretly married. There is no longer reason for concealment. I now take my rightful name."

Terry bowed acknowledgment of the introduction, and his bow was completely wasted. Juanita didn't so much as glance in his direction. Her eyes, hot with hidden emotion, were fixed upon the Chinese girl.

"I knew," Sou Ha said simply, "that you loved him. After all, does anything else matter? The fire started by a match is no hotter than that which starts from a bolt of lightning."

"Come in," Juanita invited.

They entered the softly lit apartment. The hot vitality of this dusky-skinned young woman filled it, as the vibrations of a temple gong fill a room with a resonant sound, searchingly insistent, but not loud.

The room held too many objects, yet each one of those objects in some way reflected the individuality of the woman who had selected them. A floor light filtered diffused rays through rose silk. Outside, the cold fingers of drifting fog beaded the windows. The mournful cadences of fog signals from the bay sounded a soul-chilling chorus of drab monotony. An electric heater in a corner of the room threw a warm splotch of orange light along the floor.

Juanita indicated chairs.

Sou Ha deftly crossed the room so that she seated herself in the chair which Terry Clane had been about to take. Nettled, yet trying to keep from appearing awkward, he crossed to another chair, started to lean back against the cushions and suddenly stiffened to startled attention.

In the corner, directly in front of his eyes, standing behind a table upon which were stacked newspapers, ornaments, half-filled ash trays, and a cigarette case, was an unframed canvas some three feet long by two and a half feet wide.

The dark background of the portrait matched perfectly with the deep shadows which were behind it. It was all but impossible to tell where the somber background of the canvas melted into the shadows of the corner.

The face of Jacob Mandra stared with mocking insolence from the canvas. The dominant feature of the painting was the eyes, eyes which held at once an expression of cynical distrust and a yearning desire for that which the very cynicism of the man had thrust from his life. In some unexplained manner, then, this portrait must have passed from Alma Renton to the woman who claimed to be Mandra's widow.

"You will," Sou Ha was calmly asking, "claim your rights as his widow?"

Juanita's eyes were sullenly defiant. "I have taken the bitter," she said, "and now I will have the sweet."

"There will, perhaps, be a lawsuit?" Sou Ha asked.

"With whom? He left no relatives and no will."

"You are certain—about the relatives?"

"Yes. He had many mistresses, but only one wife." She beat her chest with a passionate palm. Her voice rose as she half-screamed defiantly, "You hear me, Sou Ha? He had but one wife!"

Sou Ha, without seeming to shift her eyes, managed to glance significantly at Terry Clane.

"Many mistresses?" she inquired.

"Many mistresses. There was the rich woman who came to see him twice a week, painting his picture. Bah! There was the cashier in the restaurant; the blond usherette of the movie theater. He didn't fool me. I knew them all, from the young woman whose father's chauffeur drove her from Communist meetings to the arms of my Jacob, down to the cigarette girl in the night club. He hypnotized women. He mocked them, laughed at their weaknesses—and he *married* me!"

She faced Sou Ha and said, speaking so rapidly the words rattled in a fierce crescendo upon the ear drum: "Do you know what attracted women to him? It was because he was lonely, and after they had given themselves to him he remained more lonely than ever. They were fascinated by this, as a bird is fascinated by a snake. The vanity of woman makes her feel that the spell of masculine loneliness must dissolve in the warmth of her favors. They came to him. He did not go to them.

"At first I was no different to him than the rest. But I am different now. I *was* his wife! I *am* his widow! Let the mistresses come into court. Let them fight me! Now there will be no more slipping up the back stairs while a liveried chauffeur waits in front. Now there will be no excuses of portrait painting. Now they will have to come out in the open and fight!"

Sou Ha did not nod; only her eyes showed she had heard. "Who killed him?" she asked.

Sheer surprise showed for a moment on Juanita's face. "Why, I thought you knew. It was the mistress who painted his picture!" She spat out the words with a venom which surcharged the air with hatred.

Sou Ha arose slowly. "Perhaps it is fitting to leave you alone with your grief."

Juanita laughed bitterly.

"My grief. . . . He would have broken my heart had he lived. He was going to divorce me! I am like a moth when the light is snuffed out. Had it not happened, I would have burnt off my wings. But I loved him! I alone *really* loved him, because I alone *really* understood him. It is the nature of my race to understand those whom we love. . . . My race you ask? Ha! No one knows it. There are children who have no fathers. I am not only fatherless, but motherless. I alone know my race, just as Jacob alone knew his."

She sighed, went on in a lower voice. "It was nice

of you to come, but I can't talk calmly. I had a lover once who had his arm shot away in battle. He told me that when he looked down and saw that his arm was gone, he felt no pain. He was a fool, this lover. He told me of his war experiences, in the moonlight, when words could have been employed to better advantage. Perhaps it was because I was very young and very angry with him for this talk that what he said made such an impression upon me. I can never forget it. And now I am like that: my lover is gone and the pain is too great for me to feel. Later on I will feel the pain, and then I will throw myself through that window.

"Do I shock you, my friend? Do I shock this man who is with you? I am not sorry. You came to see me. I did not invite you. I am glad that you came, but I will not suppress myself. I have never done so, and I will not begin now. Woman was made for emotion. I know *your* race pretends it is not so. You talk of learning and say nothing of emotion, yet beneath your veneer you bubble and boil like water in a covered pot."

Sou Ha caught Terry's eye and nodded. In the doorway she gave Juanita her hand. "Good by," she said.

Juanita flung out both arms and crushed the Chinese girl to her, then stepped back and tossed her head in a gesture of abandon.

"Come to see me again," she said, "and if the window is smashed, look for me in the yard below!"

The slamming door punctuated her farewell.

Sou Ha turned to Terry Clane. "You saw the portrait?" she asked, in a low half-whisper.

Somberly, Terry Clane nodded.

# 8

TERRY CLANE TURNED HIS CAR INTO
Grand Avenue and slowed to a scant ten miles an
hour. Sou Ha, seated at his side, stared straight
through the windshield with expressionless eyes. She
had said no word since leaving Juanita Mandra's
apartment.

Seeking to fit the events of the last hour into their
proper place in the pattern of things, Terry was
grateful for her silence. The Chinese, he knew, were
like that. She had made her point and she was finished. Where a girl of his own race would have in-
dulged in a chatter of speculation, or confronted him
with a barrage of questions, Sou Ha would take ref-
uge in the sanctity of her own thoughts, and leave
him to do the same.

Ahead of them lay the weird intermarriage of the
Occident and the Orient, which is San Francisco's
Chinatown. Neon signs blazoned Chinese characters
in a crimson glare which turned the overhanging fog
bank into wine. Plate glass show windows, brilliantly
lighted with electricity, displayed delicate embroideries which had been sewed by the flickering flames
of peanut oil-lamps.

Terry slowed his car to a stop in front of one of these lighted windows. His eyes stared moodily at the silken display.

Sou Ha's voice was soft in his ear. "You are thinking," she asked, "of the painter woman?"

He shook his head without shifting his eyes and said moodily, "To tell you the truth, Embroidered Halo, I was thinking of the topsy-turvy world in which we live. The women who go blind after a few years because they must work such long hours by poor light, making these embroideries which are sold to people who are too lazy to darn a pair of stockings."

"It is the law of life," she said with the finality of a fatalist.

Terry Clane said savagely, "It is *not* the law of life. It is the law of man. It's a topsy-turvy scheme of things which has been built by piling error on error, one mistake at a time, until the completed pattern shows it's lack of logic, yet is all so inextricably mingled, one mistake flowing so easily from another, that it is impossible to tell where the trouble lies. Mark you, Sou Ha, I myself have seen a Chinese woman seated on a Hongkong sidewalk long after midnight, sewing these embroideries by the weak light of a street lamp. Two daughters lay beside her, stretched on the hard cement. One was a girl eleven or twelve years old, the other about nine. Such light as came from the street lamp was weak and reddish. The woman was bent forward, straining her eyes to see the tiny stitches she was taking. She stopped from time to time, to wipe away the water which ran from her smarting eyes, using the germ-laden cloth of her coat sleeve. Within a few months she would be blind. Perhaps that bit of embroidery, which she sold for a few cents, is one of the pieces displayed in the luxury of that lighted window."

Sou Ha's warm fingers squeezed the back of Terry Clane's hand. "I am glad, First Born, that you think of these things. But you cannot help the woman in China, and you can help your painter woman. Good night."

She opened the door of the car, slid lightly to the pavement and was gone, almost instantly swallowed in the shuffling stream of humanity which flowed ceaselessly along the narrow sidewalks.

For a long moment Terry sat there, motionless, the slip-slop of Chinese shoes, the clanging bells of the cable cars, the sing-song intonations of Cantonese conversation audible above the purring sound of his idling motor. Then he shifted gears and depressed the foot throttle.

He took precautions to make certain he was not followed, and went at once to the studio of Vera Matthews.

Alma Renton opened the door only after he had knocked twice and gently called her name. Her face was gray with fatigue. She had sought to discount this by the generous application of make-up. But an aura of weariness clinging to her skin made mockery of the crimson lips and rouged cheeks.

With a glad little cry she came to his arms and snuggled close to him.

"Oh, Terry, I'm so glad you're back! The minutes have been fighting me, and have me licked."

"You didn't answer the telephone," he said.

"I was afraid to, Terry. If it had been someone calling Vera, I didn't want to explain who I was, and why I was here; and if it had been someone calling me . . . I couldn't trust myself to talk. I mustn't see anyone until . . ."

"Until what?" he asked, as she hesitated.

"Until Cynthia comes."

"Cynthia," he said, "went to the district attorney's office."

"I know," she told him. "Sit down, Terry. There's Scotch, soda and ice on the table. Help yourself, but don't give me any."

"It might do you good," he told her.

"No," she said, "I tried it. I didn't get any lift out of it."

"That bad?" he asked, stretching out in a chair near the taboret, and dropping ice cubes into a glass.

She rested one hip on the flat arm of a Mission-style chair and watched him pour a small amount of amber liquid over the ice cubes, then hiss charged water from the siphon.

"You don't go much for liquor, do you, Terry?"

He raised his eyebrows in silent interrogation.

"You're using that drink just as a prop," she said, "a stage setting you can have to fall back on. You have something important to say, and you don't want me to realize how important it is. So you'll sit and toy with that drink, slide the tips of your fingers up and down the moist glass, and make comments which are apparently casual, yet are filled with deadly importance."

"Know me that well, Alma?" he asked.

"A woman always knows the man she loves."

"No," he said slowly, "she doesn't. That's the hell of it." He would have said something more, but she silenced him with a gesture and said, "That's something else we've got to settle, Terry, but we mustn't do it now. We *won't* do it now, so you needn't be frightened."

"Frightened?" he asked, frowning and sliding the tips of his fingers up and down the moist glass. He checked himself abruptly as he realized what he was doing, and saw the amusement in her watching eyes.

She laughed throatily and said, "I'll discuss that with you later. Terry, do you suppose anything has gone wrong with Cynthia? They've been holding her down there for hours."

"You know what time she went there?" he asked, making the question very casual indeed.

"Approximately, yes," she admitted.

"In other words, Alma, you and Cynthia knew that my apartment was being watched. When you were ready for Cynthia to tell her story, you had her come to call on me, knowing that she'd be picked up."

Alma tried to keep her face expressionless, but Clane didn't even bother to look at her. He stared moodily at the bubbles which shot upward from the drink in his glass, and went on in a low monotone, "Obviously, Cynthia had been carefully rehearsed in the story she was to tell the police. She left Mandra's apartment at two o'clock in the morning, carrying Mandra's portrait. In order to substantiate her alibi she'll have to produce the portrait. Now why didn't she leave it where she *could* produce it?"

"But she did," Alma said, puzzled.

"Where?"

"It's at my apartment."

"At *your* apartment?"

"Yes."

"You're certain?"

"Of course I'm certain."

"How did it get there?"

"By taxicab, silly."

"In which case the police will trace it back to you here."

"No. They won't trace it, Terry. They can't."

"Why can't they?"

"Because it wasn't sent directly."

Terry kept his eyes fastened on his drink. His voice was noncommittal. "Tell me about it," he said.

"There's nothing to tell. The portrait is at my apartment. That is, it *was* at my apartment. I presume it's at police headquarters now. You see, Cynthia will tell her story, and the police will pick up the portrait. Then they'll check her alibi. A young artist saw her on the stairs. They'll ask him to identify her. If he's truthful, he'll do it—and that will be all there'll be to it. Mandra was killed at around three o'clock. Cynthia left there at two o'clock."

"How does Levering figure in it?" Terry asked abruptly.

"He doesn't—except as a friend."

"What makes you so certain the police won't trace the portrait to you here?"

"Because they can't."

"What reason will Cynthia give for having the portrait at your apartment?"

"The best in the world. She took the portrait to me because she was proud of it. She wanted me to see it . . . and asked me to touch it up a little."

"And left it with you?"

"Temporarily, yes."

Terry slid his fingers up and down his glass, and said, "The police searched your apartment early this morning. They found that your bed hadn't been slept in. They would also have noted that Mandra's portrait wasn't in your apartment at that hour. They want to question you, so they're watching your apartment, and have been, ever since early this morning. The police will know exactly when that portrait was delivered, and by whom it was delivered."

She gave a quick, gasping intake of her breath.

"Hadn't thought of that?" he asked.

She shook her head, her eyes holding the helpless expression of a trapped animal.

"That's what I was afraid of," Terry said. "Just how *did* the picture get there?"

"We took the canvas from the frame and rolled it up. George concealed it under his coat. I gave him the key to my apartment. He went in there, unfastened another canvas from its frame, and tacked on this portrait of Mandra. Then he slipped out."

Terry shook his head. "Levering was taken to the office of the district attorney for questioning."

"I know, Terry; but they let him go almost at once. He wasn't there for more than fifteen minutes."

"And you've heard from him since?"

"Yes."

"How?"

"By telephone. I phoned his place two or three times. When he answered I asked him where he'd been. He told me what had happened. I told him to make certain he wasn't being followed and to come over here. Then I gave him the portrait and told him what he was to do."

Terry said slowly, "I don't trust Levering."

Alma said bitterly, "I know you don't! It's unfair. He's loyal to Cynthia and me, and he'd be loyal to you if you'd let him."

Terry shook his head. "I'm afraid you've been sold out, Alma."

"What do you mean, Terry?"

"Not over an hour ago," he said, "I saw that portrait. It was in the apartment of a woman who claimed to be Mandra's widow, a woman who hates both you and Cynthia, a woman who claims that Cynthia murdered Jacob Mandra."

Alma came up to her feet, slowly, as a prisoner

might arise at the sound of an executioner's approaching steps. "Terry!" she cried.

He nodded.

She came to him, dropped to the floor at his feet, wrapped her arms around his knees. "Terry," she said, "I'm frightened."

He nodded gravely, making no attempt to reassure her with words in which neither could have had any confidence. "Let's figure what happened," he said. "There are two possibilities. Either Levering blundered, or after the police took the portrait they gave it to Mandra's widow."

"Thanks, Terry, for eliminating the possibility that Levering deliberately double-crossed us."

They sat for several seconds in thoughtful silence.

"If Levering blundered, the police will soon be here," he said. "Are you prepared for that, Alma?"

"Yes. I'm prepared for anything so far as I'm concerned. It's Cynthia I'm worried about. I can take it. I'm not so certain about Cynthia. She's just a kid, Terry."

"No, Alma," he said slowly, "she isn't a kid. She's a woman. She's only three years younger than you are."

"I know, Terry, but in spite of all that, she's still a kid. Life hasn't licked her yet."

Terry's eyes were serious. "You can't stand between Cynthia and life. It won't work."

She looked up at him. "Terry," she said, "life licked me. I don't want it to lick Cynthia."

"How did life lick you, Alma?"

"I don't know. I guess that's something one never knows. It's not as though you could come to grips with life in a decisive battle. You can't. Life undermines your defenses, a little at a time, as insidious as decay eating into a tooth, and the first thing you know, you're beaten without even knowing there's been a battle."

He shook his head, the tips of his fingers gently smoothing the hair at her temples. "Perhaps," he told her, "you paid too great a price for success."

"What makes you think that?" she asked.

"Everyone does," he told her, stroking her hair. "That is, everyone who concentrates on being successful. You see, Alma, life is a keenly competitive game. No matter what goal you strive to attain, there are millions who are also striving toward that same goal. Of those millions, there are hundreds of thousands who have more than average aptitude. It isn't, therefore, so much a question of ability as adaptability. Those who win out are the ones who are willing to make sacrifices that the others are not."

"Do you mean that I should have been content to just drift through life?"

"No," he told her, "it isn't that, Alma. It goes farther back than that. It's a question of the goal you picked."

She looked up, caught and held his eyes. "Terry," she said, "tell me *all* of it. I want to know. Life has licked me. Life has licked almost everyone I know; but it hasn't licked you. I've tried to keep it from licking Cynthia—and now I've failed. She's like a kitten chasing a piece of crumpled paper around the room. I've loved to sit on the sidelines and watch her. She's had a complete disregard for the consequences of life, and I've wanted to keep her that way.

"You know, Terry, whenever you see a person who laughs his way through life, you can bank on it there's someone in the background who's taking the shocks, usually a mother or a father who's too indulgent, or, as in Cynthia's case, a sister.

"Cynthia's always been getting into scrapes, and I've always been getting her out. And now she's got into a scrape that . . . Well, I'm afraid I can't get her out."

"That bad?" he asked again.

She nodded, and for several silent seconds sat with her head resting on his knees. Then she said, "Go on, Terry, tell me how you've managed to keep all your spontaneity. You refuse to take life seriously, and yet, somehow you respect it, as one respects a powerful adversary. You don't underestimate it and you don't worry about it. You're still an adventurer—more so than when you went away."

"Perhaps, Alma," he said, slowly, "the trouble lies in selecting a goal. *You* wanted to be a successful painter. You wanted your success to be financial. You entered a keenly competitive field. You had a talent amounting almost to genius, but there were lots of others who had talent. *You* reached *your* goal because you made sacrifices. It's the same way with the young doctors and the young lawyers, the young business men, everyone, in fact, who enters a keenly competitive struggle. The reason I haven't sacrificed is because I'm not trying to achieve the same goal everyone else is.

"It's difficult to explain so you'll understand it, Alma. I heard of some ruins in a remote part of China where there were gold and gems to be had for the taking. But a man could only get into the country if he went as a neophyte and attached himself to a certain monastery. So I went as a neophyte. I had no real intention of doing any studying. I only wanted to get the gems and get out."

"Were the gems there?" she asked, her eyes wide with interest.

He nodded.

"And you brought some out?"

He shook his head.

"Why?"

"I don't know," he told her. "That is, I do know, but that's what's so difficult to explain. I became interested in a theory of life."

"Something they taught you in the monastery?"

"Yes."

"What was it, Terry?"

"It has to do with what we were talking about just now," he said. "It's the thing one picks in life as the measure of success. Everything in life is relative. Financial success is relative. That which is big enough to be really desired is only for the favored few. To be one of that charmed circle, one must either be smiled upon by luck or willing to out-strip his competitors by paying life a greater price.

"But if one puts a financial goal out of his mind, and chooses only to develop his own individuality, he finds that he has no outside competitors. His struggle comes from within, rather than from without. And, incidentally, as he achieves some measure of success, he finds that he's not only increased his enjoyment of life but he finds that financial success is usually thrown in for good measure."

"But how about me?" she asked.

"Money," he said, "is a false God. People worship it and it betrays them. They fight for it, get it, and in the getting of it, become selfish and arrogant. They lose health and happiness getting wealth, and then it mocks them. It's like giving gold to a starving man in the desert. He can't eat it, nor . . ."

He broke off as a vague noise of feet in the corridor resolved itself into the ominous pound of authoritative steps.

"I'm afraid, Alma, the police have back-tracked that portrait," he said, almost casually.

The spots of make-up on her face flared into garish brilliance as her skin went dead-white. "Terry!" she asked in a whisper, "*what* shall I say?"

His arm circled her waist as peremptory knuckles pounded on the door. "Say nothing," he told her cheerfully, "but say it as loquaciously as possible."

Her quivering lips sought his, clung hungrily as another knock banged on the panels of the outer door.

"Coming!" Terry called, crushing her to him in one last quick embrace; then, freeing her, he opened the door, to confront Inspector Malloy, flanked by two plain-clothes officers.

"Well, well, well!" Malloy exclaimed, unsuccessfully trying to conceal his irritation, "Fancy meeting *you* here! You certainly *do* get around."

"Come in," Clane invited. "There are ice cubes, Scotch and soda over there on the taboret. Alma will get you some glasses ... Oh, by the way, I guess you haven't met her. Miss Renton, may I present Inspector Malloy?"

Malloy's fingers groped for his hat brim, removed it. "Glad to know you," he said. "Come in, boys." The two plain-clothes men didn't take off their hats.

Terry said, "Perhaps, Inspector, you'd like to know how I happened to stumble onto Miss Renton here."

Malloy said breezily, "Oh, that's all right, Clane, quite all right. So far as I'm concerned, *I* don't care, but, of course, the district attorney might want to know. He's rather cold-blooded about business matters, you know. Didn't he tell you he was looking for Miss Renton, that she wasn't at her apartment, and her bed hadn't been slept in? And didn't you tell him you didn't have the slightest idea . . ."

"As a matter of fact," Terry interrupted smoothly, "it was that very statement which gave me my clew. Knowing that she wasn't in any of her usual haunts, I happened to remember that Vera Matthews had left town on a vacation, that she'd probably asked Alma to drop in and look after her plants and things.

"And, of course, Alma, being a painter, and the studio here being equipped with everything, it was only natural that she'd dabble around here with a few odds and ends. You see, Alma is successful and popular, and, in creative work, success and popularity make rather a bad combination. So Alma was taking advantage of an opportunity to get away from her friends. She hadn't seen the papers, and of course didn't know anything about Mandra's death, and didn't have the faintest idea that the police were looking for her. When I told her just now what had happened, and that the district attorney was looking for her, she was thunder-struck. She was just starting for the telephone to call him when . . ."

"She speaks English, doesn't she?" Malloy interrupted, his veneer of good humor crackling under the pressure of inward irritation.

"Why, certainly," Clane said.

"Well then," Malloy snapped, "we can get along without an interpreter. I'm sorry to interrupt your *tête-à-tête*, Clane; but it just happens that the district attorney has rather definite ideas about what he wants, and one of the things he wants right now is Miss Alma Renton, and one of the things neither of us wants is to have the interview colored by your pleasing personality. So we'll excuse you right now."

He nodded to one of the men, who held the door open for Terry.

Terry picked up his hat and said with dignity, "I appreciate your position, Inspector, but let me assure you that Miss Renton has nothing to conceal. Cynthia, as you know, had painted a portrait of Jacob Mandra, and it was only natural . . ."

Inspector Malloy's heavy hand clapped down on Clane's shoulder. He was once more his boisterously genial self as his booming voice drowned Clane's remarks. "Not at all, Clane, my boy, not at all! Don't worry about it in the least! Miss Renton is absolutely on the up-and-up. The district attorney only wanted to ask her a few questions. Don't try to explain, because there's nothing to explain."

And Clane found himself spun around by Inspector Malloy's arm, felt the weight of Malloy's broad shoulders pushing him toward the door.

"Awfully sorry to interrupt your chat, Clane, but this is business, and you know how business is. You can talk with her any time when the district attorney gets finished, but he's waiting for her now, and we don't want to keep him waiting."

And Clane found himself propelled out into the corridor. He turned long enough to smile a reassuring good-by to Alma, and then his view was blocked by one of the plain-clothes men who reached for the knob and swung the door. Inspector Malloy's voice reached Terry's ears through the diminishing crack in the door. "The first thing I said when the district attorney told me to bring you in, Miss Renton, was that it was just too bad . . ."

The slam of the door shut off the rest of Inspector Malloy's speech.

## 9

WHEN HE WAS HALF A DOZEN BLOCKS FROM
the apartment house where Vera Matthews had her
studio, Terry pulled his car into the curb and shut
off the motor.

Various disjointed bits of information were flying
around loose in his brain like the detached views
which are thrown on a picture screen when the film
suddenly breaks and the loose ends fly in front of the
projecting lens before the mechanism is shut off.
Terry wanted time to correlate those detached impressions.

Seated there in his car, with the motor running,
Terry fixed his eyes on the lighted speedometer, and
brought his mind to focus upon the facts in his possession.

As patiently as a trout fisherman unsnarling a
badly tangled line, Terry went over the events of the
day, only to convince himself in the end that some
important fact was being withheld from him.

Cynthia Renton had painted Mandra's portrait. A
combination of blackmail and fascination had bound
her to Mandra. But, regardless of the tie, Cynthia
would only go so far, then she would fight free.

And that turning point had evidently been reached at two o'clock in the morning, when Cynthia had taken her portrait and left Mandra's apartment, doubtless defying him to do his worst. She had been seen on the stairs by a witness . . . but *had* she been seen? The witness had observed only a woman carrying a portrait. Yet the portrait was distinctive enough, and it was only natural that Cynthia should have taken it to Alma, for appraisal.

But why should Alma have put finishing touches on Cynthia's portrait? An artist of Cynthia's individuality would hardly care to have some other painter interfering. Then there was the physical disposition of the portrait to be considered.

Alma had arranged with Levering to have that portrait taken to her apartment. In some way, it had been diverted to Juanita Mandra's apartment. Had Levering delivered the portrait to Juanita? Or had the police taken it from Alma's apartment and subsequently surrendered it to the widow? One explanation would mean a connection between Levering and the widow of the murdered man: the other that Juanita and Malloy were working hand-in-glove. Or . . .

Clane's mind suddenly realized a disquieting solution. He stared in frowning perplexity, then abruptly reached for the ignition switch of his car.

He realized now, only too clearly, the necessity of finding out just who had killed Mandra. Cynthia's story might give her a brief respite but would eventually leave her hopelessly entangled. Clane drove his car through traffic with a certain savage insistence which made others instinctively yield the right of way at the crossings. He parked his car at the curb in front of his apartment house, and recognized Cynthia's convertible coupé some hundred feet ahead. As Terry stepped to the curb the horn was tapped into brief noise.

Terry nodded his head, to indicate that he had heard the signal, but did not go at once to the car. He strolled to the lobby entrance of his apartment house, then as though he had forgotten something, turned on his heel, walked quickly to his own car and then down to where Cynthia was waiting. He pulled open the door of the car, and encountered Cynthia's upturned nose, smiling lips and flashing eyes.

"Well, Owl," she said, "let's shout."

"Why?" he asked.

"Because," she told him, gayly, "it's all over except the shouting."

He looked carefully up and down the sidewalk. "Were you followed here?" he asked.

She shook her head and said, "Not a chance. They've dropped me like a hot potato."

He regarded her with thoughtful scrutiny for a few seconds, then said, "All right, Cynthia, come on in, I want to talk with you."

"Don't be so frightfully serious, Owl," she said, "I want to make whoopee."

She pivoted about on the leather seat, pointed her feet toward him, braced her right hand against the back of the seat, the left hand on the steering wheel, and said, "Here I come, Owl."

She slid toward him, a flashing bundle of flying legs and kicking feet, as a ball player might slide into a base.

He avoided the feet, caught her around the waist, lifted her to the sidewalk.

"Listen, Owl," she said, "I've got some great news . . ."

"Save it," he told her. "Not a word until you're in my apartment. And remember, they *may* have someone planted in the lobby. As we walk through to the elevator, don't seem to be elated. Can you look downcast and worried?"

"Hell, no!" she told him. "Not now. I'm sitting on top of the world."

"Do the best you can, then," he told her, "because someone may jerk the world out from under you. Come on, let's go."

He escorted her to the apartment house. They crossed the lobby to the elevator. The face of a strange girl at the telephone switchboard regarded them in disinterested appraisal. The Filipino elevator boy nodded to Terry, and shot the car smoothly to his floor.

Cynthia, holding her face in a grim mask of tragic gloom, suddenly quivered her lips into a smile. The smile became a giggle as the elevator operator opened the sliding door, she flung an arm around Terry's waist and pulled him out into the corridor. The grinning elevator boy slid the door shut, and the cage dropped smoothly to the lobby.

"I told you I couldn't do it, Owl," she said. "Come on and buy me a drink. Where's Yat T'oy?"

"Out."

"Don't tell me the old boy's playing around," she said, as Terry fitted a key to the apartment door.

"No, I think he had a business engagement somewhere," he told her.

She tripped lightly through the door, flung off her coat, hat, and said, "I'm sorry he's out, because I wanted to see if he savvied gingerale highballs the same as he did a Tom Collins. My God, Owl, I'm famished for a drink and for a chance to be informal. I've been so mealy-mouthed and polite I'm worn out mentally."

"Are you supposed to go back again?" he asked.

"Don't be silly, Owl. Why should they want me back? I'm out—exonerated. Stubby Nash got me a lawyer, but I didn't need him. They put my alibi to the acid test and it stood up. But I had to be *such* a nice little girl that I feel like a damned hypocrite. I want to do something unconventional. How's your self-control, Terry?"

"Swell," he told her, grinning.

She eyed him appraisingly. "Yes," she admitted, "it's your strong point. Two highballs may thaw you out. I'm going to start in, Owl. It's time I busted through your reserve to see whether you've got me listed as one of the untouchables. You're altogether *too* self-contained, too self-sufficient. Women don't like it, although it attracts women to you. But their designs are sinister, Owl. That's feminine nature. We want men to get all steamed up over us. When they do, we're very coy, proper and demure. But when they don't, we start teasing the animals."

"So what am I supposed to do?" he asked.

"Mix the highballs, stupid."

He brought ice cubes, gingerale, Bourbon, Scotch and soda, mixed two drinks. She gulped hers down, tilted the empty glass toward him and said, "Rotten manners, Owl, but I've got to break loose."

He said, "Not yet, Cynthia. Wait until you're out of the woods."

"But I *am* out of the woods," she told him, and, at the shake of his head, went on, "Oh, don't be such a damn' killjoy, Owl. Snap out of it. Here, catch!"

She kicked her right foot at him. Her shoe spun through the air and missed his head by inches.

She giggled delightedly, squirmed around in the overstuffed chair until her weight was on her other hip, and kicked the other shoe. This went straight up in the air, struck the ceiling and thudded back to the floor.

She swung her legs up over the cushioned arm, and wriggled her toes.

"I warned you, Owl," she said. "I'm going to bust loose. Give me that second drink so I won't feel so deliberate. It's smart to be just a tiny bit tight, but unladylike to be forward."

He smiled at her as he sipped his Scotch and soda.

"Do I understand you're planning to be forward?" he asked.

"Well, Owl," she told him, twisting her toes, "I'm not going to be exactly backward. I've sat for hours, being a very demure little lady, and I'm quite certain there's going to be a reaction. In just a minute I'm going to think of a limerick which'll jar you loose from your dignity. Right now I can't think of one that's good enough, but it'll come."

"You mean bad enough, don't you?" he asked.

"Don't be silly, Owl. I mean good enough. After all, you know, I wouldn't want to frighten you to death with the first one and that's the way with limericks. Try to think of a clever one that'll leave 'em guessing, and the only ones which pop into your mind are . . ."

"Tell me about the questions," he interrupted, "and about the answers you gave, and about the lawyer."

She sighed.

"They wanted to know all about me and all about the handkerchief and . . ."

"Did you admit it was your handkerchief?"

"Yes, and I didn't even hesitate. I think that made a good impression. Thanks to what you'd told me, I knew they were going to pull the handkerchief trick. So, when the district attorney held it out very dramatically and very accusingly, I gave a little squeal and said, 'Why, that's *my* handkerchief,' and grabbed for it."

"They ask you where you'd lost it?"

She nodded. "I told them I couldn't tell. They asked me if I'd left it in Mandra's apartment, and I told them I might have. Then they wanted to know lots of things and I told them."

"The truth?" he asked.

"I always tell the truth." She glanced sidelong at him from beneath lowered lashes, her lips provocatively parted. "Really, Owl, do we *have* to talk about this?"

"Did you tell them about the portrait?"

"Yes, of course."

"Tell them where it was?"

"I told them Alma had it. I'd given it to her. I wanted to see what she thought of it, and perhaps have her smooth it up a little."

Terry picked up the whisky bottles and returned them to the sideboard.

She raised her feet, caught her skirt under the backs of her knees, swung around in the chair and said, "Why you stingy old walrus!"

"I'm afraid," he told her, "this is just a recess, Cynthia. How about the attorney?"

She giggled. "He has the longest neck, and the funniest horse face. He reminds me of a string bean on parade. Tell me, Owl, do string beans ever parade?"

"What's his name?"

"Oh, you know C. Renmore Howland, *the* criminal attorney, known to his intimates as 'Renny.' My Heavens, Stubby wouldn't get anything for me except the best! I'm an intimate, Owl. He told me to call him Renny."

"How does Stubby figure in this business?"

"He isn't in it. He's just standing by *me*."

"And what did Howland do?"

"Oooh, he waved his hands and talked about writs of *habeas corpus*, and stretched his neck in and out of his collar and patted me on the shoulder in a fatherly manner. . . . Honestly, Owl, that man should have been a race horse. He could have won his races by a neck without ever leaving the starting post."

"And they turned you loose when he threatened *habeas corpus?*" he asked.

She nodded and said, "But about that time they found the portrait."

"Where?"

"I don't know. I suppose Alma gave it to them. That was an awfully nice boy who met me coming down the stairs from Mandra's place, Owl. His name's Jack Winton, and he's a painter. He looked me over and said that he couldn't tell whether I was the one he'd seen coming down the stairs or not, but that he'd seen a woman who had *very* attractive ankles carrying a portrait of Mandra. I loved him for that crack about the ankles, Owl. And he gave a perfectly swell description of the portrait: dull background, the face catching high lights, and Mandra's eyes staring with that cold glint. . . . Ugh, Owl, it just doesn't seem possible the man's dead. He had such a way of controlling people and things that somehow you'd expect him to control death itself."

Terry stared steadily at her. "Cynthia," he said, "you weren't the woman Jack Winton met on the stairs. You never did carry that portrait out of Mandra's studio. But you learned somehow that this man Winton had seen a woman coming down the stairs carrying the portrait. You figured it would be swell if you could manufacture an alibi from that, and you knew that Alma, with her swiftness of execution and deft technique, could make a passable portrait in a few hours. She locked herself in Vera Matthews' studio, worked all night, and finished a portrait which you could claim was the one on which you had worked."

Her face lost its animation, became suddenly weary. She raised her chin defiantly and said, "Don't talk like that, Owl. C. Renmore Howland . . . damn it, I must remember to call him Renny . . . would sue you for slander or defamation of character or whatever it is he'd sue you for. He'd have some perfectly splendid word for it."

Terry Clane crossed to her, slid his arm around her shoulders.

"I'm sorry, Cynthia," he said, "but you and Alma both overlooked something. The woman who really has this portrait you painted hates you. She's going to bust your alibi wide open."

Cynthia grabbed his fingers, pressed them to her cheek. Hot tears dropped on the back of his hand.

"Tell me about it," he said to her.

She dabbed at her eyes with a handkerchief, laughed half-hysterically and said, "I'm not going to start bawling, Owl, it's just the let-down."

"What happened?" he asked.

"Mandra was blackmailing me."

"Over the hit-and-run business?"

"Yes."

"Money, marbles or chalk?" he asked.

"Money, marbles *and* chalk," she replied. "If you'd known Mandra better you wouldn't have asked."

"So what happened?"

"Honestly, Owl, I'd never known anyone as completely ruthless as Mandra. He fascinated me. When he wanted something, nothing on God's green earth could stand in his way. He would use any method and he played a no-limit game.

"He was crazy about the portrait. I saw that that was going to be my strongest hold over him. I decided to call his bluff last night, and told him I was going to take the portrait away with me unless that hit-and-run charge was cleaned up."

"Did you," Terry asked, "know that he was teamed up with a William Shield to blackmail wealthy car owners?"

"No, Shield is the man I hit. How it could have been *just* a blackmail scheme, Owl, I don't know, because X-rays showed a permanent injury to the spine. I really must have . . ."

"You didn't hit him at all," Terry interrupted. "An acrobat hit your car with his fist and then did a tumbling act. Later on they introduced you to Shield. Shield hadn't even been near your car. It was all a frame-up."

She stared at him steadily for several seconds and then said slowly, "Owl, is that absolutely true?"

"Absolutely."

"That," she said, "explains it. I told Mandra I was all finished, that I was going to see a lawyer, and that I was taking that portrait home with me. And then, Owl, the man actually had the audacity to drug me. We were drinking tea. God knows what he put in it. I felt things going round and round. I got to my feet, and my knees were weak. I grabbed at the side of the table, and things turned black."

"Then what?"

"When I woke up," she said, "it was around three o'clock. I had a terrific headache. I went to the room where I'd left Mandra. He was sitting there at a table, slumped over, with his head on his arms."

"Did you see a sleeve gun there?"

"No."

"Now wait a minute," Terry said, "this is important, Cynthia. Try and reconstruct the table just as you saw it."

She closed her eyes and said, "Well, of course, the thing that I keep seeing is Mandra's arm crooked over the table and his head lying on his arm. It was awful . . ."

"Was his face down?"

"No, turned slightly to one side, the eyes were open and starey, all glassy and inanimate. Ugh! Owl, *you* know how dead people are! Don't make me describe it."

"Did you scream?"

"I don't think so."

"And what else was on the table?"

"Well, let me see. There were some papers."

"Where were the papers, right in front of Mandra?"

"No, to one side."

"Do you remember what sort of papers? Were they letters, or what?"

"No, I can't remember that."

"Were they placed in piles or . . . ?"

"No, just in a scramble, as though someone had pushed them over to one side."

"As though Mandra had pushed them to one side to clear a space on the table?"

"Either that or as though someone had been looking for something and pulled them over to the corner to get away from Mandra's body."

"Was there anyone in the room except Mandra?"

"No . . . that is, I don't think so. Of course, I didn't look under the desk or in the closet, or in any of the adjoining rooms."

"What did you do?"

"I had a mad desire to get out. But, frightened as I was, I realized I mustn't let the guard see me, and know what time I had left. I felt all tight in my throat, the sensation you have when something's suffocating you and you want to fight your way through to the air. I've always been like that, Owl. If I'm putting a dress on over my head and it catches and covers my face, I want to tear the thing to pieces."

"I know how you felt," he said. "What I want to know is what you *did*."

"Well, I was there alone with Mandra. He'd been

murdered. Someone else had killed him but I didn't know if I could prove that—and I wanted to keep my name from being dragged into the thing. It was all foolish—just the blind panic which grips you sometimes and makes you want to run. I knew about this corridor door. Of course, it could be opened from the inside. Mandra had the only key which would open it from the outside. So I opened this door and ran out."

"Now, what time was that?"

"Right around three o'clock. I didn't look at my watch until after I got to Alma's apartment."

"Did you close this corridor door behind you?"

"No, I left it open."

"Why didn't you close it?"

"To tell you the truth, Owl, I thought I had, but I must have been mistaken. I don't remember clearly about what happened when I was getting out of there. I remember fighting with the bolts on the door and ripping the door open, and then being in the corridor and racing down the stairs. The natural thing for me to do was to close the door, but I guess I didn't."

"But you don't remember positively?"

"No. Why, Owl—does it make any difference?"

"It might," he told her. "Everything makes a difference. Now, did you notice whether the portrait you had painted was there?"

"No, Owl, I didn't notice—not then."

"So you ran down the stairs to the street. Did you meet anyone?"

"No."

"And what did you do?"

"I stopped in at an all-night drug store and telephoned Alma, to see if she was home. She was. George Levering was there with her. I told Alma to wait for me. I found a cab and rushed out there. I dragged Alma into the bedroom and told her all about it. It was her suggestion that we take George into our confidence and let him see what he could do."

"How long had Levering been there?" Terry asked.

"I don't know. I didn't ask."

"Wasn't that an unusual time for him to be calling on Alma?"

"He wanted money," she said, "and you know George. He can want money any time."

Terry nodded and said, "Go ahead, Cynthia, what happened after that?"

"Well, George suggested that he'd better go out on a trip of reconnoissance and see if the police had discovered the murder. He told us to wait for him and he went out and jumped in his car. He came back and told us about what had happened. This man had gone out to get something to eat and came back and found the door open, and looked inside and found Mandra's body. The police had arrived and there was a crowd around the place, not a big crowd, because of the hour, but big enough so that George could circulate around and ask questions without attracting too much attention. He found some newspaper man whom he knew, and the newspaper man had found this Jack Winton who had met the woman on the stairs carrying a portrait, so George knew all about that, and he came racing back to tell us that Winton had seen this woman leaving the apartment at two o'clock in the morning, but hadn't been able to see her face clearly enough to identify her because of the way she'd been holding the portrait. So George suggested that if we could duplicate that portrait, I could claim that I was the woman who had left at two o'clock.

"I had my original sketches in my apartment and some photographs that I'd taken when the portrait was about two-thirds completed, so with my sketches and the photograph, Alma insisted she could make a passable duplicate of the portrait and have it ready by nine or ten o'clock in the morning. Of course, it wouldn't be a finished piece of work, but I'm not a finished artist, and Alma's a very rapid worker. It was George's idea that Alma could dash off another portrait and that this would give me a perfect alibi."

"Didn't you consider the possibility that the other woman might show up with the real portrait?"

"It was a possibility, all right, but we figured she'd want to keep in the background. Of course, Owl, we were rattled, and it sounded like a good scheme at the time. You know George Levering. He's played so many crooked horse races that he figures nothing's on the level and anything can be fixed. He said this was iron-clad."

Terry started pacing the floor, his head bowed in thought.

Suddenly he whirled to Cynthia.

"If anything happens," he told her, "don't tell anyone anything. Just sit tight until you can talk with your lawyer."

Cynthia's eyes were uneasy as she stared across at Terry. "I want to get a little bit tight, Owl. When I get home Alma will be waiting for me, and Stubby will be parked on the doorstep. Oh, Owl, I don't want to see Stubby! He's so damn possessive. And he got me that lawyer, so I'll have to be grateful. I don't *want* to be grateful to Stubby. He's a damn nuisance.

"Gee, it's been an awful day! Owl, dear, you don't know what it means to have the reputation of being a good sport, and having to stand up and take it on the chin all by yourself. Alma doesn't understand me, Owl. She thinks I never have a serious moment. She loves me all right, but she feels responsible for me. She thinks that I'm just a little butterfly . . . that I waste my opportunities, squander my talents and dissipate my life."

He said, "You won't be seeing Alma for a while, Cynthia."

"What do you mean?" she asked, straightening in the chair.

"Inspector Malloy took Alma down to head-quarters with him."

"How long ago?"

"Shortly before I drove up and met you. They

were watching Alma's apartment. They found the portrait and took it down to headquarters. This witness, Jack Winton, evidently identified it. About that time, your lawyer was making a kick, and they thought, in view of Winton's testimony, they wouldn't have anything to hold you on.

"But shortly after that they managed to backtrack that portrait, and found out Alma was staying at Vera Matthews'. They wanted to talk with Alma, just on general principles."

"Owl," she cried, "you don't mean George Levering sold us out . . . Oh no, it couldn't have been that. He wouldn't do that . . . but he might have blundered somehow. Tell me, Owl, will they get rough with her?"

"Not now they won't. That will come later."

"How much later?"

"When they find the other painting," he said.

"But they mustn't find it! Don't let them, Owl! There's something we can do. There must be something."

He stared at her with fixed intensity.

"Don't look at me like that, Owl," she said impatiently, and then suddenly realized that he hadn't heard her. He was concentrating so intently for the moment he seemed to have lost all animation, while every bit of his mental energy was centered in a white-hot spot of concentration.

Fascinated, Cynthia watched him.

For the space of some seven or eight seconds he sat there. Then he said slowly, "No, they mustn't find that other portrait. It would raise the devil." He crossed over to the sideboard, returned with the whisky bottles.

"Now *that*," she observed, "is a *swell* idea!"

Terry poured whisky into her glass. She regarded the amount of amber fluid with speculative eyes.

"Owl, are you *trying* to get me tight?" she asked.

Pouring gingerale on top of the whisky he asked, "Why should I try to get you tight?"

She giggled. "Don't you *ever* read the tabloids, Terry Clane? Think of the headlines: GIRL LURED TO MAN'S APARTMENT AND PLIED WITH DRINK, SHE EXPLAINS TO ARRESTING OFFICERS."

"Officers?" he inquired.

"You know, the ones the neighbors call in when the party gets rough. And the tabloid story runs something like this: 'Really, I had no idea where we were,' pretty Miss Smith, nineteen and blond, said when interviewed by a Whosis reporter today. 'I thought we were going to the library to look at some etchings. He produced a flask of amber liquid and told me it was cold tea. My mother never lets me drink coffee, but tea is all right, she says. So I drank it. I thought it had a peculiar taste, but I drank it all, and the next I remembered was when the officers broke down the door of the apartment.'"

She held the glass up to the light and said, "When it's this color, Owl, it's plenty potent. But here goes, down the hatch."

She gulped down the drink, gravely pushed the empty glass across the table to him.

"You know, Terry, I'm inclined to co-operate. . . . Tell me, Owl, why are you trying to load me up?"

She stretched out a shapely leg, looked at the wriggling toes thoughtfully and then surveyed the graceful curves. "Terry, I believe it's time to call a halt. Every time I wiggle my toes it seems to wiggle something in my mind and make me feel like laughing."

"Why not?" he asked. "Babies wiggle their toes and laugh."

"Oooh, Owl, you're so *good* to me! I thought perhaps you'd get sore. Honestly, Owl, I really *am* going to get a teeny-weeny bit tight. I intended to stop after the second drink, but now you've started to ply me with liquor I'm going to trail along and see if you are going to take advantage of me. . . . I'm afraid you're not . . ."

She slipped from her chair, got to her feet, held out her hands in front of her, extended rigid forefingers, and went through a burlesque of trying to put them together, executing elaborate maneuvers.

He came to her, slid his arm around her waist and said, "Cut the comedy, Cynthia."

"Why should I? I get pleasure out of it. I'm in a serious-minded world. People are all too damned serious. Man is supposed to suffer with a long face and keep his mind in a lather of worry. Because I won't do it, people think I'm cuckoo.

"You've heard about the fox who had his tail cut off. He wanted all the other foxes to be the same way. Honestly, Owl, that's the way with the world. Here we have a glorious life to live, and people shut them-

selves up in stuffy offices and worry about the interest on the National debt or the high price of gasoline,
or which political party is going to have the spending
of the tax money. Wouldn't it be funny, Owl, if some
day the play-boys should get sufficiently in the ma-
jority to take over control of the government and the
banks and everyone *had* to be cheerful. They could
amend the constitution to provide that everyone
would have to drink at least one cocktail before dinner."

She was still making elaborate efforts to get her
fingertips together.

"Now," she went on, "I'm going to hold the left
one still and the right one is going to sneak up on it
like a man hunting a deer. Tell me, Owl, when you
were in China, did you . . ."

His arm tightened about her. The stray tendrils of
her unruly hair tickled his cheek and chin. He felt
the warmth of her body through the thin dress,
sensed the vibrant vitality, the spirit which refused
to take life seriously. His other hand grasped her
shoulder, swung her around to face him.

As she looked up, he bent his lips to hers.

With a little satisfied exclamation, she snuggled
her body close to his. Her right hand slid up the back
of his neck, until the fingers entwined themselves in
his hair. His arm, suddenly tightening, lifted her
shoeless feet from the floor.

Their lips were clinging in a quivering embrace
when a latch key clicked in the door.

Cynthia dropped her arms, placed her hands

against Terry's shoulder and pushed back until she was free, then turned to face the door.

Yat T'oy stood on the threshold.

"Yat T'oy," she assured him, with mock solemnity, "there are twenty-four hours in the day, seven days in the week, fifty-two weeks in the year, yet, with all that time to choose from, you had to pick *this* particular time to latchkey that door."

There were times when Yat T'oy was able to comprehend virtually everything which was said to him in English, and there was no time when he could not comprehend a situation, but now he chose to understand neither.

"No savvy," he said, blandly.

"You heap savvy Tom Collins."

"Heap savvy Tom Collins," he admitted, and his eyes, watching for an opportunity, moved significantly to Terry.

"It would be well," Yat T'oy said in Cantonese, "that the master should hear that which the servant would speak."

"Don't do that, Yat T'oy," Cynthia remonstrated. "It's as bad as whispering. You mustn't speak Chinese to your master when I'm here. Now if you hadn't come in just when you did . . . Oh, skip it!"

Terry moved toward the far end of the room. Cynthia regarded him with thoughtful scrutiny.

Terry stepped over more closely to Yat T'oy.

"The detectives," Yat T'oy said in Chinese, "inquire much about sleeve guns. They also wished to know the names of those who called upon the master during the past few days."

"What did you tell them?" Terry inquired.

"I am an old man. My eyesight is dim and my memory is poor. You are the Beneficent One who sees not the infirmities of age, but keeps me employed as a servant when I am fit for nothing save to sit in a chair and await the moment of joining my ancestors.

"Of course," Yat T'oy went on, "I was able to remember the man with the pale eyes because the detectives had followed him here, and I knew of this sister of the painter woman who is here now because they also had been aware of her, but as to other matters, my memory was very dim.

"But that of which you should be warned is that they are seeking to find the Chinese girl with whom you are friendly. The police have wide ears and they listen to the babble of many tongues. Does the Honored One wish that I shall bring more ice?"

"Yes," Terry said. "And, Yat T'oy, I have something which I must do, and of which this sister of the painter woman must know nothing. It would be well if she should sleep."

Yat T'oy's eyes were utterly without expression. "How long should she sleep?"

"Not for long. An hour, perhaps, then awake. Perhaps a little of the herb you used . . ." Terry let his voice trail into silence, and Yat T'oy said smoothly, "It is as nothing. A very small matter."

He turned and shuffled from the room. Cynthia

called after him, "Don't forget my Tom Collins, Yat T'oy!"

"Tom Collins," Yat T'oy assured her, in his broken English, "come right now, plenty soon. Heap quick. Can do!"

Terry returned to his chair. Cynthia stared across at him and said, "Listen, Owl, one more is my limit. You know me. I like to get just a little bit tight, and then I stop."

He nodded.

"Of all the miserable times for Yat T'oy to come in and interrupt us. . . . Tell me, Owl, what were you going to say—or were you going to say anything? Was it just a biological spasm, or did you . . . No, don't. Skip it. Trying to recapture a moment like that is like trying to warm up cold biscuits. It's better to throw them out and perhaps mix up another batch sometime."

Her eyes stared at him wistfully. "We *will* mix up another batch sometime, won't we, Owl?" And then, as he started to say something, she pointed a rigid forefinger at him and said, "No, stop right there! Don't answer that question."

She regarded her extended forefinger, grinning, and said, "What do you think of *that* trick, Owl? It's one I learned from C. Renmore Howland—you know, Renny for short—it's a swell trick. It pushes the words right back down your throat. I know just how it feels, because Renny pulled it on me this afternoon. You see, Owl, I don't want you to answer the question because even that is like trying to warm up the biscuits. We'll just have to . . ." Her voice choked. She helped herself to a cigarette and smoked in silence. Terry Clane, watching her, said nothing.

Yat T'oy opened the door, bearing glasses on a tray.

She mechanically took the glass nearest to her, as Yat T'oy extended the tray.

"The Chinese," Terry said, "have a custom with their last drink of making an 'umbrella' glass. Not so, Yat T'oy?"

Yat T'oy beamed upon them, the benign smile of a convivial spirit. Never by any chance would one have suspected him of having expertly drugged Cynthia Renton's drink. "Yes," he said, "Chinese say *'gahn bie, gahn bie'* and then turn bottom of glass toward ceiling, make wine glass all same like umbrella. You savvy?"

Terry said *"gahn bie, gahn bie,"* and drained his glass. Cynthia sighed, said, "Not to be outdone in Chinese etiquette, Owl, *'gahn bie, gahn bie.'* " She took a deep breath, drained her glass and returned it to the tray. Yat T'oy gravely bore the empty glasses from the room.

"That's the last one, Owl," Cynthia announced. "You know, it's funny the way people look at things. Alma would say I was just a heedless little windbag; Stubby Nash would say I was making a spectacle of myself; C. Renmore Howland—damn it, why *can't* I remember to call him Renny?—would say I was talking too damn much; but you . . . Well, Owl, you understand. That's why I can let myself go with you.

"When a girl's been all bottled up with emotion, she either has to cry, or talk, or throw things, and you'd prefer to have me talk rather than cry or throw things, wouldn't you, Owl?"

He nodded.

She grinned at him. "Good old Owl," she said. "You know, I can always count on you for the most precious thing in life: understanding. Owl, I'm frightfully low tonight, and most awfully tired of holding my chin up—no, I mean out. I want a masculine arm around me and a shoulder to snuggle up against . . . Owl, damn it, I want to try warming over those biscuits."

She sighed tremulously, smiled at him and then suddenly ceased smiling. Her eyes grew wide. "Owl!" she exclaimed, "you're drifting away from me. I can't seem to get my eyes focused. Good Lord, Owl, I'm not tight! I've taken twice that much without feeling like this . . . Owl, don't go away . . . I need you. I . . ."

He crossed to her, picked her up from the chair and held her in his arms as though she had been a child overcome by fatigue.

Her arm twisted around his neck. He felt her lips as a hot circle on his cheek, the warmth of her breath on his neck.

"Oh, Owl," she whispered, "I'm so warm . . . and cuddly . . . and happy . . .",

Yat T'oy opened the door from the bedroom.

"Bed all ready," he said.

Terry carried Cynthia into the bedroom, covered her with a light blanket, turned to Yat T'oy and said, "Under no circumstances, Yat T'oy, is she to know that I have gone out."

The Chinese servant nodded gravely. "Maybeso," he said, in the pidgin English of a servant, "she sleep one hour, no can wake up. After one hour keep on sleep but *can* wake up. You wake her up you come back. She not know you been gone."

Terry nodded, stood over the bed, staring tenderly down at the sleeping figure, a figure which suddenly seemed too small and frail to maintain an armor of facetious levity against the sledge-hammer blows of fate.

He heard a slight noise behind him and turned to see Yat T'oy's expressionless countenance staring inscrutably above the collar of an extended overcoat. "Your coat, your hat," Yat T'oy said. "Velly foggy, you no get wet."

Terry slid into his coat, pulled a dark green felt hat low on his forehead. There was something almost savage in his voice as he said to Yat T'oy, "Take care of her, Yat T'oy, until I come back."

Yat T'oy said, "Plenty heap savvy. Maybeso you like to catchum good luck, maybeso better you go out back way, catchum cab, leave your car stand in front."

# 10

THE MOURNFUL BLASTS OF FOG SIGNALS booming from the misty darkness of the Bay were as eerie as the sound of hooting owls in midnight woods.

Terry Clane turned up the collar of his overcoat, and gazed upward at the wall of the apartment house, its grim darkness broken at intervals by the orange oblongs of lighted windows. In the pauses between fog signals, he could hear the steady drip-drip of fog-bred moisture from the eaves.

It was a night of no wind. The white fog seemed to generate as spontaneously as foam on freshly drawn beer.

Terry stepped into the dark doorway. The outer door was unlocked. He pushed it open and entered the lower corridor. He noticed a ribbon of light showing from under a door marked *Manager*. He tiptoed past this door and climbed stairs.

After the misty freshness of the outer night, the odors of stale cooking assailed his nostrils with increased potency. To his ears, attuned by the spice of danger to the faintest of sounds, came the various night noises of human tenancy. From an apartment on his left sounded the shrill cachinnation of a young woman who had been drinking. A man was snoring loudly in the apartment on his right. Terry climbed the second flight of stairs. A man and a woman were quarreling in one of the front apartments. He heard the faint creak of springs as a restless sleeper stirred uneasily. The doors and partitions, he realized, were hardly thicker than paper.

Terry walked swiftly down the upper corridor, using the beam of his flashlight to guide him. Juanita Mandra's apartment was dark. No light seeped from beneath its door. Terry didn't knock. The skeleton keys, tribute to the ingenuity of Yat T'oy upon an occasion when Terry, suddenly called from Hongkong, had neglected to leave his servant the keys to his rather extensive domicile, made swift sesame of the door.

Clane had learned in the Orient that the secret of nocturnal silence lies in the exercise of infinite patience. Keying his senses to react to the faintest sound of stirring life from the interior of the apartment, he slowly twisted the knob of the door, and spent some fifteen seconds in the tedious process of discounting a squeaking hinge.

A bedroom opened to the left. He could see it but indistinctly. He used his flashlight now only to point straight down at the carpet, and kept the bulb shielded by his cupped hands.

Crouching forward so that the distance between the flashlight and the floor would be as short as possible, he moved upon noiseless feet toward the table in the corner.

The portrait of Jacob Mandra was just as he had seen it earlier in the day. Despite his shielded flashlight, there was enough lightspray to show him the somber canvas with the cynical, silver-green eyes of the dead man apparently watching him in sardonic appraisal.

Terry realized he must either move the table or reach across it and raise the portrait far enough to clear the littered ornaments on the table top, where a cloisonné vase hobnobbed with an ornamental tree composed of cemented seashells.

He doubted that Juanita would have retired, yet his every motion must necessarily be predicated upon the assumption that the bedroom contained her sleeping form. He heard an automobile grind slowly up the steep street, to come to a pulsing stop in front of the apartment house.

Terry leaned across the cluttered table, grasped the portrait of Mandra firmly at the top, and with infinite care raised it until it cleared the last clutching arm of the seashell tree. His flashlight, reposing on the table top, gave a faint illumination sufficient to show him the obstacles which he must avoid.

Holding the portrait in both hands, he stepped back from the table and slowly lowered it until its lower edge rested on the floor. A few seconds later he became conscious of pounding feet in the hallway. He grabbed frantically at the flashlight, switched it off and stood motionless.

The steps came nearer, two men, walking down the corridor.

Terry looked about for some means of escape and could find none. The steps approached the door, ceased. Heavy knuckles sent a loud knock reverberating through the room.

Terry, nerves tense, listened for the sound of creaking bed springs. The heavy knock was repeated and then the voice of Inspector Malloy said, "Open up, this is the law."

Terry's straining ears heard no sound from the bedroom. He stood motionless, hardly daring to breathe, awaiting the next move which would tell him whether Inspector Malloy had followed him to the apartment or was merely searching for Juanita.

He heard Inspector Malloy's voice say, in a rumbling monotone, "Okay, Dave. She isn't here. We'll park the car across the street and wait. You're certain you can spot her?"

A higher pitched voice said, "Of course I can spot her. I've seen her fifty times. She's dark, a swell figure, not over twenty-four or twenty-five . . ."

"And she's the one you saw with Mandra?" Inspector Malloy interrupted.

"Sure she is."

"Okay, we'll wait until she shows. I want to get in here before she has a chance to change things around any. We wait where we can spot her the minute she turns into the street. Then brace her, tell her we're the law, and that we want the low-down. We start talking on the street and rush her up the stairs and into this place. Get it?"

"Sure, I get it. But we'll have to work fast to surprise anything out of her . . ."

The men turned away from the door, started toward the stairs.

Terry, standing in the dark apartment, took stock
of the situation. Inspector Malloy and some other
man were going to be waiting where they could see
every one who entered or left the apartment house.
If Terry tried to leave before Juanita arrived, Malloy would promptly collar him. If he waited for Juanita, he would be discovered in her apartment. If he
took Mandra's portrait with him, Malloy would con-
fiscate it and demand an explanation. If he left it
where he was, Malloy would find it when he came in
with Juanita.

Terry waited until the steps had receded in the
distance. Propping the portrait against the side of
the wall, he tiptoed cautiously into the bedroom. He
sent the beam of his flashlight about in a questing
circle, then stepped to the bedroom window, opened
it and leaned out.

What he saw was not reassuring. Enough illumination was diffused by the thick white fog to show a
sheer drop stretching down farther than Terry dared
to jump. The side of the building was unrelieved by
fire-escape, porch or staircase, and, moreover, Terry
realized that, since it was constructed on a side hill,
it had no back yard and no back entrance. Stepping
into the living room, he confirmed his first impressions by peering down from those windows.

He was trapped.

Standing in front of the portrait, the attempted theft of which threatened to prove so disastrous, Terry tried to find some way out of his predicament.

He could hear the blast of fog signals, the muffled clang of a gong marking the location of a ferry pier, the noise made by distant traffic, the dripping of fog from the eaves. His racing mind took note of the smell of stale tobacco in the apartment, and, more than all, sensed the mocking stare of the painted eyes of the dead bail-bond broker.

Terry sought to exclude these things from his mind. In China he had been taught that thought has the speed of light, that it requires complete concentration for less than a second to grasp any problem of environment with which the mind can be confronted. He remembered the mental exercises of the cowled monks who were accustomed to sit on sharp stones by a roaring waterfall to practice the exclusion of marginal thoughts.

Yet here was something which was no abstract problem, but a predicament from which there seemed no way out, a predicament which involved not only Terry, but Cynthia. Staring into the mocking eyes of the portrait, Terry concentrated.

Abruptly he pocketed his flashlight, twisted the spring lock on the door, stepped out into the corridor and gently pulled the door shut behind him. He walked boldly down the two flights of stairs, pulled his hat down low on his forehead and knocked on the door marked *Manager*. A moment later the door opened to disclose a man in slippers and shirt sleeves, who breathed garlic into the corridor and surveyed Clane with glittering, hostile eyes.

"I'm looking for a vacancy," Clane said, "either a single or a double."

"A helluva time to look for vacancies," the man said, but continued to hold the door open.

"I'm sorry. I'm working, and the only time I have is during the evening. I didn't realize it was so late . . ."

A woman's voice said, "Tony, get away from that door." And the shirt-sleeved figure was jerked out of sight as though it had been a puppet in a Punch-and-Judy show.

While Terry was still marveling at the silent celerity with which the belligerent figure had been whisked into oblivion, its place at the door was taken by a thin woman, whose hatchet face, dark, swarthy skin, long, bony nose, and alert black eyes seemed appropriately framed in the six-inch opening.

"Hello," she said, "what's your name and what do you want?"

"I want an apartment."

"I've got two vacancies."

"Something on the top floor?" Terry ventured.

"Top floor back, on the right, a big single, twenty-five dollars. That includes light and water. You pay for the gas."

"I'd like to look at it," he told her.

"What do you do?"

"I'm a salesman, on a commission basis."

"One month's rent in advance."

"That'll be all right," he agreed, "if I like the apartment."

Without a word she turned away from the door. Terry heard the jangle of keys. A moment later she walked out into the corridor, a tall, bony woman, who took long, flat-footed strides toward the stairs.

Beneath the billowy folds of her skirt, her feet took the treads two at a time. Terry was hard put to it to keep up with her. As she reached the upper corridor, she strode down toward Juanita Mandra's apartment, paused at the adjoining apartment, unlocked and flung open the door, and switched on lights.

Terry saw a gloomy, single apartment, the decorations a monotone of drab cheerlessness. A musty odor clung to the place, but the room was scrupulously clean.

Terry gathered that the apartment was thoroughly cleaned only during the periods when it was unoccupied.

He voiced his thought: "Like a freshly bathed kid who's putting in an uncomfortable Sunday waiting for Monday to come so he can get dirty."

The glittering eyes looked at him searchingly.

"You may be a salesman," she said, "but you talk like an apartment manager."

He smiled, shook his head, and, lest he seem too eager, peered about in the closets and in the little kitchenette, making a critical survey; at the end of which he produced five five-dollar bills. "The name is Sam Pelton," he said.

She scribbled a receipt. "When do you want to move in?" she asked.

"Right now."

"Baggage?"

"It'll come later."

She nodded, handed him the key and said, "Good night." She pulled the door shut behind her and Terry stood, listening to the business-like plunk-kerplunk-kerplunk of her flat feet as she pounded down the corridor.

Switching out the lights in his apartment, he opened the door and stood listening, until he heard the muffled bang of a door on the lower floor.

Terry slipped across the few feet of hallway which separated him from the door of Juanita's apartment and once more his skeleton key clicked back the spring lock. Within less than ten seconds, he had picked up the portrait, tiptoed out of Juanita's apartment and gently closed the door behind him. He walked into the apartment he had just rented and switched on the lights.

Terry removed the thumb tacks and pulled the canvas from the wooden frame which had supported it. He pulled an edge of carpet loose and inserted the canvas between floor and carpet. Then, replacing the carpet, he placed a chair directly over the spot which concealed the portrait. He broke the wooden backing into several pieces, moistened his handkerchief, scrubbed the pieces carefully, so as to remove any fingerprints, and stacked them on the shelf of the closet, picking the darkest corner he could find.

He was consuming his second cigarette when once more he heard steps in the corridor and this time he detected the rich, throaty tones of Juanita Mandra.

". . . a liar. *I'm* the one that left at two o'clock with that painting. I can prove it. Why did I take it? I took it because that woman had hypnotized my husband. He was going to divorce me. . . . How do I know whether she was serious or just playing around? All I know is he . . . fascinated by her . . . didn't give a damn whether he did a little stepping . . ."

As they huddled together before the door and Juanita apparently bent over to insert her key in the lock, Terry missed some of the conversation. A moment later he heard the slam of the door.

Terry dragged a chair to the door, stood on it and listened through the open transom. From time to time he could hear bits of conversation, mostly exclamations from Juanita. Inspector Malloy's voice was, for the most part, merely a suave rumble.

"No, I don't know any Chinese girl!" Juanita half screamed. "What the hell do I care what *she* said?"

There followed the rumble of Inspector Malloy's voice, then Juanita Mandra again, "You can't pin that on me! I tell you I *had* the portrait. It's been stolen!"

Apparently they moved into the bedroom. Their voices all became a mere murmur, punctuated from time to time by an occasional isolated word which meant nothing to Terry. After some ten minutes of fruitless eavesdropping, he heard the door of Juanita's apartment open and Inspector Malloy's voice sounded as distinctly audible as though he had been at Terry's elbow. "Now don't get all excited. We're just checking up, that's all. You see we'd heard about this Chinese girl who said she was a friend of Juanita's, and naturally we got to wondering who Juanita was. It's funny you haven't any idea who that girl could have been, but, if you haven't, that's all there is to it. It's too bad about that portrait. I'm going to tell the D.A. about that. But if it was stolen, why wasn't something else taken?"

Juanita said defiantly, "I tell you the truth and you don't believe me. Come, we will go see the manager. *She* saw the portrait in my apartment. She can tell you that it was here as late as seven o'clock, when I went out. Why do you bother me? Arrest the woman who painted the portrait. I tell you she killed him!"

The door of Juanita's apartment banged shut, and Terry heard the trio pass directly beneath the open transom, heard them on the stairs, and, a few seconds later, the sound of excited conversation from the lower floor.

Because of her friendship for Sou Ha, Juanita was protecting the Chinese girl. And, in extending that protection, she had automatically thrown the cloak of her silence over Terry's visit earlier in the evening. To have referred to Terry as a witness who had seen the portrait, would have been to involve Sou Ha. Despite her desire to enmesh Cynthia Renton in the toils of the law, Juanita was protecting her Chinese friend at all costs.

Terry waited until the sounds of conversation on

the lower floor had subsided. He had fully expected that Inspector Malloy would take Juanita with him to headquarters for questioning. This would leave the coast clear for Terry's escape.

He was surprised, therefore, to hear Juanita's step on the stairs, and Inspector Malloy's booming voice, "It's too bad about that picture. I know how you must feel about it. And I'm all upset, finding that you're Mandra's widow. I wouldn't have bothered you at a time like this for anything. I'll be running along now, and we'll try to get that portrait for you. You just leave everything in my hands. You'll hear from me again."

Juanita said nothing. She was, Terry reflected, hardly the type to be impressed by Malloy's genial sympathy, a sympathy which always seemed directed toward some very definite goal.

Terry stood by the door, listening to the quick tread of Juanita's feet in the corridor, the sound of her key in the lock. Slowly, he climbed down from the chair on which he had been standing. Inspector Malloy had traced Juanita, had learned of the portrait which she had left in her apartment. He had taken steps to check up on that portrait, and *then had gone away!*

Why?

Was he setting some trap for Juanita? Had he, perhaps, something else in mind, something more important than the checking of Juanita's story? In that case, Malloy's sudden departure would have to do with Cynthia Renton or with Terry Clane, and in either event it boded no good. Juanita had admitted her relationship with Mandra, had admitted that she was the woman who had been seen coming down the stairs at two o'clock in the morning, carrying the portrait of the dead bail-bond broker. She had insisted that portrait had been in her possession as late as seven o'clock; and, more to the point, she had produced evidence tending to prove it.

This made her a most important witness. It also brought her into the case as a logical suspect. If she had had that portrait at seven o'clock, as she claimed, then Cynthia's alibi must be founded upon a forged portrait. If she hadn't had the portrait, her admission that she had been at Mandra's apartment at two o'clock in the morning would make her one of the last persons to have seen Mandra alive. In either event, the logical thing would have been for Malloy to have taken her to headquarters for questioning. Yet he had contented himself with apologizing for intruding upon her grief, had expressed his sympathies for the loss of the portrait—and had gone away.

Malloy's action was, on the face of it, so completely inconsistent with the man's character that Terry feared a trap, and, until he knew more of that trap, he was afraid to leave the apartment house.

He smoked several cigarettes, sitting, tense, excitedly expectant, waiting for some event of major importance to take place, yet not having the slightest idea what that event would be.

He prowled around his own apartment, trying to

find some better means of disposing of the portrait and the broken bits of wood. He could find none. To have tried to burn either the canvas or the wood would have been to fill the apartment house with smoke. To have pitched bits of wood out of the window, might or might not have been a good move. He could only tell with the coming of daylight. Yet long before daylight he must find some way of leaving.

Standing in the closet where he had concealed the bits of wood, he became conscious of the sounds of motion. Puzzled, apprehensive, he opened the closet door and made a cautious appraisal of his apartment. It seemed to be just as he had left it, and he could no longer hear the sounds of motion. He returned to the closet, and this time was able to locate the source of the sounds. Juanita was moving about in her apartment, and the back wall of Terry's closet was as a sounding board, transmitting noises from the adjoining apartment. Evidently it backed up to a closet in Juanita's apartment, and either the door of that closet was open, or else she was moving about in the closet itself.

Terry was wishing he had discovered this listening post during Inspector Malloy's visit, when he heard the sound of quick, pounding steps in the corridor. That would be Inspector Malloy coming back. Was he, perhaps, coming to Terry's apartment? Terry listened in an agony of suspense. The steps passed his door, knuckles rapped on Juanita's door.

Terry heard the door open, heard Juanita Mandra

say "What is it?" and then heard the close-clipped accents of Doctor Sedler's voice saying, "You're the widow of Jacob Mandra?"

"Yes. Who are you?"

"My name's Grigsby. I was a business associate of your husband. We had some joint investments that I wanted to discuss with you."

"I don't want to talk about money."

"This is important."

"No. I do no talking. Not now."

"You don't want some other woman to take what is rightfully yours, do you?" Dr. Sedler asked.

That question proved the key to the situation. Juanita said, "Come in."

Terry heard the sound of the door closing, and returned at once to the vantage point of his closet. He found that he could hear the conversation almost as easily as though he had been in the room with the speakers.

"Jake and I were partners," Dr. Sedler was explaining. "His unfortunate death has left matters in confusion. I can understand your grief. I, too, cared for Jake. He was a strong character, peculiar, but likable, once you got to know him. He had many good points. . . ."

"Your business?" Juanita interrupted.

"We had an interest in an automobile insurance company. Not in the insurance itself, but in settling accidental losses which were incurred and in which we were subrogated. It's too complicated for me to explain the details. But there were several cases pending at the time of Jake's death. There's a chance to make some adjustments which will bring money into the estate. But, before I can make those adjustments, I'll have to know just what Jake had done. I'd been out of town for a couple of weeks. I flew back as soon as I read of his death. . . . Now if you'll get his books we can look up . . . well, for instance there's a Cynthia Renton who's paid twenty thousand dollars. I can't get the proper releases until I can prove that payment, and . . ."

"Renton?" Juanita interrupted. "Cynthia Renton?"

"Yes."

"She is the one who killed Jake."

Dr. Sedler said in the crisp voice of a professional man, "That is a startling statement. But I'm not interested in *who* killed him. I want to . . ."

"But *I*," Juanita cried, "am interested in that!"

"I'm sorry. This is a business matter . . ."

"A business of murder. She killed him! She shot him with that sleeve gun, and then she lied to the police! She claimed that *she* was the woman who left Jake's apartment at two o'clock, carrying the portrait. I'll find her and choke the words down her throat. I'll twist her lies into a rope to braid around her neck. I'll . . ."

"Now listen," Sedler interrupted, "I've got to know about what settlements Jake had made. This other stuff of yours is for the police. This of mine is business. It's something we're both interested in. Where are his books?"

ERLE STANLEY GARDNER

Juanita's laugh was scornful.

"Where are his books? You come here and ask me that. *You* say your name is Grigsby and you and my husband were partners. My husband had no partners. Grigsby! And you want to see his books! Do you think I am a fool?"

Sedler's voice was so low that Terry Clane, his ear pressed against the paper-thin wall, could barely hear what was said. "Shut up. Don't blab it to the whole apartment house. You've heard your husband speak of Dr. Sedler."

"What if I have?"

"I'm Sedler."

Her laugh was scornful. Terry heard the rustle of motion, the sound of whispers, and then Sedler saying, "I guess that proves it, doesn't it?"

Juanita's voice was surly and defiant. "What do you want?"

"You know what I want. Jake double-crossed me."

"You lie!"

"I'm not lying. I tell you I can prove it. He collected twenty thousand dollars . . ."

Juanita drowned out his voice. "I know nothing of his business affairs. I know that he had some arrangement with a Dr. Sedler. You seem to be that one. I know nothing about the business which you had with my husband. But I do know that Jake said you were a crook and he distrusted you . . ."

"Shut up, you little fool!" Sedler exclaimed, his voice booming through the thin partition of the closet. "Lower your voice and come down to earth.

202

We're in this thing together. You can't double-cross me. I know too much. I know all about the sleeve gun that killed Jake. I got that gun for him. I know it was in his apartment the night of the murder. *And I know how that sleeve gun was returned!* Now would you rather get Jake's books for me, and play fair for a change, or . . ."

Terry's straining ears heard that unmistakable smacking sound which comes when flesh strikes flesh. He heard Juanita give a choking cry, heard her panting fiercely, and was able to hear the little exclamations with which she interspersed her efforts.

"That's my answer . . . damn you . . . get out! . . . I'll claw out your eyes. . . . You dragged Jake into . . . You devil—Let me go. . . . Let me go. . . ."

Terry heard the sound of bodies bumping against furniture, heard Sedler's gasping voice calling out the names which men of a certain type invariably use as words of abuse to women. Then he heard Sedler exclaim, "So, you're going to try that, eh? Get a load of this!"

There was the solid sound of a blow, and then the thud of something falling. Steps across the room, and Inspector Malloy's voice, "Well, well, what's happening here? No you don't, Buddy! If it's fight you want . . ."

Inspector Malloy's voice was swallowed into the grunting preliminary of physical effort. Terry heard a terrific blow, a crash and Malloy's voice saying, "Get the bracelets on him, Dave, and take a look at the woman. Then we'll just have a look around. . . ."

Juanita, Malloy, the man called Dave, and Dr. Sedler were all closeted in that apartment. If Terry was going to reach Cynthia before it was too late, he must take advantage of that opportunity. It might be hours before another presented itself. He wanted to know what was going to happen next in that apartment, but he also wanted to get to Cynthia.

He left his point of vantage in the closet, tiptoed silently out into the hallway, down the stairs and out into the fog-filled darkness of the wet street.

## 11

MAN IS PRONE TO ATTACH TOO MUCH IM-
portance to the spectacular, and not enough to the
cumulative effect of the little things. Terry, having
won his way to the street, having ascertained that
Inspector Malloy's trap had clamped down upon
Doctor Sedler, was filled with elation. He had removed the original portrait from Juanita's apartment. Cynthia's alibi remained as good as gold save
as it had been impeached by the testimony of the
manager of the apartment house who had seen the
portrait in Juanita's apartment as late as seven
o'clock that evening. But Cynthia had been able to
back up *her* claims by the physical production of an
actual portrait. Juanita had not. Until Malloy could
establish the existence of that other portrait by in-
disputable evidence, he would move very cautiously.
And, by sowing the seeds of suspicion in the minds
of the conspirators who had been a part of Mandra's
blackmail ring, Terry had opened the door for Inspector Malloy to unearth and expose Mandra's sinister activities. Moreover, since every one connected
with those activities believed that the others had been
guilty of deceit, the stage was all set for confessions,

accusations and recriminations which would be of far-reaching importance.

Having accomplished so much, Terry had but to reach Cynthia in advance of Malloy and see that she understood the situation. And he found himself balked by the absurdly simple fact that he could find no effective means of transportation.

The hour was late. The neighborhood was one in which cruising cabs seldom ventured. It was, moreover, foggy and the steep, hilly pavements were wet and slippery. Even walking must be attempted with circumspection. Stores were closed. Nor could Terry pound on the door of a private residence or apartment house and ask to use the telephone. This section of the city was tenanted for the most part by a poorer class of Latin peoples who lived in terror of nocturnal visitors. So Terry, thinking every time he had negotiated one wet, slippery block that he would find a cab at the next block, or, at least, some place from which he could put in a telephone call, continued to hurry through the fog. Twice he tried to signal passing automobiles, thinking that by explaining his predicament to a motorist he might secure a lift to a better lighted, more prosperous district where he could find a cruising cab. In both instances the cars he signaled veered off, and whipping beads of muddy moisture thrown from the whirling tires spatted Terry's clothes and face in a coldly discouraging shower.

There was a night club half a dozen blocks away. Terry had visited it two weeks earlier. He knew he would find a cab there, and, as a last resort, set himself the task of negotiating those six blocks—and the night club was closed. A raid had left the building dark and tenantless. Finally, Terry found a little beer parlor. He was able to telephone, and, a few minutes later, a cab came hissing through the darkness in response to his call. But Terry's wrist watch showed him that more time had been lost than he cared to contemplate.

He gave the driver the number of an apartment house a block from the place where he maintained his residence. If Malloy had closed in on the place, Terry didn't want to come driving up in a cab and plump himself into Malloy's hands.

Terry paid off his cab, walked rapidly toward his apartment house. No suspicious-looking cars were parked in front of the place. A casual glance through the windows of the lobby showed no one whom Terry could not account for. Reassured, he opened the lobby door and entered the lighted interior. The elevator cage was descending. As Terry moved toward it, it slid to a stop and the door opened. An athletic young man with heavy shoulders, a waist which was just a trifle too thick, a pugnacious jaw and hands which were clenched into fists, stood belligerently in the doorway of the elevator.

Terry inspected the blue serge, pin-stripe suit, the golf-club tie pin, the hostile gray eyes, and said casually, "Mr. Nash, I believe."

Stubby Nash launched into invectives. "A hell of a friend *you* turned out to be!" he blazed.

"Of yours?" Terry asked.

"Of everyone."

"I don't think," Terry told him, "I've ever made any particular claim to your friendship in the past. I certainly don't care to do so now."

"You're a hell of a friend for Cynthia, then, if you want it that way."

"And you, I take it, are censoring Cynthia's friendships? Doubtless that will give her *great* pleasure."

Nash pushed forward. Terry gave no ground, but swung slightly to one side. Nash said in a low voice, "Never mind what Cynthia wants. *I* know a rotter when I see one. You've dragged her into a hell of a mess, and now you're keeping her in your apartment."

Terry, looking over Stubby Nash's shoulder, saw a police car slide to a stop at the curb. The door opened and Inspector Malloy bounded to the curb. Behind him other men spewed forth, and separated. Malloy barged into the lobby of the apartment house and grinned broadly as he took in the situation.

Stubby Nash said, "If you won't understand words, you may understand this! . . ." and swung his fist.

Terry stepped smoothly back, shot up a deft hand, plucked Stubby's blow out of the air, diverted it into glancing futility, and heard Inspector Malloy say, "Now, now! That's no way to do, boys! I wouldn't want to have to arrest you. That'd be too bad! Come on, boys, into that elevator. I want to talk with you."

His broad shoulders pushed them back into the cage. Two plain-clothes officers, following Malloy into the lobby, came crowding in after the inspector.

"Who the hell are *you?*" Stubby Nash demanded.

Inspector Malloy flipped back the lapel of his coat, gave Nash a glimpse of a gold shield, indicated the two plain-clothes men and said, "A couple of assistants."

Nash was breathing rapidly from rage, and his exertion. "I'm Nash," he said, "and I . . ."

"Yes, yes," Malloy interrupted, "I know all about you, Nash. You're a friend of Miss Cynthia's. You retained a lawyer for her. Glad to see such devotion. The first thing I said when I heard about you and what you'd done was that it was too bad you'd had to do it. If you'd only have come directly to me in the first place we could have fixed things all up. It's too bad you didn't. . . . But right now, my business is with Mr. Clane. I'm going to search your apartment, Clane."

Terry said grimly, "Not without a warrant."

Malloy beamed. "Do you know, Clane, what I told the boys at headquarters when I telephoned in for them to meet me here? Well, I told them I fancied your nerves would be getting worn a bit thin, and that it was just too bad we had to intrude on you again tonight. You've had rather a long day, rather a strenuous day. It began when you were summoned to the D.A.'s office early this morning, and it's been keeping up ever since. I told the boys I wouldn't blame you a bit for refusing to let us in without a warrant, and I told them to get a warrant and meet me here. It's just too bad, Clane, but it's something I have to do."

Clane said wearily, "Yes, I knew it would be too bad. What specifically are you searching for, Inspector?"

"A portrait of Jacob Mandra. It was stolen from the apartment of Juanita Mandra some time after seven o'clock this evening. Of course, Clane, that doesn't mean we suspect you of any crime. It merely means that we want to take a look through your apartment. Just a matter of form, you know. But when you consider that the murder weapon had been taken from your apartment, you must realize that it's only reasonable to suppose some of the other things that figured in the crime might be hidden there."

"Did the portrait figure in the murder?" Terry asked.

"I'm afraid it did," Malloy told him.

"You can't let them in there *now!*" Stubby expostulated to Clane.

Inspector Malloy seized on the remark. "Not *now?*" he asked Stubby. "And why not *now?* What's the reason *this* particular time is so inopportune?"

Nash lowered his eyes, said nothing.

The elevator came to a stop, and Inspector Malloy said, breezily, "Well, here we are. After all, it's just a formality. Come on, boys, and we'll get it over with as quickly as possible and let Mr. Clane get some sleep. . . . And why shouldn't we search the place *now*, Nash?"

Stubby avoided his eyes.

"I wonder if you're referring to the presence of some other person in Clane's apartment," Malloy said musingly, walking down the corridor, his hand on Nash's elbow.

"I think, Inspector," Clane remarked, "you've gone about far enough along that line. Suppose you show me the search warrant."

"By all means," Malloy agreed cordially. "Here it is, Clane. Just a formality, of course; but one of those little formalities which are sometimes so necessary. You'll notice that it's all in order. And there's an endorsement that it may be served in the nighttime. Notice that, please. You see, I left Juanita Mandra's apartment and went directly to a telephone. I called headquarters and told them to get a search warrant for your apartment. Then I went back to Mrs. Mandra's place. She's his widow, all right. She was married to him. Rather a bundle of emotions, that girl, but then, you wouldn't know her. She's a dancer. . . . Well, well, here we are. Perhaps you'd better explain to that Chinese servant of yours that we're free to go all through the place, Clane. Those Orientals are sometimes a little slow about understanding our laws, and I'd hate to have any misunderstanding. You see, these boys of mine are a little quick on the trigger. . . . No, no, Nash, that's just an expression. . . . I didn't mean they'd pull a gun, but they swing a wicked fist on occasion, and I'd hate to have any misunderstandings, particularly since Mr. Clane's been so willing to co-operate with us all along."

Terry didn't open the door of the apartment, but rang the bell. When Yat T'oy answered the bell, Terry said to him, "These men alla-same policee men. Must come make search this place . . . Oh, hell, Inspector, I can't explain it to him in English. I'll have to tell him so he can understand. . . ." And Terry, switching abruptly to Chinese, said, "Get the painter woman out of here, while I keep these men . . ."

He was able to say no more. Inspector Malloy pushed past him into the apartment, sending Yat T'oy spinning back against the wall. "Come on, boys," Malloy said to the plain-clothes men. "The warrant's been served. You can go ahead explaining to the Chink while we make the search, Clane."

Clane tried to reach the bedroom before the members of the searching party, but the men spread out as though they had carefully rehearsed every move. With ruthless efficiency, they ransacked the place, going through closets, trunks, files, peering behind pictures, in drawers, even moving out clothes from the closets.

Terry managed to enter the bedroom as the men were piling things onto his bed. The bed was freshly made. The pillows were smoothed into perfect mounds of unwrinkled white.

Inspector Malloy said to Stubby Nash, "How did you know Miss Renton was here?"

Clane interrupted the question. "I thought your warrant was to search for a portrait of Mandra, Inspector."

"That's right, Clane, that's right. But, do you know, I had an idea we'd find Cynthia Renton here, and we want to question her. There's nothing in the law which says you can't find two things while you're searching for one."

Clane said hotly, "That's a hell of a trick!"

"Now, now," Malloy soothed, "your nerves are all ragged, Clane. I don't blame you. You've had a hard day. But if you'll just tell us where Miss Renton is . . . You see, I happen to know she's here, and Nash knows it, too. She couldn't have gone, and yet . . ." He paused, frankly puzzled.

"The fire-escape," one of the men suggested.

Malloy shook his head. "A man's watching it at the bottom. Another man's watching the roof."

"Did you," Terry asked, as one who is mildly interested in the answer, "have any *particular* reason to think she'd be here?"

Malloy said nothing, but Stubby Nash said, "You damn well know she's here. You've compromised her good name and spoiled her chances of getting out of this mess. Someone should punch you in the jaw."

"Since you're showing such remarkable powers of observation, not to say clairvoyance," Terry suggested, "perhaps you can go further and supply the name of the person who should punch me in the jaw."

Malloy, stepping between them, said, "That'll do, boys! That'll do."

Stubby sneered. "That's not going to stand in my way when I meet you again."

"I should most certainly hope not," Terry agreed.

Stubby turned wrathfully away.

Inspector Malloy fixed Terry Clane with forceful eyes. "Look here, Clane, you'll admit Miss Renton was at your apartment earlier in the evening."

"I'll admit nothing."

"But she *was* here."

"Are you certain?"

"Of course I'm certain."

"Then why ask me to admit it?"

"Because I want to find out just where you stand."

Terry shrugged his shoulders.

"You won't admit it?"

"No."

"You'll deny it on your word of honor?"

Terry said with dignity, "If you're *quite* finished, I think I'll get some sleep."

"We're a long ways from finished," Malloy said, turning away. "Nash, you stay with me. I don't want you two getting into a fight."

"Is Nash, perhaps, one of your deputies?" Terry asked.

"What do you mean by that, Clane?"

"I mean that you're here as an officer. Nash isn't *my* guest. If you're responsible for him, you'd better deputize him so I can hold you accountable for any damage he may do."

Malloy frowned, then grinned at Stubby. "He's

got you there, Nash," he admitted. "I'm afraid you'll have to step out. Just wait outside in the corridor. I want to talk with you. No, no . . . he's right, Nash. This is his apartment. Some other time you can say what you have to say to him. Not now. And, besides, I want to talk with you first."

He escorted Stubby to the corridor and returned to the search. Thirty minutes later the men finished ransacking the apartment and acknowledged defeat. But Malloy refused to be shaken from his booming cordiality. "It's too bad, Clane. I hated to do it. But you'll remember I told you right at the start it was just a matter of form. It's too bad you got mixed into the business in the first place . . . all over the theft of that gun, too! Well, good night!"

The men shuffled out into the corridor. Terry looked at Yat T'oy with raised eyebrows.

Yat T'oy's voice showed no emotion. "The woman," he said in Cantonese, "climbed up the fire-escape."

"*Up* the fire-escape!" Terry exclaimed.

Yat T'oy gravely nodded.

"And where the devil did she go after she went *up* the fire-escape?"

"I am but a servant," Yat T'oy told him, "and these things are beyond me."

Terry went to the fire-escape and looked out. It stretched down into the milky darkness, up into the swirling mists of moisture. He realized that the detectives must have made a similar inspection. The answer was beyond him. He still suspected Yat T'oy of having pulled a fast one, but the servant's face was as blank as the front walls which camouflage the houses of Chinese millionaires.

Terry locked the door of his bedroom, donned his pajamas, turned out the lights, and was just getting into bed, when he sensed that some vaguely indistinct object was perched on the fire-escape outside of his window.

He reached for the light with a start, to hear Cynthia Renton's voice chanting in a soft monotone:

"But when all the world is asleep at night
    And nowhere is there a breath of light
Mister Owl comes out, spreads his wings for
    flight,
        Tahoo, tah-o-o-o-o-o-o-o, says the owl in the
        tree."

"What the devil are you doing out there?" Terry asked.

"Getting my clothes wet," she confessed. "This fire-escape is sopping. Are you going to invite me in?"

Without waiting for him to say anything, she climbed in through the window.

Terry switched on the light.

"Oo, Owl," she moaned, "I've got a headache!"

He thrust his feet into slippers, went into the bathroom and returned with a Bromo Seltzer, which she drank eagerly.

"If you'd been Mandra," she said, "I'd accuse you of having drugged me. I went out like a light."

"Never mind about that now," he said. "The point is, how did you get out of here, and where have you been?"

She giggled. "Stubby Nash came up and pounded on the door and tried to get Yat T'oy to let him in. The argument woke me up, Owl, and there I was, lying in your bed! What a predicament, Owl. And Stubby's *so* narrow-minded! So I got up and made the bed and wanted to get out. Then I heard you having an argument with Malloy as you came walking down the hall. I climbed out the fire-escape. I realized they'd have men in the alley, so I couldn't go *down* the fire-escape, but it was foggy enough so I could climb *up* without being seen. I was afraid to go clean up to the roof because they might have men there. The man in the apartment above you had his window open. I crawled in and sat down in a chair."

"Was *he* there?"

"Lord bless you, yes. He was in bed and snoring like a freight train on an up-grade."

"And you calmly sat there all this time?"

"There was nothing calm about it at all. I was shivering in my boots. . . . Wouldn't it be just *like* Stubby to go ahead and spill the beans?"

"How did he know you were here?"

"He just suspected it. It's that rotten, jealous nature of his. I'm going to tell him where he gets off, in words of one syllable. He isn't engaged to me, and has no right to pull a stunt like that. He should know better. . . . Tell me, Owl, why did you get me tight?"

"I didn't get you tight."

"You plied me with liquor."

"You said you wanted a drink."

She tilted her head to one side, surveying him as a bird might survey some strange bug. "It's the Oriental in you, Terry, you won't answer a straightforward question. You've become like the Heathen Chinee, with ways that are dark and tricks that are vain. You drugged me so I wouldn't know what you were doing. Tell me, Owl, what *were* you doing?"

"What makes you think I was doing something?"

"But you were. You went out somewhere and did some dire, dark deed. Come on, Owl, 'fess up."

Terry was about to reply, when he heard the sound of pounding knuckles on the corridor door and Stubby Nash's voice shouted, "Cynthia's in there! Let me in. I demand it! The cops have gone, and we're going to have this out, man to man."

"That damn fool," Cynthia said critically, "is going to wake the house up. Open the door, Terry, I'm going to tell him plenty."

Terry strode to the door, snapped back the bolt, opened it and in a voice cold with fury said, "Is there any way we can keep you from making such a confounded fool of yourself?"

Stubby whirled on him. "Damn you!" he cried, "keep out of my business and let my girl alone!"

Terry saw cumulative hatred welling up in the man's eyes. The right shoulder swung back, then he saw Stubby's fist coming in a wild swing toward his jaw.

Terry jerked back. The blow missed his jaw by inches.

"Shut up," he cautioned. "Are you completely crazy? Those officers may still be around here."

"I'll show you who's crazy!" Stubby yelled, as he came swinging forward.

Terry caught a glimpse of the grinning face of Inspector Malloy, standing in the doorway of an adjoining apartment.

"Well," Terry grunted, "at least I'll have *one* satisfaction."

He stepped swiftly to one side, with the agile motion of a trained boxer, and swung a blow which was as perfectly timed as the golf swing of a professional.

As his fist thudded on the side of Stubby's jaw, sending him backward and down, Inspector Malloy sauntered into the room and said, "That'll be about enough of that. You, Miss Renton, are under arrest. And there's just a chance, Clane, that *you'll* have a permanent change of address if you keep on monkeying with buzz saws."

Terry turned so he could watch Stubby Nash, who had propped himself to a sitting position and was stroking his jaw, his punch-groggy eyes glassy and unfocused. "And there's more where that came from, Nash," he said.

Inspector Malloy nodded to Cynthia. "Come on, sister," he commanded.

"I presume, of course," Terry observed, "you have some grounds for your action. I believe Miss Renton has an attorney who will see that her legal rights are protected."

Malloy grinned.

"It would have been a swell scheme if it had worked," he said, "but it just happens that this Juanita woman was the one who went down the stairs of the apartment house at two o'clock in the morning carrying Mandra's portrait. That leaves Miss Renton's alibi all full of holes."

"You have found the portrait you refer to and can prove it was the one taken by the woman you call Juanita?"

Malloy's face showed irritation.

"Otherwise," Terry went on, holding the flame to the end of a cigarette with a hand which showed not the slightest sign of trembling, "C. Renmore Howland would have but little difficulty in convincing a jury that the police had been more than usually credulous."

He knew by the swift flicker of expression which crossed Inspector Malloy's face that his shot had told, but Malloy gave no other sign of weakening as he escorted Cynthia to the elevator, with a rather dazed Stubby Nash stumbling along behind.

# 12

ALMA'S EYES GAVE NO INDICATION THAT she had been crying. Watching her, Terry decided the manifestations of grief would come later. Just then she was in the position of one who had work to do and couldn't take time out to indulge in emotions.

"Terry," she said, "we're depending on you. I just came from visiting Cynthia in jail."

There was no outward curiosity upon the face of Yat T'oy as he shuffled into the room, bearing drinks.

Terry said, "How do things look for her, Alma?"

"In some ways rather bad."

"Has she made any statements?"

"Not after she was arrested. She refused to say a word unless Renny Howland was there. Of course, she made a statement to the district attorney when she was first questioned."

"In which she said she carried the painting away with her?"

Alma's face showed a swift shadow of discouragement.

"Yes," she said. "Oh, Terry, why *didn't* I get in touch with you before we got into the mess! It looked like such an easy way out at the time, I didn't figure what must inevitably follow."

"Cheer up," Terry told her. "I think we'll come out all right yet."

"Have you heard anything more?"

He shook his head.

"They're going to do something with you. Terry?"

"I suppose so. But in the meantime they're giving me the mental third degree of letting me wonder just when they're going to strike."

"They'll arrest you?"

He nodded, smiled and said, "Sure. Why not?"

"Can they prove anything?"

"Not a thing," he said cheerfully. "Inspector Malloy insists there have been some very remarkable coincidences connecting me with the case. So far, that's all he can prove—merely remarkable coincidences."

"So far, Terry?" she asked.

He nodded.

"But suppose . . . well . . . suppose he should be able to get some proof?"

"Then," Terry said, "he would be confronted with something of a dilemma. He'd have two murderers instead of one, and he wouldn't know just which was which. That's why he's concentrating on Cynthia first. If he can't pin it on her, he'll switch to me, but he knows how important it is to have public opinion with him in a murder case, so he's holding Cynthia under suspicion at the present time and mentioning to newspaper men that one of her close friends is being kept under surveillance."

"But, Terry," she said, her eyes staring at him in

steady appraisal, "how about this Juanita? She swears that *she* had the portrait Cynthia painted. She swears *she* was the woman who went down the stairs at two o'clock in the morning."

Terry Clane clinked the ice in his glass and said, "So what?"

"And she claims someone stole the portrait from her."

"Most interesting," Terry remarked. "It's a shame she hasn't the portrait to back up her story."

Alma lowered her voice.

"Terry," she said, "you know and I know that she really *did* have that portrait."

Terry said, "Personally, I wouldn't put too much reliance in her statement. She's too emotional and high-strung, and she has the devil of a temper. No telling what a woman like that would do."

"Terry, you're making fun of me. You know and I know . . ."

"Nothing," he interrupted. "We can only surmise."

He sipped his drink.

She shrugged her shoulders and said, "Well, if you won't be frank with me, you won't."

"I'm always frank," he told her.

"But baffling," she charged. "Terry, don't sit there grinning like a Cheshire Cat, this is serious. You're taking it as too much of a joke."

"Almost the same words that Inspector Malloy used," Clane observed. "By the way, Cynthia's law-

yer rang me up and said he'd like to have me stop at
his office this afternoon for a conference. What does
he want? Do you know?"

"No. He told me to come, too. He said things
looked pretty black, and we were all going to have
to pull together to get Cynthia out of it."

"Laying the foundation for a bigger retainer?"
Terry asked.

"I don't think so. Stubby Nash gave him a check.
I don't know how much it was, but I think it was
ample."

"How does Cynthia feel about that?"

"She doesn't like it. She told me she was going to
pay her own legal fees."

"There's just a chance," Clane said musingly,
"this lawyer might do more harm than good."

"How do you mean, Terry?"

"Events," Terry said slowly, "are like a jigsaw
puzzle. Each piece fits into some other piece, and if
the pieces don't fit, the puzzle doesn't work. If the
police can't get all the pieces they may not be able
to put the puzzle together, but if they get *too many*
pieces, and then put the whole thing together, they'll
be able to detect those which are spurious."

Alma's forehead showed lines of worry. "I've been
thinking of that, Terry. I wonder if you could talk
with Howland when you see him this afternoon."

He nodded slowly.

"Terry," she said, "we're in a position where we've
all got to be frank. Cynthia needs you, and I need
you. And, somehow, you're both holding back because

of me. I care so much for both of you . . . and I'm like a wall, standing between you.

"Terry, I want you to talk to me and tell me the truth. You've said things from time to time which didn't sound so dreadfully important at the time. Lots of them impressed me as being unsound ideas. Lately I've realized how terribly right you were."

He studied her and said, "Such as what, Alma?"

"You said once that the underlying relationship between the sexes was one of hostility. What did you mean by that, Terry?"

"Just what I said. To the extent that sex enters into companionship, there's an underlying hostility. Real, frank friendships can only be had when the sex element is either entirely absent or else taken for granted."

"Isn't that a cynical way of looking at life, Terry?" she asked.

"Perhaps."

"Terry," she said, "I came to tell you something."

"What?"

"You're fighting yourself."

"I?" He raised his brows.

"Yes, you."

He became facetious and said, "Well, it should be a good even money bet. Which do you think will win, Alma, myself or me?"

"Don't kid me, Terry," she said, "you know what I'm trying to say, and you're afraid to have me say it."

Slowly he set down his glass and said, "Go ahead, Alma. . . . Perhaps you're right."

"You were in love with me when you went to China," she said, not as one asking a question, but as one making a statement, with a note of calm certainty in her voice.

"Yes," he said, dropping his hand to his glass and sliding the tips of his fingers up and down the moist surface.

"Why did you go, Terry?"

"You were married to Bob," he said slowly, "and Bob was my best friend. Then there was that night in my apartment . . . and I found out that I loved you and . . . well, things like that can't be lived down, ever."

"Don't be such a Sir Galahad, Terry. You know, or should know, that the old double standard has become pretty obsolete. The really intellectual people know that sometimes circumstances . . . the sudden rush of emotion . . . a few drinks . . . Oh, Terry, you're making it hard for me to say."

"Bob was my best friend," he said. "I was madly in love with you. It's all right for you to look back on it and think it was circumstances . . . I don't know how you looked at it at the time, but I know how I felt about it."

"And so you went to China," she said softly.

"I went to China," he agreed. "I sailed the next day and I didn't let anyone know my address. I deliberately closed a chapter of my life."

"And Bob died within six months . . . and there

was a report that you were dead, and I never believed it, Terry. I kept your picture on my dresser for those long years. You were there with me . . . watching me . . . the last thing when I turned out the light at night, the first thing in the morning."

"And Bob died without knowing?" he asked.

She nodded and said slowly, "All this was seven years ago, Terry. You went away just seven years ago."

"And now," he said, "I'm back, Alma."

There was almost a sob in her voice, but she went bravely on, "No, Terry, you're not back. Why pretend that you are? The Terry who went away never came back. He couldn't, Terry, because he was such a strange, visionary Terry. He loved the wife of his friend—and he went into self-imposed exile. And he never came back. Another Terry came back. Those years did things to you, and they did things to me. You went away, Terry. You were in love with me, and I was in love with you. I thought it was my duty to be loyal to Bob. I fought against my feeling for you, just as you thought it was your duty to be loyal to him and fought against your feeling for me. But the fact remains that you went away.

"Bob died. I concentrated on my career. You concentrated on forgetting. You became an adventurer. I became a plodder. . . . No, don't interrupt, Terry, I'm a plodder, I know it. I'm a slave to my success.

"You told me once that the world levied a price for everything the world gave us, that the price of success was always more than the purchaser was prepared to pay. In some ways, Terry, you were right—that's the worst of you, you're always right.

"When you came back, it was a different Terry, one who had taught himself to adventure, to seek the thrill of new experiences. You found a different Alma, one who had become fairly successful. Some call me famous.

"For years, Terry, I'd been stifling all of my impulses, concentrating every bit of my energy upon achieving success. I achieved it, and while I was achieving it, I was losing my ability to laugh, to live and to *love*.

"I didn't realize it consciously, but subconsciously I did. That's why I encouraged Cynthia to play. I liked to watch her getting a kick out of life. I even went so far, Terry, as to get something of a martyr's complex, thinking that girls like Cynthia who caught the masculine fancy always seemed to be able to play with life without getting their fingers burnt, but that always in the background must be some woman with a maternal instinct watching over them, standing between them and the blows which the world would strike."

"Alma," Terry said, getting to his feet, standing by his chair, staring across and down at her, "you're unjust—unjust to yourself and . . ."

"Don't, Terry!" she interrupted. "Don't stop me now. I've got started and I must finish. You came back—Terry Clane, the adventurer. You'd sailed into the far ports, seen strange people, and had adventures—and liked them.

"You found Alma Renton a serious painter, rapidly winning international acclaim. And you found Cynthia, a happy, carefree play-girl, who, nevertheless, had enough sense of restraint and responsibility to be decent, who laughed at life because she refused to be crushed by it. And she appealed to the adventurer in you. But you were loyal, Terry, not to me, but to your memory of me. I still love you, but I love my career more. I'm too ploddingly methodical to appeal to you in the way Cynthia does. I think and plan and plod, while Cynthia lives and laughs and loves.

"I came to tell you, Terry, to quit fighting with yourself. I'm not a machine, I'm a woman. I *want* to to have a home, a garden. I *want* to plan meals, I *want* a husband, I *want* children. But I know that I can never have them, Terry. Too long now I've concentrated every bit of energy I have, toward perfecting my painting. Now it's grown to be bigger than I am. It's bigger than the woman in me, bigger than the maternal instinct, bigger than anything else in life."

She ceased talking, and for a long moment Terry stood silent. Then he said slowly, "And so?"

"And so," she said, "I want you to know that you mustn't let any mistaken loyalty to me stand between you and Cynthia."

"How much," he said, "of what you have just said was said for yourself, and how much was said for Cynthia?"

She shook her head, jumped to her feet and said,

"Terry, don't cross-examine me. I've told you. I've told you the truth. Now I've got that off my chest, I must go. And you *will* go to see Howland, won't you. Terry? It may mean a lot to Cynthia."

She crossed to the door before he could stop her. Her hand reached for the knob, fumbled about in a groping search.

"Alma," he said, reaching for her, "you're crying. Come back here."

As he took her shoulders in tender hands, the knob turned from the other side. She stepped back into his arms, keeping her tear-flooded eyes averted. The door opened.

Yat T'oy's imperturbable eyes stared calmly at Terry.

"Embroidered Halo," he said in Cantonese, "awaits you. I have taken her into your bedroom, that she may not know the painter woman is here. It is important that you go to her at once."

# 13

TWIN RED SPOTS SHOWED ON SOU HA'S cheeks. Her eyes glittered with emotion, but she affected the elaborate casualness of flippant youth.

"Hi, Wise One," she said.

"Hello, Sunshine," he answered, matching her tone, while his eyes studied the dilated nostrils, the tense rigidity of her pose and the evasion of her manner. "What'll it be this time, melon seeds or highballs?"

She shook her head, made a little gesture with her hand, as though checking him. She was like some wild thing approaching a suspicious object, ready at any moment to turn and bound into flight.

"You were at Juanita's apartment sometime after our visit, and before midnight?" she asked.

He remained silent and motionless.

"Why did you go there?"

He shrugged his shoulders and said, "I'll not lie to you, Embroidered Halo."

She said slowly, "It is unfortunate Juanita hated the painter woman."

"Time spent in contemplating misfortunes is time wasted," he told her. "Unless one may thereby change the bad to the good."

"Do you, then, love her that much?" she asked.

He purposely misunderstood her. "Juanita?" he inquired, raising his eyebrows.

She was impatient, and showed it in her voice. "The painter woman. Do not avoid the question."

He moved toward her. "What is it, Sou Ha? What's wrong?"

She backed away from him, her face utterly impassive save for the slightly dilated nostrils and those two tell-tale spots of dusky red beneath the satiny smoothness of the skin.

"Tell me," she demanded.

His eyes were narrowed now. "I will," he said, "answer your question with a question. . . ."

"You will," she told him, "answer my question with deeds, not with words. I have come to tell you the truth. *I* am the one who killed Jacob Mandra. He tried to blackmail me. He demanded that I should make my father cease fighting this opium ring, otherwise he would show that I had crippled a man by hitting him with my automobile. He said I was drunk, and some doctor also claimed I was drunk."

He watched her in frowning concentration.

"And what did you do?"

"I placed the seal of silence on his lips. The man was evil, and I killed him."

"With what?"

"With your sleeve gun."

"Where did you get it?"

"From the case in your apartment. Afterwards Yat T'oy saw it was gone and locked the door, lest you should accuse him of carelessness when you discovered its loss. I tied it to my arm and pressed my arm down on the table top as Mandra leered across at me. He was evil, I killed him, and my soul knows no regret."

He studied her thoughtfully.

"Where was he sitting?"

"At the table where the body was found."

"Was the portrait there in the room at the time you killed him?"

"No, certainly not. Juanita had taken that with her when she left at two o'clock."

"Where was the painter woman?"

"Asleep in another room. I think she had been drugged. She did not waken, but she stirred uneasily. Her black bag lay on the table at Mandra's elbow."

"Did you leave through the corridor door?"

"No, I left as I entered."

He regarded her with narrowed eyes. "Whom have you told of this?"

"No one save you."

"Why do you tell me?"

"So that you can save the painter woman if it becomes necessary—but only if you have to do it to save her. Otherwise I am proud of what I did. My race does not regard such an act as being wicked. He was evil. He needed to die. The law could not touch him. I sent him to his ancestors."

"Look here, Sou Ha, do you know what this means?"

"I am not a child."

233

"But why do you tell me of this? *I* want to protect you. I know the man was evil."

"You also want to protect this painter woman?"

"Yes."

"And to protect me?"

"Yes."

She laughed bitterly and said, "I am not of your race. You love her. Protect her. If it becomes necessary, surrender me to your law. I have placed my life in your keeping."

She turned and sought the door. And Terry Clane knew enough of his Chinese not to interrupt the dignity of her exit by word or gesture.

It was as she gently closed the bedroom door that Terry, moodily contemplating the opposite wall, noted that one of the pictures was slightly tilted. His training in the Orient had taught him to notice details and to appreciate the hidden significance of those things which would appear trivial to the casual eye. He strode to the picture. Looking on the floor directly beneath it, he detected several bits of plaster dust. He gently tilted the picture. Behind it was a sinister dark object, a concealed microphone, looking as malevolently omnipotent as the unblinking eye of a serpent.

Terry gently replaced the picture, walked quickly back to the center of the room and, speaking in a naturally conversational tone of voice, his face turned toward the empty chair which Sou Ha had just vacated, said, "No, Sou Ha, wait a minute. I have something to tell you, a confession of my own. But

I must make it in my own way, and you mustn't interrupt me. You promise? That's fine.

"I am going to tell you something of Mandra, something which, perhaps, you already know, since he tried to blackmail you. Mandra and a Dr. Sedler were working together, hand in glove. There were two others in the game, but they were small fry, one was a man with a serious spinal injury, the other an acrobatic tumbler.

"This combination was supposed to be working together, but the individuals were actually double-crossing each other. Mandra collected twenty thousand dollars from one victim. He held out on the others. Dr. Sedler heard of this and became angry. He sought out Mandra to demand an accounting. Mandra was cold, sneering and triumphant. Sedler determined to kill him.

"Now, that leads up to my own connection with the case, but first, in order that you may understand exactly what I have done, I want you to know just how I feel toward this painter woman. . . . No, don't interrupt me, Sou Ha, you promised, you know. . . . Sit back there and listen to me. . . . Look at me, Sou Ha. . . . There, that's better.

"You think that I am in love with the painter woman. And when you say the painter woman, you mean Alma. Please believe me when I tell you that I am *not* in love with Alma. Remember that much can happen in seven years . . . and remember that I have a confession to make, not in regard to my feelings for the painter woman, but in regard to the murder."

Terry paused to take a deep breath. Mechanically he wiped a handkerchief across his forehead. He knew now how a radio announcer must feel, talking against time when something goes wrong with a program schedule, striving to hold his listeners with an improvised patter.

Terry moved over to the window and looked down at the sidewalk. He saw Sou Ha cross the strip of cement, enter her car and drive out from the curb, unmolested. As nearly as Terry could tell, she was not followed.

But Inspector Malloy was waiting somewhere at the other end of that dictograph wire. One thing, and ore thing alone, would hold him to continued inactivity, Terry's repeated assertion that he was about to make a "confession." And even that bait would soon grow stale. Sou Ha must be given every opportunity to get away.

Terry turned back toward the dictograph. "Now, Sou Ha, you must realize that Mandra was a man of many interests. In some of those interests he had crossed you and your father. But how about me? Isn't it possible that I, too, was a victim of that same hoax which Mandra played upon automobile drivers who had taken a drink or two? Isn't it possible that I, myself, had reason to wish both Mandra and Sedler out of the way? And how about Sedler? Think for a moment of his position. *Think*, I say!"

Terry paused. He realized he wasn't doing so well. He dared not actually implicate himself, yet nothing short of a confession would stay Malloy's hand.

Sooner or later the Inspector would realize Terry was talking against time. . . . He was seized with a sudden inspiration. . . . "Wait right there, Sou Ha, and think this matter over. I am going to step into the next room and get some papers which will furnish definite proof of what I have to say. When you see these papers, you will realize . . . But sit there and wait. Do not move."

Terry walked to the door which led to his bedroom, jerked it open, slammed it shut with an audible bang, and waited. He had not long to wait. As he heard a commotion at the door of the apartment, he opened a drawer in his desk, started rummaging through some papers. He heard Yat T'oy's voice screaming, "No can come! No can come in!" Then the sound of swift struggle, and the door opened to disclose Inspector Malloy's broad, capable shoulders pushing their way into the room.

Terry looked up with a start of surprise. "Why, Inspector," he said, "what brings you here?"

Malloy was cordial as ever, but there was a glint in his eyes which belied the geniality of his manner. "Well, Clane," he said, "it's getting so I'm calling on you in so many different capacities I hardly know how to keep them separated, myself. Now, for instance, there's the theft of your sleeve gun. In one of my capacities I'm trying to help you find out who stole that. And then there's my capacity as investigator. In the one capacity I'm helping you—a friend, as it were. In the other capacity I'm causing you some inconvenience by doing my duty."

"I see," Clane said, "and which is it this time?"

"Oh, this time I'm a friend! I got an idea about that sleeve gun business. You know, I'd like to nail the one who stole that, and I think I'm getting close. Of course, I can't guarantee results, but I think I'm making progress."

"And just what did you want?" Terry asked.

"Thought I'd take a look through the place, if you don't mind, and see just how many exits and entrances there were. Perhaps some of the doors will show evidences of having been pried open with a jimmy. You know, Clane, it's just the usual routine investigation."

"You're making it at a rather late hour, aren't you, Inspector?"

"Well," Malloy admitted, "I've been a busy man. You know that, Clane. Now let's see, suppose we begin with the bedroom? I'd like to take a look in there . . . and, oh, yes, tell that Chink of yours not to get so vehement when I drop in. He seems to think I'm trying to rob you or something."

"Perhaps," Terry said, "he doesn't fully appreciate these different capacities in which you call."

Malloy grinned and nodded. "That must be it," he said. "In the meantime, how about taking a look in that bedroom, Clane?"

Yat T'oy, watching Terry, his wrinkled, inscrutable countenance as fixed in its expression as though it had been carved from old ivory, said in Chinese, "There are men in the hallway, men who search the alley, men who are watching the fire escape. And this man is evil, First Born. His mouth speaks the words of friendship, but his hand is the hand of an enemy, clenched to strike."

Terry answered him in the same language, "The best way to confuse a trapper is to walk around the trap, pretending, the while, that you do not know it is there."

Malloy, his hand on the doorknob, his forehead creased in a scowl, said, "I guess I'll have to learn Chinese if I'm going to keep up with you, Clane."

Terry laughed. "I thought you wanted me to explain to him the different capacities in which you called."

Malloy jerked open the door, surveyed the empty bedroom without surprise. "I'll take a look around," he announced, and proceeded to make a complete search of the place, while Terry, standing at the window, noticed the men who were stationed at various points of vantage about the sidewalk, and heard the tramp of feet in the corridor.

Malloy had quite evidently taken over some adjoining apartment as field headquarters. The wire from the dictograph must run into that apartment, and Malloy had been holding enough men there to "sew up the place" whenever the occasion might demand.

As it was gradually forced home upon Malloy's consciousness that the bird had flown the cage he had so carefully constructed, his face darkened, but he still kept his genial manner.

"Now is there any possible means of getting in or out of this apartment that you haven't shown me,

Clane?" he asked. "You know, in solving a theft, it's important to figure out just how the thief came in, and just how he went out."

Terry, knowing the real reason for the question, achieved an inward chuckle as he said, with a perfectly serious countenance, "No, Inspector, there's no way of getting in or out that you haven't seen."

Malloy frowned. "Funny about that Renton woman last night," he said. "She certainly pulled a rabbit-in-the-hat trick on us, didn't she?"

"Rabbit-in-the-hat?" Terry asked.

"You know what I mean. We thought she was here. We frisked the place and she wasn't here. We went out, and there she was, right in your bedroom."

"Did you really think she was here?" Terry asked. "*I* thought you were searching for the portrait, and Stubby Nash was the one who thought she was here. As it happens, she came in shortly after you went out, Inspector."

Malloy's eyes stared with disconcerting steadiness. "I hadn't gone far," he said.

"Perhaps," Terry told him, with unsmiling gravity, "she didn't have far to come."

Malloy said, "I'll just take another look in that bedroom of yours, if you don't mind, Clane. There may be a secret exit there you don't know anything about."

"Exit?" Terry asked. "You mean an entrance, don't you?"

"Same thing," Malloy said, and strode into the bedroom, where he put in a full half hour pounding and thumping the walls. At the end of that time, very embarrassed and angry beneath the veneer of his genial friendliness, he left the apartment.

Terry frowningly considered the situation.

Malloy wasn't ready to spring his trap until he knew it would catch someone other than Terry Clane. He was sure of Clane, and could get him at any time. He had wanted the Chinese girl whom he had heard confess to the murder, but he wasn't as yet ready to show his hand and admit that he had overheard that confession. He wanted to get the girl first, and, since she had eluded him, he intended to keep that dictograph under cover, hoping to enmesh Terry still further.

But Sou Ha had given Malloy plenty of material to work on. She had let it out that Terry not only knew Juanita, but had gone to call on her; moreover, she had accused him of calling once more upon Mandra's widow, *between seven o'clock and midnight!* And Malloy knew that Mandra's portrait had been stolen between those hours.

Terry might have managed to slip Sou Ha through Malloy's clutches, but it wouldn't take Malloy long to get busy on the leads the Chinese girl had given. And Inspector Malloy, regardless of how big a nuisance he might be, was most certainly nobody's fool.

# 14

C. RENMORE HOWLAND MAINTAINED AN IM-
pressive suite of offices. Stenographers clattered away
at busy typewriters. Clerks bustled importantly
about. Howland, occupying an inner shrine, which
could be reached only after passing two formidable
secretaries, consented to see Terry Clane, after the
manner of royalty conferring a favor upon a fortunate suppliant.

His voice was unctuously smooth.

"Miss Renton spoke of you to me. She said she
knew you would stand by her and do everything in
your power. You have, I believe, a legal education,
Mr. Clane?"

Terry nodded, noticing the lawyer's long neck and
bony features. He thought of Cynthia's remarks that
the man should have been a race horse.

Howland consulted his wristwatch and said, "The
other witnesses will be here within a quarter of an
hour. I believe you wished to talk with me before
their arrival?"

"Yes," Terry said, "I have some news for you, and
it isn't very pleasant news. I'm afraid it's going to
affect Cynthia's case."

Howland raised inquiring eyebrows, while Terry went on, "You see, Cynthia's alibi will hold water for a while, and then it will blow up with a bang. It was an alibi which looked genuine at first. That's why the police turned her loose. Then they uncovered other evidence. . . . Frankly, they discovered the widow of Jacob Mandra who swore that *she* was the one who had left Mandra's apartment at two in the morning, carrying the portrait. *She* was the one the witness met on the stairs. So far, she hasn't been able to produce the portrait she was carrying, but . . ."

The lawyer's horse face broke into a big-toothed grin. "Now, don't let that disturb you in the least, Mr. Clane. I knew it would be only a matter of time until the police would uncover that original portrait; and I've already discounted that fact. Cynthia has told me her entire story. Thanks to her interview with you, she realized the necessity for telling me the truth. I have all of the facts in my possession."

"Well," Terry said, "here's one fact you didn't have. That original portrait vanished from Juanita Mandra's apartment between seven o'clock and midnight last night. So far, the police haven't been able to find the portrait nor figure out how it was taken. Due to the fact that Inspector Malloy placed a dictograph in my apartment, he was able to overhear some conversation which gave him some very definite clews. I have every reason to believe he'll not only find that original portrait, but will unearth evidence which will connect me with its theft."

The big teeth vanished as the lawyer pursed his

lips. "Well, now, *that's* something new. That makes things look pretty black."

"For Cynthia?" Terry asked.

"No, for you."

"It won't hurt Cynthia's case?"

Howland said impressively, "Mr. Clane, Cynthia hasn't talked *too* much. Whenever I can contact my clients early enough, it is almost impossible to convict them. Remember, the state has to prove its case beyond all reasonable doubt. That gives the defendant a wide margin."

"Just what are you getting at?" Terry asked.

"If the situation develops along certain lines," Howland said, watching him keenly, "I might intimate to the newspapers that *you* were the one who had killed Mandra. The fact that the murder was committed with *your* sleeve gun, the fact that *you* stole the portrait from Juanita . . . Oh, I could make up a very convincing argument. What would be your attitude on that?"

"It's okay by me," Terry said, "if it will save Cynthia."

Howland scowled, then said slowly, "No. Now that I come to consider the facts more carefully, I can see that it won't do. The reading public would realize you had stolen that portrait to protect Cynthia. For me, as her lawyer, to make a suggestion of that sort would be to alienate the sympathies of the newspaper readers—and the sympathies of the newspaper readers are very important. Perhaps you have noticed how infrequently an attractive young woman is convicted of crime, Mr. Clane?"

Clane said dryly, "Isn't it better to become fully familiar with the facts before mapping out a defense?"

"Not necessarily. One only needs to secure a verdict of acquittal. The means don't matter so much. You'd be surprised, Mr. Clane, to find out how much higher value is placed by jurors upon the honor of young women with attractive legs, than on the honor of women who cannot cross their knees in a witness chair to advantage."

The lawyer's smile became a leer.

Terry said shortly, "Look here, that leg defense is used by every trollop who's guilty of emotional murder. It wins her a verdict, but she's forever after covered with slime. Now you don't need to do that with Cynthia. Cynthia didn't kill him. Here's something for you to investigate: a Dr. Sedler, William Shield, and a Fred Stevens were all working with Mandra in a blackmail racket. I heard Dr. Sedler make some very incriminating statements about where that sleeve gun came from. Malloy's working on that angle of the case, but he isn't following it up. He's trying to pin the crime on Cynthia. Naturally, he isn't going to start digging up facts which will prove her innocent. But *you* can do it. I'll give you Sedler's address, and tell you where Shield and Stevens can be found. They're all guilty of criminal conspiracy in a blackmail racket, so it won't be hard for you to get detectives who can make them . . ."

Howland interrupted, "Never mind that angle, Mr. Clane. It won't be necessary."

"Why won't it be necessary?"

"Because the state can never convict Cynthia Renton."

"To hell with that," Terry said. "I want Cynthia to prove that she's innocent, by proving just who *did* kill Mandra. Getting an acquittal won't be enough."

Howland slowly shook his head and said, "I never try to prove who did commit a murder. I content myself with showing the state has failed to prove my client did it. It's much easier to punch holes in the Prosecution's theory of the case than it is to work out another theory of the case the Prosecution can't punch holes in. Always keep the defendant in the position of being the injured party, always keep yourself in the position of being the one who is shooting holes into the other man's case. That keeps the jurors from weighing one theory against the other. A defendant should never advance a theory. And, when the defendant is a young and attractive woman she should always give the jurors a chance to sympathize with her desperate struggles."

"What desperate struggles?" Clane asked ominously.

"Struggles to save herself from a fate worse than death," the lawyer said smugly.

Terry's voice was toneless. "I see. Would you mind telling me just what kind of a defense you *are* going to make?"

The lawyer raised his eyebrows, gestured with the

palms of his hands. "*I*," he said, "am not going to make *any* defense. I will act as Miss Renton's attorney and interrogate the witnesses. The witnesses will, of course, testify to the facts upon which the defense will be predicated."

"Never mind beating about the bush," Terry said. "I want to know . . ."

Howland checked him with a gesture.

"Permit me to complete my thought, Mr. Clane," he said, in a voice which seemed to slide smoothly from an oiled tongue. "When the witnesses are assembled this afternoon *I shall first tell them Miss Renton's story of what actually happened*. I think the witnesses are all very friendly to her. I think they want to see her acquitted. I think they will do everything in their power—remembering, of course, to tell the truth, and only the truth.

"I think you'll agree with me that the original story Miss Renton told was most unfortunate. I am very much afraid a jury would be inclined to convict her, as the evidence *now* stands, if she told that story to them. But the real facts of the case are these: Miss Renton was painting Mandra's portrait. He brought some very considerable pressure to bear upon her in order to get her to paint that portrait, blackmailed her, in fact. Miss Cynthia Renton is a very talented painter. But she did not have the technique of her sister, Alma, who is internationally known as an artist. So, Cynthia took her sketches to Alma, asked Alma to create another portrait of Mr. Mandra. When the two portraits were finished, she wanted to place them side by side so that Mr. Mandra could take his choice.

"After all, you know, Cynthia is something of a child, and she is inclined to discount her own very marked skill with the brush.

"On the night of the murder, her picture was completed. Alma had also completed her portrait. Cynthia took *both* pictures with her to Mr. Mandra's apartment. She showed him both. He selected one— the one, as it happened, which Cynthia herself had painted. The other portrait was to go back to Alma.

"Mr. Mandra had some other appointments. He kept Cynthia waiting. He gave her a drugged drink. Think of it! This monster *drugged* her! She fell asleep, dozing in a big easy chair.

"Now, bear this in mind, as this is important. Jacob Mandra wanted to secure a sleeve gun, was, in fact, *very* anxious to get one. He had secured one. We don't know where it came from. The Prosecution will perhaps claim that it was *your* sleeve gun. As to that, I understand you can make no definite identification. You can only say that the gun they will show you is a gun which is similar to yours, and that yours is missing. You do not know how long yours had been gone, nor by whom it had been taken. A sleeve gun, however, was lying upon Mr. Mandra's desk. And, when Cynthia awoke, she saw Mandra toying with the gun. He had even inserted a dart in the weapon.

"Cynthia, awakening with a start, looked for the portrait Mandra had chosen. It was gone. She asked him what had become of it. Mandra told her he had given it to a certain woman. He had wanted the portrait as a gift for this woman.

"It was at this time Mandra became amorously insulting. He showed himself in his true character as a sinister blackmailer, a despoiler of virtue. It then became apparent that the pressure he had brought to bear upon Cynthia was not so much for the purpose of getting her to paint his portrait as to get her in his power. She was young, fresh and virtuous, an unplucked fruit, a budding flower! And Mandra was a roué who had sipped honey from so many flowers that his taste had become cloyed. This fresh young thing aroused not the manhood in him, but the beast in him. So depraved had he become, that, in place of wanting to protect the virtue of this young woman, he wanted to strip her of that most priceless possession. And he knew that he could do it only by the use of drugs and of force. So he conspired to get her in his apartment, alone with him, at the unconventional hour of three o'clock in the morning."

The lawyer was working himself up to an emotional climax. His voice rose in volume. The vibrant timbre of it filled the room.

"Miss Renton had taken the sleeve gun in her hand to examine it. In picking it up from the table, she had no idea that it was a weapon. Mandra's emotions got the better of him. He suddenly disclosed himself in his true colors. He made his leering proposal. Cynthia drew back. Mandra reached for her and grabbed her. They struggled. Mandra ripped the dress from Cynthia's shoulder. She screamed and tried to pull back. Mandra's hands were wet with perspiration from his struggles and from those unclean thoughts which had possessed his mind. Those wet hands slipped down the smooth skin of Cynthia's bare arms, caught her wrists, then her fingers, and gripped them with crushing force.

"She screamed because he was cutting the fingers of her right hand on the brass catch which protruded downward from the sleeve gun.

"Poor innocent child, she didn't know the deadly nature of that weapon, nor did she know that Mandra's grip was pressing a catch which would release an instrument of death. She screamed with pain. Mandra's grip tightened. Suddenly there was a whirring noise. She felt the jar of a recoil. Mandra sank back in his chair. She looked at him. He was dead."

Howland paused dramatically.

"You're not going to have her put on that defense!" Clane exclaimed.

"I'm afraid you misunderstand me," Howland rejoined. "*I* am only acting as her attorney."

"But that story won't hang together."

"On the contrary, it is the only story which *will* hang together. Miss Renton was *very* ill-advised in connection with her original story—*very* ill-advised.

"After Juanita Mandra left her husband's apartment carrying the painting, she took a cab to her apartment. That is the point Cynthia overlooked; yet it is the thing which occurred to me the moment

I realized what must have happened. That is the trouble with the lay mind, Mr. Clane, it doesn't reason far enough. It deals only with one thing at a time. As a lawyer, it instantly occurred to me that the person who had taken this portrait from Mandra's apartment certainly wouldn't go walking down the street like a sandwich man, carrying an oil painting pushed out in front. It was logical to suppose that this person must have called a cab. And the same line of reasoning occurred to the police. This man, Malloy, is deep and clever as the very devil. He too started searching for a cab driver who had picked up a fare near Mandra's apartment. It wasn't a difficult search. The cab driver was found. Late last night he identified Juanita as the one whom he had picked up. The time was six minutes past two o'clock in the morning. The address to which he drove her was the address of her apartment. She paid him by taking a twenty-dollar bill from her stocking. It was what she called her 'mad money.' Naturally, the portrait, the woman, the stocking, and having to change twenty dollars, made an impression on the cab driver. In view of those facts, you can see how suicidal it would be for Miss Renton to try to stay with her original story. And she must change it in such a way it will attract widespread interest, arouse sympathies.

"Now this story which I have outlined *will* hang together. It cannot be disproved, and it has certain advantages. Miss Renton is a very attractive young woman. Sitting on the witness stand, her face covered with her hands, her legs covered only by the sheerest of hose, she can sob out her story—and she will win an acquittal."

Howland beamed at Clane.

"And you're having these witnesses come here so you can drill them to corroborate *that* story?" Clane asked.

Howland frowned. "I'm afraid," he said, "that for all of your legal education, you don't understand the position of an attorney, Mr. Clane. I am acting as Miss Renton's representative. *She* has told me that this is what happened. I shall, of course, go over the facts with the witnesses, with a view to seeing that her story is corroborated. I shall not ask any witness to falsify. In fact, I would not permit a witness to do so, *if I knew it*. I will, however, tell the witnesses *first* what Miss Renton has told me. I will outline to them that we, all of us, wish to see her acquitted. I will explain to them that, in view of the general survey I have made of the evidence, I have reason to believe it is very fortunate Miss Renton has finally told me the truth, because I think *this is the only story which will stand up*.

"Juries like to hear these stories of struggle—a strong man grappling with a woman. And, of course, the mechanical operation of the sleeve gun is such that Miss Renton's story will carry conviction, particularly when one considers that this young and unsophisticated woman was in the clutches of a lecherous despoiler of virtue, a libertine of the most depraved character."

Clane pushed back his chair.

"You're just smooth enough," he said, "so there's no way of reaching you. Alma Renton will lie to protect her sister. George Levering will say anything you tell him to. But, by God, you're not going to do it! I think something of Cynthia. I think a hell of a lot of her. I'm not going to let her be put in such a position. She's a fine, clean kid. You spew the slime of your shyster tactics all over her and she'll be something that stinks by the time you've dragged her through the salacious atmosphere of this trial. A jury may turn her loose, but no one will believe her. You'll crush her character to win a verdict! Her legs will have been in every tabloid in the city! You make me sick!"

Howland got to his feet, and said sneeringly, "And so, Sir Galahad, you are going to charge to the rescue, I suppose! Your sweet innocence is sublime."

"Sit down!" Clane interrupted, slamming his hand down on the lawyer's shoulder and pushing him back into the big swivel chair. "If I could gain anything by smashing your dirty mouth, I'd do it. I presume you've completely hypnotized Cynthia . . . Oh hell, what's the use!"

He whirled on his heel, strode to the door which led to the corridor, and jerked it open.

He was just stepping into the corridor when a secretary, entering Howland's private office, said, "Miss Alma Renton and Mr. George Levering."

Howland controlled himself with an effort, to say,

"I think you'd better stay just a moment, Mr. Clane
and . . ."

Terry banged the door shut.

As Terry reached the street, a newsboy thrust a
paper in front of his face.

"All about the Mandra murder! Read about it!"

Terry purchased the paper, stepped back from the
stream of pedestrian traffic to scan the headlines.

# PROMINENT PAIR IMPLICATED
# IN MANDRA MURDER

## POLICE SEARCH FOR MYSTERIOUS CHINESE GIRL

### Speedy Solution Certain, District Attorney Declares

Terry skimmed hastily through the newspaper account, which hinted at a sinister background of midnight meetings, of beautiful mistresses, of a vast, far-
flung web which snared beautiful women, while in the
center of the web, like some huge spider hypnotizing
his victims with the compelling power of his silver-
green eyes, Jacob Mandra lured women to their doom.

The newspaper account went on to state:

"The sleeve gun is now considered by police to have
been taken from the apartment of Mr. Terrance Clane,
a mysterious adventurer who spent years in a monastery
in Southern China and who, according to the district
attorney's office, will have to do considerable explaining
before he, himself, is free of suspicion.

"It was pointed out that Miss Renton, the beautiful artist who had been painting Mandra's portrait and who tried juggling portraits to build up an alibi and confuse the police, undoubtedly had ample opportunity to take this death-dealing instrument from Clane's collection, either with or without his consent.

"Police pointed out that finding Miss Renton in the apartment of Terry Clane at an early hour this morning was amply sufficient to raise an 'inference' that she might have taken the sleeve gun either with Clane's consent or without his knowledge.

"Terry Clane, the mysterious and romantic figure who was entertaining Miss Renton while clad only in pajamas and slippers, furnishes a mysterious angle to the case.

"According to Inspector James Malloy of the homicide squad, Clane has thus far offered no satisfactory explanation of how the sleeve gun happened to have been discovered in a chair which he had occupied in the district attorney's office when being questioned the morning after the murder.

"An outstanding feature of the case is that a young and attractive woman was seen by Jack Winton, a young artist, leaving Mandra's apartment at two o'clock in the morning of the murder. This young woman was carrying a portrait of the dead man, done in oils. Apparently the paint on the canvas was still wet, and the woman was holding the portrait out in front of her in such a manner that it concealed her features from the young artist who was climbing the stairs, but the stairs were steep, and, looking up those stairs, Winton was able to see what he has described as 'a damn good-looking pair of ankles' beneath the lower edge of the portrait.

"Since police have fixed Mandra's death as having taken place sometime after two-thirty and before three-five in the morning, it is apparent that the young woman Winton met on the stairs at two o'clock must, obviously, have left Mandra's apartment at least half an hour before the murder was committed.

"Miss Cynthia Renton, when first interrogated by Parker Dixon, the district attorney, insisted that she was this woman, and produced a portrait of Mandra to prove her contention. Winton, after inspecting Miss Renton's neatly turned ankles, and examining the portrait, stated he was convinced she was the young woman whom he had met. Miss Renton was thereupon released from custody.

"Subsequently, Juanita Mandra, the widow of the dead broker, claimed *she* was the woman Winton had seen on the stairs. While she has so far been unable to produce a portrait to corroborate her story, police have located a cab driver who drove her from Mandra's apartment to the address where she lives, and who remembers the occasion very clearly, and distinctly remembers the portrait the young woman was carrying. Police have found one other witness who swears she saw this portrait in Juanita's apartment as late as seven o'clock last night. Since the portrait produced by Cynthia Renton was in the hands of the police at that hour, it is apparent that this witness either must be mistaken, which police think unlikely, or that there were *two* identical portraits of Mandra. The portrait which Juanita Mandra insists was in her apartment as late as seven o'clock in the evening had disappeared by the time Inspector Malloy arrived, shortly after midnight. Juanita Mandra claims it had been stolen.

"Juanita Mandra, herself a colorful personality, an

exotic dancer in one of the downtown night clubs, was secretly married to Mandra more than two years ago. She insists that the ceremony, despite its secrecy, was perfectly legal, and detectives checking up her story are inclined to agree with her.

"Since Cynthia Renton is the artist who painted Mandra's portrait, police point out that she would well have been able to duplicate the portrait in order to establish an alibi. Juanita Mandra, on the other hand, is concededly incapable of executing any such striking canvas as the work in question. There is also Miss Alma Renton, an artist of international reputation, sister of Cynthia Renton, who is being questioned by the police.

"The authorities insist that they will shortly uncover the portrait which Juanita Mandra claims was stolen from her apartment. They feel that this will have been accomplished before another twenty-four hours have passed, and state that when such a discovery is made their case against Cynthia Renton will be iron-clad.

"It is a case filled with colorful, exotic characters, moving against bizarre backgrounds. Not the least colorful of the personalities involved is Mr. Terry Clane, an adventurer who has recently returned from an extended stay in China. It is reputed he spent much of that time studying in a hidden monastery in a mountainous region where the old ruins of an ancient city were filled with gold and gems which had remained undisturbed through the centuries. Clane is able to speak Chinese fluently, and police insist that they overheard a conversation between Clane and a young Chinese woman who was in Clane's apartment, in which this beautiful young Oriental accused Clane of having stolen Mandra's portrait from Juanita's apartment. As yet, the police have not taken Clane into custody, but Inspector Malloy states that if there is any evidence uncovered connecting Clane with the mysterious disappearance of the portrait from the dancer's apartment, Clane will be arrested and charged not only with being an accessory in the murder of Mandra, but with the crime of breaking and entering as well.

"Cynthia Renton is represented by C. Renmore Howland, the noted criminal attorney whose boast is that he has never yet lost a murder case. Those who are acquainted with the tactics of this forceful lawyer insist that the witness, Winton, will be cross-examined as to his identification of Miss Renton's legs. These insiders also claim the true story of what happened in Mandra's apartment the night of the murder has not yet been told; that Howland will soon release, either himself, or through his client, a story of innocent youth lured into a compromising position, of a desperate struggle between a man of the world on the one hand, and an adventurous but unsullied girl (continued on page 3)."

Terry turned the page of the newspaper, but didn't resume reading the article. He stood staring at the reproduction of the portrait, watching the cynical, leering eyes which, even in the newspaper reproduction of the portrait, seemed so coldly dominant.

Terry realized that, despite the obstacles he had thrown in the way of the police, it would be but a matter of hours before they had separated the wheat from the chaff. There remained Sou Ha's confession to consider. Inspector Malloy had doubtless had that confession taken down in shorthand, yet he had not mentioned it in the interview he had given to a representative of the press.

Why?

Terry had heard many stories of police methods. He had heard of evidence being suppressed in order to secure convictions. If Sou Ha should be arrested and should repudiate her confession, there would be numerous legal obstacles in the way of her conviction. It would, for one thing, be difficult to secure any corroborating evidence, whereas, so far as Cynthia was concerned, her attempt to switch portraits, her contradictory statements, her futile effort to manufacture an alibi, all would tell against her heavily.

Was it possible, Terry wondered, the police would deliberately ignore what they had heard Sou Ha confess in order to convict Cynthia? He had heard of such things being done. Standing there on the sidewalk, heedless of the roar of traffic, Terry brought his mind to a sharp focus upon the problem which confronted him.

Clane's entire period of concentration didn't occupy more than a few seconds, yet, in those few seconds, he reached a conclusion which would have startled Inspector Malloy, could that individual have but peered into the recesses of Clane's mind. There was one logical deduction to be made from the known facts, which had so far escaped everyone.

Terry abruptly snapped the newspaper together, folded it, thrust it under his arm, entered a nearby drug store and telephoned C. Renmore Howland's office.

"There's a Mr. Levering in conference with Mr. Howland," he told the girl who answered the telephone. "It's imperative that I speak with him at once."

"What is your name?"

"Ben Marker, an attorney in the Cutler Building," he told her. "Get Mr. Levering at once. It's *most* important."

He heard a click on the line, then the sound of low voices as though rather a heated argument were progressing in a whispered undertone a few inches from the transmitter. Then Levering's voice said cautiously, "Hello, what is it?"

Terry made his voice sound harshly belligerent.

"I'm Ben Marker, an attorney in the Cutler Building. I'm taking charge of the affairs of a certain William Shield. Shield has assigned all his property to me, and, looking over his papers, I find he has a claim against you on a hit-and-run charge. My client has an injured spine because you smashed into him when you were driving a car while intoxicated and I want some money and I want it fast, otherwise I'll sue."

Levering was surprised into betrayal.

"You can't do that," he explained. "That's all settled. It's completely fixed up."

"Do you hold Shield's written release?"

"Not exactly that, but it's all cleaned up, it's all taken care of."

"The hell it is," Terry said. "I want some money out of you and I'm going to get it."

Levering suddenly became conscious of his surroundings.

"I can't talk with you now," he said, "but I can explain the entire situation to your satisfaction. If you'll only talk with your client, he'll explain exactly how it is. You don't want to press this thing. It wouldn't look good for him. I have your name. I'll call you later. Good-by."

The telephone slammed in Terry's ear.

Clane broke the connection at his end, and turned from the telephone to encounter the genial smile of Inspector Malloy.

"Well now, Mr. Clane," the Inspector said, "what have you been up to? Co-operating with us again?"

"What do *you* want?" Clane asked, but the impatience of his tone failed to ruffle the Inspector's breezy good nature.

"It's too bad to inconvenience you again," Malloy said, "but the district attorney wants to see you. The first thing I said when he told me to bring you in was . . ."

"Ain't that too bad!" Terry interrupted.

Malloy's face showed hurt surprise.

"You see," Terry grinned, "I had a dictograph into the district attorney's office."

Malloy frowned and said, "One of these days you and your accomplice, Cynthia Renton, will learn that a murder case isn't an occasion for making wise cracks. How come you're not attending the conference of witnesses in Howland's office?"

"I walked out on Howland," Terry said.

"Yes, we know you did. Why?"

Terry shrugged his shoulders.

"Oh well," Malloy observed, "we'll pick the others up as soon as Howland gets done with them, so you can meet *all* of your friends. We've got a tip that Howland's getting ready to pull one of his fast ones."

"So you're going to interrogate all of his witnesses and beat him to the punch?" Terry asked.

Inspector Malloy's voice showed hurt reproach. "Why, Mr. Clane," he said, "we wouldn't do anything like that. We wouldn't interfere with the witnesses for the Defense. We don't want to talk with them because they're witnesses; we just want to go over the facts of the case with them in view of certain new developments which have been uncovered."

"More facts?" Terry asked.

Malloy's grin was triumphant. "Well," he said, "we got to wondering just how that portrait of Mandra could have left Juanita's apartment, so we started to check up on the apartment house where she lives, and bless my soul, if we didn't discover that a young nan had rented the adjoining apartment. That young man's description checked with yours, Clane.

"You could have knocked me over with a feather when the manager of the apartment house described this young man. But duty is duty, and I went up and searched that apartment. We couldn't find any clothes or any evidence that the place had been occupied, except some bits of wood on a shelf in the closet. They were innocent looking bits of wood, but when we fitted them together we found that they'd originally been the board backing of a painting, with thumb tacks stuck in the side. So then we got to prowling around, looking under the carpet and places like that, and we found the portrait of Mandra which had been stolen from Juanita's apartment. Juanita identified it. The taxi driver identified it. The manager of the apartment house identified it."

Inspector Malloy stared accusingly at Terry Clane.

Clane sighed. "And so we go to see the district attorney once more, is that it?"

"Those were my instructions."

"Do we take a taxicab?"

"If you pay for it."

"And if I don't?"

"That," Malloy announced, "would be too bad. It would be . . ."

Terry held up his hand. "Taxi!" he called.

# 15

PARKER DIXON SMILED WITH HIS LIPS. HIS eyes were as coldly watchful as those of a pugilist studying an opponent in the ring.

"I'm afraid, Mr. Clane," he said, "that you haven't been entirely frank with me." And he glanced across the room to where a shorthand reporter was seated at a small table, taking down everything that was said.

Terry said, "I've tried to co-operate."

"Co-operate?" Dixon asked.

"Yes."

"With whom?" the district attorney demanded, a trace of irritation showing in his voice.

"I've tried to co-operate with you and Inspector Malloy," Terry assured him.

"A little more co-operation such as you have given us would have plunged the case into hopeless confusion. There was, for instance, the rather mysterious manner in which this Chinese girl disappeared from your apartment. How do you explain that?"

"As I told you earlier," Terry said, "co-operation implies a mutual objective definitely known to both parties. Therefore, I might as well ask why *you*

264

didn't tell *me* you had planted a dictograph in *my* apartment."

Inspector Malloy said, "You can bounce words off of him like rubber balls off a handball court, Dixon, it doesn't bother him! Nothing fazes him. He looks sweet and innocent but he moves around like a greased pig in . . ."

"Never mind, Jim," the district attorney interrupted, without taking his eyes from Clane. "Incidentally, Mr. Clane, I didn't call you in to engage in a verbal exchange. I called you in to give you one last chance to give a satisfactory account of your connection with the Mandra murder and to explain your subsequent activities, particularly your theft of Mandra's portrait from the apartment of his widow.

"Please understand, Mr. Clane, I am not seeking information *now*. I *have* the information. I am giving you one last chance to justify your actions."

Terry remained silent.

"Do I gather," Dixon said, "that you have nothing to add to what you have said?"

"If you'll specify just what points you want me to declare myself on, I'll be glad to answer questions," Terry told him.

"Why did you leave Howland's office this afternoon before the others arrived?"

"I had a difference of opinion with Mr. Howland."

"What about?"

"About a matter which has nothing whatever to do with the facts of the case."

"Did it have something to do with Miss Renton's defense? With her testimony, perhaps?"

Clane raised his eyebrows. "Is it possible," he inquired coldly, "that you have summoned me here to interrogate me concerning Mr. Howland's plans for Miss Renton's defense?"

Dixon acknowledged he had lost a point by lowering his eyes, but a moment later he had raised them to stare searchingly at Clane.

"I'm going to have Alma Renton and Mr. George Levering brought in here," he said. "My men picked them up as they left Howland's office. I'm going to interrogate them concerning the substitution of paintings. I want you to be present at that conversation. If anything is said which doesn't coincide with your recollection, I'd be glad to have you advise me. I don't want to make any threats, Mr. Clane, but I think I am justified in saying that the only thing which can possibly keep you from being charged with a very serious crime is the question of your intent."

"Therefore," Terry said, smiling cheerfully, "if I assist you in making a case against Alma as an accessory you'll know my intentions are all right, and I probably won't be arrested, whereas, if I don't do so, you'll know my intentions are wrong and prosecute *me* as an accessory. Is that right?"

"I didn't say that," Dixon retorted.

"You didn't *say* that, but isn't that the idea you wished to convey?"

The district attorney shrugged his shoulders and said, "I think, Mr. Clane, that we have pursued this phase of the conversation quite far enough. After all, I think you understand your own position and I am now quite certain that you appreciate mine."

He slid his finger along the desk to the push button, and a moment later, apparently in response to the signal, a young woman opened the door and Alma Renton and George Levering were ushered into the room.

"Be seated," the district attorney invited. "You both know Mr. Clane, of course. I want to ask a few questions."

"The understanding being," Clane warned, in a slow, amused drawl, "that if you don't answer those questions truly and correctly, I'm to interpolate a word here and there. That's the price I'm being asked to pay for my own freedom."

Alma glanced swiftly at him and said, "Terry!" her voice sharp with incredulity.

Levering nodded his head, and there was something of smirking satisfaction in the gesture, as though he were saying, "You may surprise Alma by turning stool pigeon but you haven't surprised me."

Dixon leveled his eyes at Alma Renton.

"When did you first know your sister had murdered Mandra?" he asked.

Terry's comment came with the effortless ease of a polished toastmaster recalling a well-worn story.

"Permit me to make a correction, Mr. Dixon. She *didn't* know her sister had murdered Mandra for the simple reason that her sister *didn't* commit the murder."

The district attorney's eyes shifted to Terry.

"That remark, Mr. Clane, indicates a knowledge on your part of who *did* murder Mandra."

Terry nodded.

Dixon's finger slid once more to the button on his desk. This time he rang twice. "Perhaps," he said, "you'd like to tell us the identity of the Chinese girl who called on you at your apartment earlier this afternoon."

"No," Terry said slowly, "I'm afraid I can't give you any help on that, Mr. Dixon."

He noticed a sly, sardonic expression in the district attorney's eyes, and was therefore not entirely unprepared for that which followed. A door was flung open with dramatic swiftness. A uniformed officer escorted Sou Ha into the room.

The Chinese girl stood very erect, very quiet and very dignified, her manner indicating that her mind had achieved a calmly unruffled tranquility.

"Is this the girl?" Dixon asked.

Slowly Terry Clane got to his feet.

"That," he said, "is the girl."

"And I believe, Mr. Clane, she confessed in some detail to the murder of Mandra, but explained to you that she was leaving the knowledge of her guilt with you in the nature of a trust, not to be used unless you found it was quite necessary to save Cynthia Renton."

It was Sou Ha who spoke. "That is true," she said calmly, "the man was evil and I killed him."

Alma Renton's gasping intake of breath knifed

the moment of tense silence which followed Sou Ha's statement.

"And do you wish me to make a correction on *that?*" Terry asked.

"You have done quite enough, Mr. Clane," Dixon said.

"Perhaps," Clane suggested, "I could do still more with a question or two." And without waiting for permission, he said to Sou Ha, "Where was Cynthia Renton when you killed Mandra?"

"On the couch in another room, asleep," Sou Ha said, in the toneless voice of a fatalist facing a supreme crisis.

"What was Mandra doing?"

She looked at him for a moment with inscrutable eyes. Her face was expressionless and yet a barrier seemed to have been thrown up between them.

"The time has come," he told her, "for you to answer these questions. In no other way can I save the painter woman."

"Mandra," she said, "was seated at the table. He had the sleeve gun in his hand. I recognized it. It was the sleeve gun which you had kept in your glass-covered case."

"What else was on the table?" he asked.

"A woman's hand bag. I think it was the hand bag of the painter woman."

Parker Dixon exchanged a swiftly significant glance with Inspector Malloy. The district attorney's eyes held a glint of triumph. Malloy was frowning thoughtfully.

"What color was the hand bag?"

"Black."

Clane glanced at Alma Renton. "Would Cynthia have carried a black bag?" he asked.

"No," she said, "she hates black. Her hand bag was brown—a dark brown."

Clane turned back to Sou Ha. "Where did Mandra get this sleeve gun?" he asked.

"In some way it came from your house."

"*How* did he get it?"

"As to that I do not know."

Dixon turned to the shorthand reporter and said, "Are you getting this, Miss Stokely?"

"Every word," the young woman said.

"Go right ahead, Mr. Clane," Dixon invited smilingly, "you're doing splendidly. Your co-operation was a bit tardy but, now you've started, you're making up for lost time."

"I take it," Clane asked, with a swift glance at Sou Ha, "this will clear Cynthia Renton?"

"There are one or two other matters to be straightened out," the district attorney pointed out. "We can't afford to overlook some of your activities, Clane. Take that portrait, for instance."

"Yes," Clane said, "I appreciate the spot I'm in, but since confessions are in order, I think we'll all come clean. One of the first things to clear up is the matter of these counterfeit portraits. I think you, Levering, had better explain that."

Levering looked repentant. "I'm sorry I did what I did," he admitted. "I'm going to make a clean breast of it. Now that this Chinese girl has confessed, I can do it. I was with Alma. Cynthia came to us and told us her story. She'd been drugged. When she awakened, Mandra was dead. I wanted to keep her out of it, so I suggested I could scout around a bit and find out what had happened. I did so and discovered that a witness had seen some woman leaving Mandra's apartment carrying the portrait Cynthia had painted. I asked Alma if she could duplicate such a portrait from Cynthia's sketches. She said she could, so I suggested we make the counterfeit portrait, put it in Cynthia's apartment, and give Cynthia that two o'clock alibi."

Dixon's eyes stared at Levering in unflattering appraisal.

"How long had *you* been with Alma Renton before Cynthia's arrival?"

"I can't give you the exact number of minutes."

"Wasn't it rather an unusual hour for you to call on her?"

"Not exactly. I'd been confronted with an emergency . . . That is, I had to see her in regard to a business matter."

"Meaning you wanted her to give you some more gambling money?" Clane asked.

"You can keep out of this!" Levering blazed. "I don't know who made you guardian for the Renton girls, anyway. Trying to protect this Chink, you've involved them in a dirty scandal."

"That will do," Dixon said sternly. "Your own conduct is far from blameless, Mr. Levering."

"And now," Terry said, "I think it's my turn, so I'll make a confession. The murder, gentlemen, was committed with *my* sleeve gun."

"So you're satisfied it's your sleeve gun now, are you?" Dixon asked.

"I'm morally certain of it. I always have been."

"You didn't seem anxious to identify it."

"I was a little conservative."

"Very well, go ahead," Dixon said.

"Well," Clane observed thoughtfully, his eyes flickering in swift appraisal over the faces which were turned toward him, "one of the important questions to be considered is: How did that sleeve gun get into Mandra's possession? The next question is: How did it get *here?* How do *you* account for that, Sou Ha?"

"I know nothing further," she said.

"What did you do with the sleeve gun after you killed Mandra?"

"I tried to return it to your collection. The door of the case was locked and so I . . ."

She hesitated.

"So you what?" Terry asked.

"I have finished," she said with calm dignity. "So much I will tell and then I tell no more."

Clane nodded and said to the district attorney, "Let's see if we can't reason out an answer to those two questions—first, how the sleeve gun got into Mandra's possession; second, how it happened to be found in your office. We'll begin by taking Mandra's character and his desires into consideration.

"We must remember Mandra was *very* anxious to get a sleeve gun. It's a weapon which is very typical of his collection. One which is both rare and valuable. Therefore, Mandra was willing to go to any lengths to secure a genuine, authentic, antique sleeve gun.

"Our knowledge of Mandra's character is that he didn't stop when once he had made up his mind. He didn't limit himself to orthodox methods. *Someone* took that sleeve gun from my apartment and transferred it to Mandra's possession. Perhaps the best way of determining who that someone was, is by considering how the sleeve gun came into *your* possession.

"That gun was put here by someone who had been *unexpectedly* brought to this office. If he'd known in advance he was coming here, he naturally wouldn't have carried the gun with him. I gather, therefore, that the person who brought the gun here was someone who was picked up by your man as he was leaving my apartment; since everyone who left my apartment was unexpectedly placed under restraint and brought here.

"The question arises why that person should have had the sleeve gun in his possession on leaving my apartment. There is one answer, and, as I see it, only one answer. That person had stolen the gun from my collection, knowing that it would be some time before I would miss it, in the ordinary course of things. He was anxious to return it after the murder, just as he had been anxious to take it before the murder. He wanted to replace it in the glass-enclosed case where

I keep many of my curios, but he didn't have the chance to do so because Yat T'oy had locked the door, which was customarily kept unlocked. He therefore decided he'd try it again at a later date, left my apartment and was picked up by officers with the sleeve gun still in his possession. Now, that person *couldn't* have been Sou Ha because, as Sou Ha has suddenly realized, *she* didn't come to this office prior to the time the sleeve gun was found. It's at that point the circumstances cease to corroborate the confession she has made. Therefore, it becomes increasingly important to find out who brought that sleeve gun here.

"Now, gentlemen, there was only one person in my apartment who had any opportunity to try to return that sleeve gun."

Terry paused, whirled, and extended a dramatic forefinger at Levering.

"You, George," he said, "tried to return that sleeve gun and you were baffled by a locked door. And you were whisked up to the district attorney's office before you had any chance to get rid of the weapon. You managed to wipe all the fingerprints off of it with your handkerchief while you were waiting in the outer office here, but you didn't have a chance to hide it until you had entered this room.

"Now then," Terry demanded, staring into Levering's pale eyes, "*where did you get that sleeve gun?*"

Levering stared with wide, apprehensive eyes at Terry as though hypnotized. Parker Dixon's urbanity of expression gave way to a puzzled frown, while his lips forgot their ready smile. Alma Renton shifted startled eyes from Terry to Levering.

Terry said slowly and impressively, "*I'll* answer that question for you, Levering. I'll tell you where you got that gun. You got it from William Shield. You stole that gun for Shield in the first place. Shield and Mandra were engaged in a racket by which they framed hit-and-run charges on a carefully selected list of people who were accustomed to drive their cars after taking one or two cocktails. You were picked to be one of their victims because, through Alma, you had access to my apartment. Mandra didn't blackmail you for money. He blackmailed you for my sleeve gun. The price you had to pay for escaping prosecution on a hit-and-run charge was the stealing of that sleeve gun. It was understood Mandra was going to have a duplicate gun made and let you return that duplicate to my collection. You were convinced the substitution could be made before the absence of the sleeve gun had been noticed.

"But a murder was committed with that sleeve gun. The dart had buried itself in Mandra's heart, and couldn't be recovered by the murderer. The authorities were certain to learn the nature of the murder weapon when they recovered that dart at the postmortem. Therefore, since *I* had not known that my sleeve gun was missing, it became vitally important to the murderer to have that gun returned to its position in the cabinet before I missed it. So Shield once more brought pressure to bear upon you to *return* that gun."

Dixon interrupted. "Just a moment, Mr. Clane," he said, "we're going to keep this straight as we go along. Why should Shield seek to protect this Chinese girl?"

Terry said, "He wasn't trying to protect her. Let's use our heads, gentlemen, and not overlook the most significant fact in this entire case. The testimony of the impartial, disinterested witnesses shows that when the woman who took the painting from Mandra's apartment was seen on the stairs she was holding the canvas away from her in both hands, one hand resting on each side of the canvas. It's impossible, under those circumstances, for the woman to have carried *both* the canvas and her purse. This is particularly true when we consider that the paint on the portrait was still wet."

Dixon's face showed sudden interest.

"Therefore, you mean . . ."

"Therefore, I mean that that woman must have returned for her purse," Clane said. "She's the only person we've so far discovered who *must* have had the key to that corridor door, with the possible exception of Shield, or his associates.

"Now, Shield or his associates wouldn't have gone to Mandra's apartment at that hour of the morning unless they'd planned a premeditated murder, and, if they *had* planned a premeditated murder, they'd have brought a weapon. The person who killed Mandra was one who became seized with a *sudden* impulse to kill. By a fortuitous chain of circumstance, the weapon was ready at hand. The crime, therefore, was one of emotion. Now we know Juanita left that apartment at two o'clock in the morning, carrying this portrait. We know she didn't have her purse with her then, since she paid the cab driver from 'mad money' she took from her stocking. We have established, furthermore, that the crime was one, not of premeditation, but of emotion and impulse. We have established the fact that some woman's purse was lying on the table in front of Jacob Mandra when Juanita left in a jealous rage at two o'clock in the morning. That purse was seen by Sou Ha at two-forty-five. We know the purse wasn't there when the body was discovered. What more logical, therefore, than to assume Juanita Mandra, remembering when she was called on to pay off her taxicab in front of her apartment that she had left her purse behind her, paid off the cab driver from her 'mad money,' took the portrait up to her apartment, and later summoned another cab and went back after her purse?

"Since she was Mandra's wife, and since she admits she went to Mandra's apartment on the occasion of taking the portrait, and wasn't seen by the doorkeeper, it follows that she *must* have had a key to that corridor door. She returned to get her purse. That was some time between two-forty-five, when Sou Ha left, and a few minutes after three, when the body was discovered. She is the one who killed Mandra. She killed him in a jealous rage because she knew Mandra was contemplating divorce proceedings. She is just the type who would do such a thing. She snatched up the weapon which was on the table, released the dart which entered Mandra's heart, then rushed from the apartment. She returned the murder weapon to Shield. Shield returned it to Levering, and Levering was caught making a clumsy attempt to return that weapon to my collection.

"At the time of the murder, Cynthia Renton, who was asleep in an adjoining room, was awakened by the noise made by Juanita in leaving the apartment, and, slowly rousing to consciousness, came out, to find the dead body of Mandra.

"Now then, Levering, it's time for *you* to tell the truth. And, just to keep from taking an unfair advantage, I'm letting you know *I* was the one who telephoned you in Howland's office and trapped you into an admission that Shield had framed you on a hit-and-run charge, and that you'd settled with him.

"When I started figuring out what *must* have happened, knowing Mandra's methods, knowing how badly he wanted a sleeve gun, knowing that he had a blackmail system by which he could pick his victims at will, I realized you *must* have been the one whom he had used in procuring that sleeve gun; and I trapped you into admitting it."

Terry Clane, ignoring the white, strained faces of the startled witnesses, stared steadily in grim accusation into Levering's pale eyes.

Levering's entire conception of the case suddenly executed a topsy-turvy revolution and he was unable to keep what was going on within his mind from showing on his face. District Attorney Dixon, experienced in reading faces under emotional stress, needed but one look at Levering to reach an instantaneous decision.

"Young man," he said solemnly, "a shorthand reporter is taking down what's being said here. I'm not making any promises and I'm not making any threats, but within the next two minutes you're going to decide definitely whether you're running with the hare or with the hounds. Your part in this matter has been decidedly culpable. It remains for you to say whether it becomes more or less culpable from now on."

George Levering ran his forefinger about the inside of the neckband of his shirt. He was breathing heavily, as though he had been running.

"Yes, sir," he said, after a moment, "I'll tell my story."

## 16

CYNTHIA RENTON LOOKED DOWN UPON THE
surface of the King Alphonse she had been sipping.
The film of thick cream which covered the dark
liqueur was in a state of wild agitation.

"What makes it do that, Owl?" she asked.

"Do what?" Terry asked.

"The cream," she explained, "on the *Crème de
Cacao*. It looks as though it might be boiling, only
there aren't any bubbles coming up. It's like storm
clouds when they're whipped by a wind."

"I don't know," he told her.

She ceased to look at the liqueur, raised her eyes
to his.

The floor show was over. It was during the lull between dances, with the orchestra silent. Waiters and
bus boys were scurrying about. Well-modulated
voices, in animated conversation, filled the night club
with a murmur which was punctuated by the sound
of silverware against plates and saucers.

"So-o-o-o," she said, "feet of clay after all, eh?"

Terry raised his eyebrows in silent interrogation.

"Like all gods," she said, "you have feet of clay.
I've finally found something you don't know."

She laughed then, and reaching across the table, squeezed his hand. "Owl, you put it across for me, didn't you?"

He twisted his hand under hers, to give it an answering squeeze.

"But I feel sorry for Juanita, Terry," she said. "You can't blame her. God knows, Mandra needed killing, and she's a fiery, unconventional creature of emotions. She shouldn't be subject to the same rules which control other people. I'm like her, myself. I see the thing from her angle."

"I understand," Terry said, "that she's retained your friend, C. Renmore Howland, to defend her."

"Good old Renny," Cynthia laughed. "You should have seen the smug way he went about getting me to commit perjury. *My* story, he said, would get me hung. There was only one story that would get me off, and I must be very dramatic in the way I told it to the jury—tears at just the right time, and no leg when I was putting on the tears, but, in between times, plenty of leg for the jury. And sobs and leg for the newspaper photographers. Terry, he said jurors paid more attention to legs than alibis. Was he right?"

"He should know," Terry said, laughing. "I've never been on a jury, but, if I were, I know how *I'd* feel."

She looked at him with roguish eyes and said demurely, "You'd acquit me, Owl. Renny became so interested during my dress rehearsal, he couldn't keep his mind on his perjury."

With a quick motion, she leaned across the table toward him. "Tell me, Terry, what about that little Chinese girl?"

"Sou Ha," he said, "has given me her friendship, and when the Chinese give you their friendship, they give for keeps. Sou Ha thought you really *had* killed Mandra and that I was in love with you. She wanted me to be happy. Therefore, she confessed to a murder she had never committed. It was, of course, a crazy thing to do, looking at it from our viewpoint. But she's Chinese, and to her it seemed perfectly logical."

Cynthia, suddenly serious, said, "Terry Clane, no matter what happens, you're never going to betray the friendship of that Chinese girl."

His frown was puzzled. "Why, of course not, Cynthia. What makes you think I'd even consider such an idea?"

"Because," she told him, "you're getting ready to make the plunge. . . . Terry, promise me one thing . . . No, wait a minute, I know a better way than that. I'll ask you a question and you'll promise to answer it in Chinese. How's that?"

"What's the question?"

"When you marry Alma," she said, her eyes wistful, but her voice racing on with that little lilt of whimsical humor which was so characteristic of her, "will you please remember that she has some rather conventional ideas; will you please let her own you, body and soul, so you can't have any outside friendships; will you please promise never to play around at all, but look at life as a sober, serious business, to drop the little Chinese girl from your list of close friends, to lose as much of your spontaneity as possible, and always treat *me* as a little, scatterbrained sister. . . . Tell me the answer in Chinese, Owl."

"Why in Chinese, Cynthia?"

She laughed, and there was a little catch in her laugh, despite the hard smile on her lips. "Because there's no word for 'yes' in Chinese, silly. Oh, Owl, *please* don't get serious and lose your ability to take life as an adventure!"

He pressed his lips together and made a humming sound.

"What's that?" she asked.

"Chinese for 'no,' " he told her, smilingly, his eyes tender. "You see, the Chinese negative is expressed by simply prefixing that *m-m-m* sound to any word or sentence."

"My," she said, "it must be easy for a Chinese girl to say 'no.' She could say it with her mouth closed!"

Terry dismissed her remark with a mere nod and went on, "And, by way of further answer to your question, I'm not going to marry Alma."

Her eyes widened with consternation. "Not going . . . to marry Alma? Oh, Owl, but you *must!* It would break her heart. You love her and she loves you. You *do* love her, don't you, Owl?"

"In a way—yes."

"Then *why* aren't you going to marry her, Owl?"

"Because," he said, gripping her fingers, his voice suddenly husky, "I'm going to marry you."

"You . . . you're . . . Oh, Owl, no . . . please! Alma . . ."

"Wants me to," he interrupted. "She's too wrapped up in a career to take time out to be a wife. She didn't really analyze it until this thing came up, and then . . ."

Cynthia stared at him with startled eyes, suddenly scraped back her chair.

"Come on, Owl," she said. "If you've got anything like that to say to me, you're going to say it where we aren't surrounded by a whole mess of strange people, and . . . and where lipstick smears won't be so damned conspicuous. Come on, Owl. . . . Gee, I hope I'm not taking the aggressive in this thing, but you come on!"

A puzzled waiter rushed after them, caught them halfway to the door, and stared incredulously at the bill Terry pushed into his palm. At the check stand, there was a slight delay while the attendant was getting Cynthia's fur coat. A newsboy temptingly displayed a folded front page. "Read about de moider, Mister," he invited.

"Oh, Owl, look! There's Juanita's picture, and . . ."

Terry handed the boy a half dollar, grabbed the paper. Cynthia looked over his shoulder. Suddenly she giggled. "Look!" she exclaimed.

Terry, who had been reading the headlines: "POLO PLAYER ADMITS BEING TOOL IN MANDRA MURDER. . . . SPORTSMAN PROCURES MURDER WEAPON FOR DARING DANCER," lowered his eyes to the place Cynthia was indicating. Juanita's picture had been taken in front of her cell. Below it appeared the caption: "JUANITA MANDRA, THE BEAUTIFUL DANCER, WIDOW OF THE MURDERED MAN, TELLS HER STORY FOR THE FIRST TIME: 'WE HAD DECIDED TO SEPARATE,' THE DANCER SAID TEARFULLY. 'I WAS FINISHED WITH HIM BECAUSE OF HIS INFIDELITIES. I WENT TO HIS APARTMENT TO GET SOME OF MY THINGS. THIS SLEEVE GUN WAS LYING ON THE TABLE. NOT KNOWING WHAT IT WAS, I PICKED IT UP. HE GRABBED ME, STRUGGLED WITH ME, RIPPED MY GOWN FROM MY SHOULDERS. I DREW BACK, FIGHTING TO FREE MYSELF. I AM SATISFIED NOW, MY HUSBAND HAD INTENDED TO KILL ME WITH THAT SLEEVE GUN. HIS HANDS WERE MOIST WITH PERSPIRATION. THEY SLIPPED DOWN MY BARE ARMS. HIS FINGERS CLOSED ABOUT MINE, PRESSING THE CATCH OF THE SLEEVE GUN. I SCREAMED BECAUSE THE CATCH WAS CUTTING INTO MY FLESH. SUDDENLY THERE WAS A WHIRRING SOUND. SOMETHING JARRED IN MY HAND. JACOB FELL BACK. EVEN THEN I DIDN'T KNOW THAT. . . .' (Read the full story of what transpired on page 3, column 2.)"

The hat check girl brought Cynthia's coat and Terry slipped it over her smooth shoulders. She nestled against the soft fur and laughed.

"Good old Renny. He'll make it stick. Isn't it a swell break for Juanita that Renny had already thought up that story, studied up on sleeve guns and had it all rehearsed? You should have seen the methodical way he ironed out all the weak points in the story!"

She studied the photograph, looking at Juanita's legs with the critical appraisal which one woman gives to the feminine charms of another.

"At that, Owl," she said, "the arguments by which she expects to sway the jury aren't any better than mine."

**(The End)**

## *AN ACKNOWLEDGMENT*

The Chinese characters in this book are fictitious, but the background is not. Such inaccuracies as exist are due to my own inability to concentrate upon that which has been shown me, and, in turn, to depict that which I have seen.

Cultured Chinese rarely mingle with foreigners, are particularly inaccessible to the "Tourist." That I am privileged to enjoy the friendship of many of this group is a source of constant gratification. Their loyalty to friendship, the patience with which they have condoned my many errors has created a lasting impression upon me.

It is hard for them to understand a memory which is less than photographic. My clumsy attempts at mastering their language, my glaring breaches of Chinese etiquette must have provoked both mirth and embarrassment. That I have never seen evidences of either is typical of their innate courtesy.

Lest some of the things in this book seem exaggerated, may I observe that the most scholarly talk on concentration I have ever listened to was by a Chinese; that the one man I have met who seemed to have a perfect command of the English language, summoning with effortless ease the words by which he expressed the most subtle nuances of meaning, was Chinese; that the most satisfactory friendships I have ever enjoyed were with Chinese.

China is a large nation. Its people comprise many classes. Too much has been written of the more accessible lower classes; too little of the aloof Chinese aristocrat, who considers the true teacher with a respect akin to reverence. I am not a novelist. I wish that I were. But lest the reader consider the Chinese atmosphere in this book overdrawn, I assure him that I have known the exact counterpart of the characters described. I have had Chinese friends unhesitatingly risk their lives in my behalf. I am indebted to them for a most fascinating system of mental discipline, and I herewith make public acknowledgment of that indebtedness.

E. S. G.

>>> If you've enjoyed this book and would like to discover more great vintage crime and thriller titles, as well as the most exciting crime and thriller authors writing today, visit: >>>

## The Murder Room
### Where Criminal Minds Meet

**themurderroom.com**

9 781471 909467